IN THE LAP OF THE GODS

TED TAYLER

Vinci Books

vinci-books.com

Published by Vinci Books Ltd in 2026

1

Copyright © Ted Tayler 2016

The author has asserted their moral right to be identified as the author of this work in accordance with the Copyright, Designs and Patents Act 1988. This work is a work of fiction. Names, characters, places and incidents are the product of the author's imagination or are used fictitiously. Any resemblance to actual persons, living or dead, places and incidents is entirely coincidental.
All rights reserved. No part of this publication may be copied, reproduced, distributed, stored in any retrieval system, or transmitted in any form or by any means, including photocopying, recording, or other electronic or mechanical methods, nor used as a source for any form of machine learning including AI datasets, without the prior written permission of the publisher.
The publisher and the author have made every effort to obtain permissions for any third party material used in this book and to comply with copyright law. Any queries in this respect should be brought to the attention of the publisher and any omissions will be corrected in future editions.
A CIP catalogue record for this book is available from the British Library.
Paperback ISBN: 9781036700522

The EU GPSR authorised representative is Logos Europe, 9 rue Nicolas Poussion, 17000 La Rochelle, France
contact@logoseurope.eu

By Ted Tayler

The Phoenix

The Olympus Project
Gold, Silver and Bombs
Nothing Is Ever Forever
In the Lap of the Gods
The Price of Treachery
A New Dawn
Something Wicked Draws Near
Evil Always Finds A Way
Revenge Comes in Many Colours
Three Weeks in September
A Frequent Peal of Bells
Larcombe Manor

The Freeman Files

Fatal Decision
Last Orders
Pressure Point
Deadly Formula
Final Deal
Barking Mad
Creature Discomforts

Silent Terror
Night Train
All Things Bright
Buried Secrets
A Genuine Mistake
Strange Beginnings
Dead Reckoning
A Normal November
Into the Sunlight
Tame the Storm
One True Friend
Whispered Truths
A Morning Murder
Quick to Anger
Red Herring Season
Gathering Clouds
Still Standing

Chapter One

Saturday, June 29th, 2013

"This is modern policing, is it?" thought DS Phil Hounsell as he watched two police officers walking through the crowds with giant sunflowers attached to their helmets. Day Three of Glastonbury 2013, and he was visiting the police command centre at Worthy Farm.

The police had been present on the Festival site since 1989; these days, the Festival became a large town in its own right for the few days in June when it occupied this quiet part of Somerset.

As a senior detective in the Avon and Somerset service, Phil was assigned many duties in these austere times. Just his luck; this year, his name came out of the hat for a Worthy weekend.

He would rather endure a few hours' root canal work or a shopping trip with Erica and the children than this duty. Anything other than being at Festival HQ. Despite the well-documented history of mud in the previous years, the weather gods smiled on Worthy Farm this year.

A brief shower last evening did nothing to change the conditions underfoot. Nor had it dampened the spirits of the great crowd of revellers, hell-bent on enjoying what had become one of the highlights of an English summer.

Phil perused the reports from the opening days and glanced too at the events of Saturday so far. Everything was 'par for the course'. The expected number of searches at the entrances to uncover items that might be 'used illegally or offensively'. Somewhere in the command centre or back at Portishead, there would be a collection of laser pens, fireworks, questionable knives and sharp instruments. With the penchant of festival-goers for a chemically enhanced glow accompanying the music, you could also guarantee to stumble across a stash of confiscated drugs.

The CCTV coverage was extensive; throughout the weekend, officers monitored those images for public safety, crowd management, and crime prevention. Phil tore his eyes away from the mind-numbing reports and switched back to the screens.

He spotted the two giant sunflowers again. The local lads from the neighbourhood patrol were photographing a couple of scantily clad females. They looked young; the girls did too.

"Nice work if you can get it." thought Phil.

This 'touchy-feely' policing was fine and dandy but jibed with Phil's 'old school' approach. Phil wanted criminals off the streets and banged up, if possible, for a long time. He had frequently expressed those views, and his superiors knew where he stood. But, unfortunately, those superiors also understood precisely where he was going - nowhere.

He felt himself slipping gently into the long grass, perhaps thinking he wouldn't notice. Phil glanced at the young girls as they wandered on from their brief encounter with the Flowerpot Men and felt every one of his forty-seven years.

"Only three more summers," he thought, "and I can get the hell out of this charade. I prefer to wear jeans and a t-shirt to do something useful."

Phil knew they had plain-clothes officers on the ground, plus the uniforms the CCTV images now showed. Their main targets were thieves and drug dealers. So far, it had been quiet. Fingers crossed, it stayed that way. Phil sighed; he was bored to tears. The stuffy atmosphere in the room was causing his eyelids to droop. He needed to get up and stretch his legs before he nodded off to sleep.

He searched for a chaperone. No way would you persuade him to go out there alone. Walking alone around a site populated by well over one hundred thousand people was his idea of hell. A door opened, and a constable poked his head inside.

"I'm on the ice cream run; what can I get you, Sir?"

Phil jumped out of his chair and headed for the door.

"I'll come with you; this sunshine might not last much longer. We are in England, after all."

As they emerged into the sunlit site, close by the farmhouse, Phil checked out his companion, the same age as himself and yet still a constable. That seemed curious.

"Been in long?" he asked.

"Since eight o'clock this morning, Sir."

"No, sorry; I meant been on the job long."

"Eight years, Sir, and a paramedic before that. I joined the RAF straight from school but didn't enjoy it much, so I got out and tried various jobs until I found something I enjoyed. I worked as a traffic warden, a zookeeper, and a security guard out at Cribb's Causeway."

All relatively uniform, thought Phil. He had his answer. If his mother had let him have a dressing-up box as a nipper, he would have got it out of his system by the time he reached sixteen. He might have made something of his life. The further they walked, the bigger the crowd became. It proved difficult to stay together.

"Over here, Sir," called his companion as they neared an ice-cream stall, "what do you prefer?"

Phil made his way back through a sea of people and elected for a choc-ice; not that he particularly liked them, but with its wrapper, he hoped it gave him half a chance of polishing it off without getting his suit plastered.

"Cheers," said Phil as his guide handed over the ice cream, "what's your name, by the way?"

"Wayne, Sir."

"OK, Wayne, how many orders have we to carry back to HQ?"

"Eleven."

"Terrific," Phil could foresee problems.

Wayne had made this trip before; he had a system. Phil spotted the man-bag strapped across Wayne's chest but didn't pass a comment. Phil had met several gay officers during his career and always resisted saying things that might get misconstrued. Wayne fished out plastic vending cup holders from his bag. Each triangle was designed to hold six cups. The resourceful Wayne had modified the openings to accept a cornet and even a lollipop.

"Hey, Presto," said Phil, impressed at the ingenuity.

"E-bay," said Wayne, not getting the reference.

Phil finished his choc-ice before they reached the command centre. He held the door open for Wayne, and ten grateful people inside soon got chilled relief from the warm conditions. Wayne started to devour his Magnum. He eyed Phil.

"Do you want to carry on having a walk around, Sir?" he said, with a shiny chin.

Phil looked at the constable. He sensed his desperation to get back outside, mingle with the crowds and listen to the music. Well, it was marginally better than being stuck in this place.

"After you, Wayne; you know your way."

As they walked back to the site, Wayne gave Phil a running commentary on what had happened yesterday and what lay in store for the fans today.

"Glastonbury isn't just the music; it's the people too. I arrived early yesterday, and things were grim — the usual long queues for the showers and the toilets. But, by lunchtime, as last night's hangovers had disappeared and today's cider started taking hold, the mood lifted, and you saw a few smiles. Then the music starts, and you see smiles all the way, no matter what the weather's doing."

"How many times have you been here, Wayne?" asked Phil.

"This is my twelfth Festival. I've done three as a copper, three as a paramedic and six as a punter."

"I'm impressed," said Phil, "I'm a virgin. You'll never catch me in a tent; I don't queue for showers or toilets, and I'm not a great music fan. Of course, I enjoy a few songs I hear now and then, but I couldn't tell you who sang them for the life of me."

"You could always go 'glamping' over the far side if you didn't want to rough it with the great unwashed," said Wayne with a laugh.

Phil eased past a swaying teenager who looked as if his

day could only get worse and thought of his wife. Erica would probably enjoy the Festival experience, but it wasn't something he wanted to bring up at the breakfast table. He shuddered as the contents of the teenager's stomach hit the grass behind him.

"No fear. Give me a warm bed, with a shower and a loo five yards away, thanks," said Phil.

Wayne ploughed on, regardless. He adopted his tour guide persona, for which a uniform was available, and pointed out various attractions. Based on the crowds, they negotiated as they passed; they lived up to their name. Wayne interspersed this information with brief reviews of the performances he witnessed. Occasionally, Wayne shouted these observations over people's heads as the two policemen zigzagged their way through the vast site.

"Over there, you've got Arcadia, the giant spider. After midnight, it belches fireballs into the night sky, and they hold a rave. See that marquee? It's where you can queue up to complain that Glasto isn't what it used to be. The place is quiet, though. So who will hang around here when you can have a good time? Dizzee Rascal smashed it yesterday; he did a crazy set. The Arctic Monkeys sounded great, too—lots of lights, smoke and lasers. Bill Wyman played somewhere too, but you can't be in two places at once, can you?"

"Bill Wyman? Wasn't he with the Stones? Now that's a band I have heard before. What happened to them, I wonder?" shouted Phil.

Wayne gave him a sympathetic look.

"You don't have much of a clue about music, do you, Sir? The Stones are the main attraction tonight on the Pyramid Stage. They're still belting it out after fifty years on the road. That's the Pyramid over there. Can you see the big screen? That big voice and a bigger smile belong to Laura Mvula; she's superb."

Phil Hounsell glanced over towards the stage. He couldn't see or hear much at this distance, but she sounded okay. If only there hadn't been so many people around them. He was no longer watching where he was going. The inevitable happened. His shoulder collided with a man moving fast in the opposite direction with his female companion.

"Sorry," said Phil, turning to apologise for his clumsiness.

The man was arm in arm with his attractive partner; they hardly broke stride. The man grunted at Phil but didn't turn around again, and in seconds, the crowds swallowed them.

Phil massaged his shoulder.

"You can't beat meeting the public face-to-face, can you, Sir?" said a grinning Wayne.

"My fault for not watching where I was going," muttered Phil as his shoulder regained feeling.

"A smart couple, I thought. I guess those two come from the same neck of the woods as Mick Jagger and his entourage, enjoying the benefits of a more glamorous outdoor living style. I doubt they put up their tents as I have had to over the years. How the other half lives, eh?"

Phil didn't reply.

"Everything okay, Sir?" asked Wayne. The two men were now side-by-side and back in step.

"The woman is definitely out of the top drawer. But there's something about the bloke. Just seeing how he walked and made his way through the crowd. It was a familiar gait. No doubt I'll remember in time."

"I never recognised them; if they've been on the telly,

I've missed them," said Wayne, slowing as they neared one of the many food stalls.

Phil could smell heaven. He put thoughts of Erica's caustic comments relating to his growing waistline and why his shoulder hurt out of his head.

"A great idea, Wayne; it's rude not to check that these people are providing food to an acceptable standard. We're truly serving the public for the next ten minutes."

As Phil and Wayne chose what was very unhealthy but tasty food from a limited menu, the two festival-goers they had been discussing strode further and further away. For now, they were unaware of their identity.

Annabelle Grace Fox was indeed a lady, as the police officers surmised. She liked her creature comforts. Her companion that sunny afternoon was Colin Bailey. His features were subtly altered by cosmetic surgery on two occasions in the past decade; no way Phil Hounsell would have recognised him even if he had caught his eye as they bumped into one another.

What distinguishes an excellent detective from the run-of-the-mill plodders is the millions of details they have stored away in those tiny grey cells. Despite his loss of enthusiasm for the job he used to love, Phil Hounsell still behaved like a dog with a squeaky Christmas toy. He would search among those grey cells until he remembered who walked that way; and where their paths had crossed. Then, in time, the name would come to him.

Phil and Wayne spent the rest of the afternoon and evening moving across the site, gradually threading their way closer to the main stage. More by Wayne's design than any wish on Phil Hounsell's part to have his ears battered by the sound system. Wayne loved his music.

The crowd noise grew louder and louder as the main

attraction of the day was due to begin. The Stones were to make their long-awaited appearance.

As they took the stage, the Phoenix raised itself and belched fire for the Stones.

That was not a metaphor, nor a reference to the vigilante killer in the same corner of the site with Athena. Instead, it was the sculpture of a vast bird perched on top of the symbolic Pyramid stage. With its enormous moving wings, the Phoenix announced the Festival's return after a two-year absence.

Meanwhile, the human Phoenix and his partner Athena stood in the crowd as the Rolling Stones opened with 'Jumping Jack Flash'. The standout songs for Colin Bailey were 'Paint It Black', 'Gimme Shelter', and the encore 'You Can't Always Get What You Want'. Athena danced with Phoenix for most of the set. Then, suddenly, she saw her and her partner on the big screen as the cameras panned around the crowds between numbers.

Phoenix turned away and shielded his face by moving Athena in front of him.

Phil Hounsell watched the show and listened. He saw the crowd scenes on the screen. Phil prayed the director of those camera shots wouldn't pick on him. Phil didn't need the hassle of his superiors thinking he was out on a 'jolly', enjoying himself when he was supposed to be doing a proper job.

As the set ended and the Festival wound down until the final day, he reflected on what he had seen; a one hundred thousand crowd, the Stones and lots of fireworks.

Phil turned to Wayne. "No doubt it will be three times as many in ten years that swear they came here. Good fireworks, though."

"Did you clock that bloke that pulled his girlfriend in

front of him when the cameras picked him out, Sir?" said Wayne. "That seemed odd."

"What did he look like?" asked Phil, who had to admit the incident never registered.

"I reckon it was that couple from this afternoon," Wayne said.

"I need to remember who he reminded me of," said Phil. "I knew he had something to hide. We'll keep an eye out tomorrow, and if possible, I want to have a word."

On Sunday, the day started slowly again, and the atmosphere and the excitement built and built. Phil was back on duty, and once he checked that everything was shipshape in the control centre, he went to find Wayne.

"Okay, Wayne, anything you can tell me?

"A baby got delivered during the Stone's set last night; mother and baby are doing well. It was a case of 'Gimme Gas and Air' rather than 'Gimme Shelter'. I understand. Prince Harry also visited the ground last evening, enjoying life as usual. He was mostly on rum & coke."

"Coke from a bottle, I trust?"

"So I heard, Sir," said Wayne with a smile. "Brucie's on this afternoon, so that should be a riot."

Oddly enough, Phil reckoned it might be; you can't buy experience, can you? The day rocked and rolled along without the two policemen catching sight of their person of interest. As night fell and the final act took to the stage, The Phoenix belched fire again to welcome Mumford & Sons. Phil resigned himself to watching them round things off for another year. If they kept to the timetable, it would end; just before midnight.

Phoenix and Athena were still on the site and enjoying a quiet day together. Athena wanted to revisit the Pyramid stage, but Phoenix preferred his clothes cut from a heavier cloth. He endured the afternoon's offerings. Somehow, he persuaded Athena to go off-piste for a while and take in the Smashing Pumpkins, the Heavy from their home city, and they even caught a French band with a highly original name, Phoenix.

They were too lightweight for Colin Bailey. Athena enjoyed them; Colin sulked throughout their set, wishing this Eavis bloke could have booked Judas Priest or Iron Maiden for the main stage. Great memories of nights in the Crown from his youth and on tour with Maiden's Hair in 2010 came rushing back.

While Phil Hounsell and Wayne suffered a bout of indie folk-rock sickness, Athena and Phoenix made plans to pack their things, empty the yurt and drive back to Larcombe Manor. Just after midnight, Phil gave up the ghost and said farewell to Wayne. He drove towards Bath but never closed the gap between him and Athena in her high-end Range Rover.

As Phil put the key in the door just after one in the morning, he made a note to don his thinking cap later for that elusive face.

Erica and the kids were fast asleep. Oh well, with luck, that was his last weekend on Glastonbury duty. So the only thing to do tonight was to get a few hours' sleep before that alarm shattered the silence at seven o'clock.

Monday, July 1st, 2013

Getting out of bed on a Monday morning can be challenging.

On one side of the old Roman city of Bath, Phil Hounsell padded to the bathroom, trying not to disturb his wife, Erica. He glanced towards the two bedrooms where Shaun and Tracey still lay fast asleep. Phil knew from experience that as soon as they heard him get in the shower, they would scramble downstairs to snatch a few minutes watching television before they began the countdown to the school run.

Erica usually awoke by half-past seven; either she heard her husband creeping around, despite his best efforts, or the kids had started arguing over which channel to watch. Once in a blue moon, she didn't stir until the alarm on her mobile phone shattered the relative quiet with a few bars of 'Sweet Child of Mine'.

The routine and order Erica established when she reached the kitchen got them through this rigmarole every weekday morning. As Phil stepped out of the shower and gathered his wits and shaving kit, things downstairs grew calmer by the minute. Erica had awoken. Phil looked in the mirror, lathered his face and started shaving. His mind drifted back over the weekend at Glastonbury and to the day ahead at Portishead.

Phil attempted to recall that French phrase that said the more things change, the more they stay the same, but it wouldn't come to him. He finished up in the bathroom and wandered back to the bedroom to get dressed, ready for work. By the time he reached the kitchen, the first coffee cup and his bowl of cornflakes should be waiting. The tried and trusted routine all over again.

Erica would be wide awake, bright-eyed and bushy-tailed, all set to pack him off to work so she could go to the bathroom herself. Shaun and Tracey were always eager to tell their Dad everything that had happened over the weekend and what they expected of him over the coming days. There were those summer fetes, end-of-year plays and other occasions he was probably due to miss, no doubt, because of the job.

Phil entered the kitchen, and three faces turned to greet him.

"Ha-ha. Cut yourself again, Dad," sniggered Shaun.

"Don't worry, darling," said Erica, "there's another clean shirt ready in the wardrobe."

Phil sipped his coffee and sighed. Then, as he wolfed down his breakfast and carried his mug back upstairs to repair his face and change his shirt, it came to him; 'plus ca change, plus la meme chose.'

Yeah, that was right, he thought as he drained his mug. He picked up the car keys, went downstairs, kissed Erica goodbye and waved at the kids, who had already flopped on the sofa watching the box. He barely noticed the glorious summer's day outside the house as he got into his car and headed for Portishead.

Elsewhere in Bath, Zara Wheeler was also experiencing those same Monday morning blues. Ever since that chance meeting with Rusty on the streets of Bristol during the terrorist attack on the Royal visit last November, her weekends, her whole life, had been transformed.

Gone was the cosy but loveless time spent with Toby Drysdale, her long-time colleague from her days at Manvers Street police station. Gone were the hours spent alone at home with her cats and a bottle of Chardonnay, pining over her boss Phil Hounsell. Rusty had changed that.

Zara was an intelligent young woman. She appreciated that Rusty had secrets. In those first few weeks of their relationship, it had been wonderful discovering things about one another in the bedroom. Zara had no complaints in that department. Rusty was a robust, athletic and capable lover; they spent much of their time together in bed.

Although she wanted to learn so many other things about her partner, Zara understood that Rusty needed to be sure he could trust her before revealing anything he did when they were apart. It was clear he was in the SAS or a special ops unit that targeted terror threats on the UK mainland. That much was clear from his presence in Bristol, where he suddenly appeared to stop her from checking the boot of a suspicious car. Rusty's prompt action saved her life.

The details of which branch of the secret services he was attached to were unimportant; she just wanted to know he would be coming home to her safe and well for years to come.

One Sunday evening in late January, they had curled up on the sofa with a glass of wine.

"It's easy enough to work out why they call you Rusty," said Zara, "but what did your parents name you? Are they still alive?"

"My mother died when I was twenty-five. She had cervical cancer. She and my dad split up five or six years earlier. So I've no idea whether he's dead or alive."

"Really?" she asked, "Aren't you in touch with him?"

Rusty snorted.

"I joined as soon as possible to escape from the bullying bastard. My father treated my mother as a servant, not a wife. He was a regular soldier and demanded everything in his life be regular, too; mealtimes, sex, you get the picture. If not, she got knocked around. I felt guilty leaving her with him, but I need to to get away. If I'd stayed, I'd have killed him. So when she wrote to say she'd escaped and found peace in a women's refuge, I was happy for her. Unfortunately, she never lived long enough to enjoy her freedom. She always used the name she christened me in her letters,

David. That was his name too, which is why I never use it. David Scott. That was me until my first few weeks as a boy soldier. After that, the red hair branded me as Rusty, and that was good enough for me."

Zara had cradled Rusty's head on her shoulder and kissed his closely cropped hair. More small details emerged over the following weeks as he told Zara where he had been in his early time in the army. He mentioned operations he had been involved in and made her laugh at a few of the lighter moments he and his young colleagues shared when they were on leave in far-flung places worldwide.

Eventually, she learned he had applied for the SAS, where his real soldiering began. Of course, he couldn't tell her where he had served or what he had experienced. But he could say he was already an old hand in the first intake of the Special Reconnaissance Regiment in 2005.

"This red hair is often associated with people with a short fuse and a fiery temper Zara. The discipline drummed into me from day one in the army keeps it under control most of the time. But, now and then, someone winds me up so tight I explode — every corner of British society suffered at the hands of the idiots that preach liberalism and appeasement. Even in a proud, action-based organisation like the SAS, some officers should never have had the honour. These officers are weak and spineless. Instead of getting in amongst the bad guys and sorting them out permanently as soon as they arrive on the scene, every step has to be weighed, risk-assessed and rubber-stamped by faceless mandarins before anything is allowed to happen. We were on a mission deep in bandit country, and I headed a team of seven. A sandstorm struck without warning, and two of my lads separated from the group. A young colonel sat thousands of miles away and ordered us to pull out. He was still wet behind the ears and had never seen any real action. He didn't want to risk us being captured by hanging around searching for them. He said they were capable of finding their way home. We never left anyone behind on one of those missions, Zara. When we got back to base and debriefed the confusion, we learned that their bodies were found by the Americans, who had their special forces on the ground there. My two lads survived for a few days in the searing heat but died when their water ran out. I stormed out of the room after I got the news and tracked down the superior officer responsible. He ended up in the hospital with a broken jaw, and they dismissed me from the service. That was back in 2009."

Zara listened in silence to what had been the longest speech she had heard from Rusty.

"I don't blame you for lashing out," she had said. "I joined the police force to make a difference, but we've both suffered from the same disease strangling the fight against terrorism and crime. My career has been 'on hold' since I rescued little Grace from the floodwaters last year. I can't face being side-lined into crowd control and pointless PR exercises until I collect my pension."

Rusty had shut down after that for a while. Zara bided her time before she tried to get him to open up about what he had been doing for the past three years. Then, over the Spring Bank Holiday weekend, they travelled north to her parent's home and spent hours walking in the countryside near her hometown of Durham.

"Can you tell me what you do now, Rusty?" she asked as they stood on a hillside looking across a wooded valley. The sun was gathering strength and warmth so that gradually everything around them woke up after a cold and lengthy winter prolonged by the coldest spring in fifty years.

Rusty had gathered his coat about him and thrust his hands deeper into his pockets. He had known that this day would come. Rusty drip-fed snippets of information to Zara over the months, and time was running out. He had promised Phoenix that he would resolve the situation within six months. Rusty had to decide whether now was the right moment. He resolved to plough ahead.

"I work for someone in the private sector. The people approached me a few months after the SAS showed me the door. This outfit operates how our security services should, but you need to understand that what I tell you goes no further. It will change your life forever. You know how I feel about you. I want us to share the rest of our lives. Bringing you into the fold alongside my colleagues and superiors is the only way for that to happen. Will you trust me?"

Zara stood on tiptoe and kissed him.

"If it means we're together, then I'll go anywhere, Rusty. I need you to promise that you and whoever you work for aren't involved in any criminal activity."

Rusty smiled.

"A typical copper to the last," he said "start with the difficult question. I can guarantee that villains and terrorists are the opposite of my employers. Criminals work outside the law. We work in a somewhat grey area. Maybe that goes on in an area above the law. But we prefer to consider that the law has become so lax of late that we are merely operating at its rightful level."

Zara and Rusty had continued their afternoon walk and spoke nothing more on the matter for a few days. Then, finally, the couple returned to Bath and were at her home, preparing to return to work the following day. Rusty was in the shower. The door opened, and a naked Zara joined him.

"To what do I owe this pleasant surprise?" he asked.

"I've made my decision," said Zara, wrapping her arms around him. "I'll hand in my resignation, which will set me free from these mundane non-jobs they keep assigning me. Then, in four weeks, I'm all yours."

Rusty grinned.

"I think you can already tell that waiting four weeks won't be an option for that young lady."

Minutes later, they were under the duvet, and any thoughts of resignation forms were forgotten until the morning. After an early breakfast, Zara drove into the Police HQ at Portishead and started the ball rolling. She chatted to Toby Drysdale to let him know her decision. She had been nervous about Phil Hounsell finding out; she wasn't sure of his reaction. Toby had plenty of questions, and Zara knew this would be a familiar pattern over the coming weeks.

"Why on earth are you leaving, Zara? Where will you go? Has someone been head-hunting you already?" Toby asked, concerned about his friend leaving.

Zara had thought long and hard about answering these questions; she had to be firm in her decision to leave yet guarded about where she was working next. She needed to be vague on that front but not so ambiguous that it might draw attention to the possible hidden nature of her future job. A delicate balance, but Zara was confident she could cope.

"I have to leave, Toby," she had replied "ever since we did the right thing and pulled baby Grace from that car, They've shunted me into a corner. My ambitions for further promotions and a dream of becoming a Chief Constable one day ended. There's no way they'll consider me for any significant advancement in the future. I'm not sure where

I'll go eventually; I'll take time to review my options. I reckon I deserve a short holiday."

Zara had asked Toby not to spread her news around the building. She knew the cat would be out of the bag soon enough, but every day of the twenty-eight, it remained a secret was a bonus. Zara had downloaded a copy of Form 232 and provided the required written notice of her intention to leave the organisation. So far, she hadn't handed it to her Department Head.

Thank goodness that wasn't Phil Hounsell these days. Since that night in Bristol and the subsequent fall-out, they spent less time increasingly in contact at work.

After filling in the form, she then took a few days wondering about Toby's second question. Where *would* she go? What would they ask of her? Rusty must be based somewhere near Bath or Bristol, that much she realised. Otherwise, he wouldn't always be able to find his way to her house or Portishead without prior warning.

The same as her, he wasn't doing a nine-to-five job. Now and then, he told her he'd be 'off the grid' for a few days. He never said where. Zara never asked.

In a month, they were due to be living and working together. As Zara had driven home after work that Friday, she had waited for Rusty to drop by so that she could ask him. That evening, the ground fell from under her feet, and she wondered what she was getting involved in.

The pair had shared a meal and a bottle of wine, and then as they relaxed listening to music, she plucked up the courage to pose a few questions.

"Can I ask for a few details, Rusty?" she began.

"What do you need to know, sweetheart?" Rusty had replied.

"Where will I be working? Will I be able to continue to

live here, or do I need to move? What salary can I expect to receive? What type of work will they expect me to carry out?

"Woah, steady Zara; let's take these one at a time, shall we? Firstly, you already know the place where we'll be working. We'll live together, but if you want to keep this place, rent it out or sell it, that's up to you. Based on what I know of the salary structure in the organisation, I reckon you will receive something around twenty per cent above the figure you earn now. As for the work, I recommended you for attachment to the intelligence section. The team there needs strengthening; being a woman will help. We're thin on the ground in that area at Olympus. As well as gathering intelligence, we'll increasingly need a sharp mind like yours to develop strategies to fight cybercrime and cyberterrorism. Do you think that could keep you gainfully occupied while I'm off hunting down the villains you identify for me?"

A dim light went on in the corner of Zara's brain as Rusty was speaking. Then, when he had finished, she jumped up from the sofa.

"It's Larcombe Manor, isn't it?" she squealed. "I bloody knew that place was suspicious. That shower gave me the run around when I was there last September chasing up that ICO enquiry. So they did have something to hide with that bloke Garry Burns."

Rusty held his breath; had that been one step too far, too soon?

Chapter Two

Colin Bailey and his partner Annabelle Fox slept late at Larcombe Manor that same Monday morning after the Glastonbury glamping weekend. But, despite the relative luxury of their festival accommodation, nothing compared to the sumptuous surroundings of home.

Since Erebus vacated his suite of apartments and sailed away to a well-earned retirement in Ibiza, Athena and Phoenix had remodelled his rooms to suit their taste. But, in deference to the older man's history with the Georgian house and the memory of his beloved wife Elizabeth and daughter Helen, Athena kept a selection of photographs and ornaments on a table next to one of the large windows that overlooked the rolling lawns leading to the woods on the perimeter of the estate.

Phoenix had been sad to leave his old quarters in the stable block even though compensations were full-time with his partner. He missed those hours alone with the thoughts he always valued so highly as a young man; the extra leadership responsibilities within the Olympus organisation were time-consuming. He yearned to get back to direct action. He longed to have a chance for a little 'street cleaning' — the good old days.

There was no going back, though. As soon as Phoenix had been dragged away from his hidey-hole in the New Year, Athena arranged to extend Rusty's quarters next door in readiness for the planned new arrival. If Zara Wheeler decided to join the organisation, it was only right they should be together. Athena knew too that keeping Phoenix in the Manor House, a comfortable distance from the stable block and the operations room beneath the ice-house, where Zara would be working, was her absolute priority.

It wasn't merely a selfish wish; she was head of the Olympus Project at Larcombe Manor. She shared a post with Phoenix, and she was eager to have her partner at her side when they reported to the organisation's upper echelons in London. The nuts and bolts of the operation Phoenix always got involved in must be left to more junior staff. Athena understood, too, that Garry Burns and Colin Bailey looked alarmingly alike. Phoenix and Zara Wheeler had a shared history and needed to be kept apart for as long as possible. Perhaps in the fullness of time, her assimilation into the Olympus family would be such that they could reveal his true identity.

As Annabelle Fox and Colin Bailey slept undisturbed by the Monday morning blues that troubled many others on the other side of Bath, DS Phil Hounsell drove to Portishead with bits of tissue on his chin. All the fun of the Festival was behind him, and another meaningless working week beckoned. As his car idled in the building traffic, he dreamt of lazy retirement days with nothing more taxing than deciding which shorts to wear or which golden beach to visit and sunbathe.

In the Lap of the Gods

Meanwhile, Zara Wheeler sat in her car a few hundred yards behind him, praying that now that the Divisional Commander had signed off on her resignation, the remaining items on her exit checklist would be dealt with quickly.

Zara still promised herself that short holiday. The shock of discovering that Larcombe Manor was her new home continued to make her brain hurt. Her decision to leave the police service, though, remained rock solid.

God, how she hated that word. Service my eye. What was wrong with a police *force* that knew when to apply a firm hand where needed? But, as the days ticked remorselessly on towards her final Friday at Portishead, Zara was only too happy to quit that tiresome pussy-footing around behind her. She wanted to see real progress in fighting crime and ridding the country of all the evil that strangled it. Working alongside Rusty might well give her that opportunity.

Zara had eventually calmed down after her initial outburst that Sunday evening when Rusty dropped the bombshell about the Olympus Project. He filled in most of the blanks to appease her and get her to take the time to think before giving him her final decision.

Rusty explained how a wealthy group of similar-minded patriots joined forces around 2008 because the nation they loved was going to the dogs. These men and women came up with the idea of masking the Project's true nature with a charitable organisation treating veterans with PTSD. Larcombe was their HQ in the UK, and it housed many more on its grounds that the Charity Commissioners or visiting local police personnel never got to see.

Rusty had kept quite a few details back. She understood that. If her final decision was to reject a move to Larcombe, she needed to pursue a different career path. However, rusty assured her that no matter how the coin fell, their relationship would be unaffected; it would carry on as it had done for the past six months, with them getting together whenever their busy schedules permitted.

The only difference was that Zara now knew the secret behind the Olympus Project. That fact was the most significant cause of the questions banging around in her brain and leaving her sleepless nights. Would Rusty keep her close because he loved her, or did he need to guard against her passing that red-hot information to her soon-to-be former colleagues? She briefly wondered if she was in any danger.

Zara had dismissed that thought from her mind without question. She loved Rusty unconditionally and knew that feeling was mutual. Rusty would make it work somehow; of that, Zara had no doubt. The holiday she promised herself gave her enough time to sort those Olympus issues out in her head. But, for now, she needed to deal with the last few tasks on that exit checklist and, if possible, avoid Phil Hounsell before making her escape from the job she had come to detest.

Zara spotted Phil's car in the car park. He had arrived on the site already. She parked far enough away to be comfortable that they didn't cross paths later in the day when heading home. Then she made her way inside the building to her office. There were exit interviews on the cards this week with superiors to endure. Also, she needed to finalise her details with the finance department and then arrange to return the paraphernalia she'd acquired over the years. Her phone, laptop, ID access badges, parking permits, uniform, warrant card, pocketbook and other odds and ends must be handed over.

Zara knew full well where to lay her hands on ninety-nine per cent of it already, but a couple of items might need tracking down. She had few belongings to gather and put in a cardboard box. Anything relating to the cases Zara currently worked on, which these days were few, could be transferred to whoever took them on after her departure. She peered around her office over the top of her glasses. Zara reckoned it would be easier to walk away from all this than she'd thought.

Of course, she would miss a few people at Portishead. Toby Drysdale, for one, had been friends for ages, lovers for a brief period. She gazed across at Angela Chambers had once sat and realised how much she still missed her murdered colleague. She searched through her desk, wondering if a memento remained somewhere of Angela that she might take back home, wherever that might be so that she could keep her memory alive. But, unfortunately, there didn't appear to be anything.

Her hand rested on a folder at the bottom of a drawer. Zara knew at once what it contained. That photograph of Garry Burns. She opened the file and inspected the picture for the umpteenth time. Should she pass this on to someone? There was no point; nothing more had surfaced via the ICO after Portishead reported back with the results of the interviews she carried out at Larcombe last September.

The ICO had covered their backsides by raising a concern; the police found little unusual. Water under the bridge. As Zara took one last look at Garry Burns, she wondered whether he left to go travelling. Perhaps he was out there somewhere putting the world to rights for Olympus. She hesitated as she prepared to shred the photograph and copy of the paperwork gathered that day.

Had she begun to cross the line between sticking to the letter of the law and aligning herself with Rusty? In that grey area operating outside and above the law along with his colleagues?

Zara pressed the button.

DS Phil Hounsell caught up on news of yet another ram raid as he sat in his office on the other side of the building. Last year there were several similar robberies. A gang from somewhere in the country; they had never learned whether they came from the capital, or the Midlands. They had travelled along the M5 as it crossed his patch and paid fleeting but profitable visits to a collection of small towns bordering the motorway.

They spent many working hours at the crime scenes. Those had included jewellers and other stores that stocked high-end clothing. The target might be a relatively isolated ATM in the smaller towns that they crudely smashed from its housing and spirited away to be opened and emptied elsewhere. The amounts of money varied, but the sum now ran into the millions of pounds accumulatively. There was increasing pressure from his superiors to get this gang out of commission. Phil read the details of the recent attack in Taunton, where dozens of designer handbags worth tens of thousands disappeared from one of the town centre's premier stores.

Residents described hearing a massive bang as raiders hit the flagship branch on North Street, crashing a car through the reinforced windows of the store.

One local woman from a nearby flat said, 'I heard a huge crash like a giant door slamming. It was a very unusual noise, and when I checked what happened later, I saw police and tape all hanging around the shop.'

A neighbouring camera store owner who lived in rooms above his business said, 'I heard a terrible scraping of metal and then the crash. I knew straight away that it was a ramraid. Thieves have raided the business several times.'

The raid took place around half past four in the morning. The raiders used a stolen Audi to smash through the glass and steal bags that retailed up to two thousand pounds. Typical of this gang's *modus operandi*, they abandoned the Audi where it lay jammed in the shop storefront and used another stolen car to cover the trip to the motorway. Officers found a burnt-out Vauxhall Zafira on the road leading to Junction 25 of the M5.

Traffic on the arterial routes at that time of day is light but considering that the gang could have transferred to any vehicle, maybe a high-performance BMW or even a people carrier, it didn't help much. Unless they drew attention to themselves by driving like lunatics at high speed, Phil could tell this mob was too clever by half to commit that schoolboy error.

There appeared to be a lot more reading matter on the subject. Phil had already read enough. The score in the game currently: – Ram Raiders 1 Police Leads Nil.

Events that week carried on in much the same vein. Zara went through all the hoops required to secure a speedy and relatively amicable release from the job that had become her private hell. Phil Hounsell continued to search for ways to break down the stubborn defence that the ramraid gang and the villains behind the other cases on his desk constructed. The Police score remained resolutely at nil. Both officers welcomed the weekend with open arms; Zara couldn't wait for Monday to come around again so she could start her last week. But, on the other hand, Phil dreaded the prospect of more setbacks and stern faces from his superiors.

Monday, July 8th, 2013

Phil Hounsell avoided the shaving mishaps at the start of this new week, but it had hardly started before his mood darkened. Mid-morning on Tuesday hadn't arrived yet, and disenchantment had set in already. Phil flicked through the dozen or so items in his in-tray. There were a few reports to skip-read and sign; he would end up rubber-stamping holiday requests, even though he knew it promised to leave his team more stretched than usual. Notification of confirmation of Form 232? What's this? One lucky beggar must have decided enough was enough and handed in their papers. No doubt, off to pastures new for a lot less stress and a good deal more money?

Before he read it, he got up and walked over to get himself a coffee. He checked to see how soft the biscuits had become in his top drawer and decided they might still be safe to eat. Phil took a bite out of his hobnob and read.

"Bloody hell," he shouted, almost choking on his biscuit. He started coughing and gulped steaming hot coffee. That didn't help matters. "Zara Wheeler? Where the hell is she off to, I wonder?"

Phil raced through the form, searching for details, but they were few and far between. Her actual leaving date was almost upon them as it seemed she planned to take a week's holiday as part of her notice. The Divisional Commander and the ACC were interviewing her this week. Although they regretted that such an excellent young officer had decided to end her career, they agreed not to be bloody-minded and make her work every last minute.

Phil sat back in his chair and reread the information while finishing his coffee. He was confident that her leaving the service related to her superiors' response regarding the rescue of that little mite during the floods; it wasn't her being pissed off with his reaction after they slept together during the Kelly family trial in Bristol. But either way, he wasn't sure how he felt about seeing her go.

Ever since he'd clapped eyes on her in that incident room in Durham three years ago, they had been working closely together. What happened in Bristol had been inevitable; he could have handled things better. He shouldn't have insisted they stay overnight in the first place and resisted her advances when they returned to the hotel. There had been so many opportunities to do the right thing before and after the event. Instead, Phil failed to act upon them. Deep down, he knew that was because he wanted her just as much as she had wanted him that night. Once they got it out of their system, they avoided one another as far as possible, both in Bath and here at Portishead.

So much so that she had decided to leave. Zara had completed her forms and was almost through the leaving process without him even hearing a whisper. So much for the grapevine. Phil Hounsell pushed his chair away from his desk and walked towards his office door. He was determined to have a final chat with Zara Wheeler before the end of the week. He couldn't let her slink out of his life for good without at least saying goodbye.

Zara eyed the small cardboard box on her desk. So far, it only contained her Queen's Gallantry Medal, a few certificates for long-forgotten training course achievements and a calendar that Tracey Hounsell made for her at school. It was in 2012 when she and the Hounsell family were on better terms. Nevertheless, it possessed that innocent charm that kids convey to each item they bring home from school after completing a craft project, and Zara couldn't bear to throw it away just yet.

Her first meeting of the week with the Divisional Commander was thirty minutes away; her door swung open, and a flustered DI Phil Hounsell loomed in the doorway.

"So you're off on Friday then, Zara?" he said. "You didn't think to keep me in the loop, though? What brought on this urge to leave? Where are you going?"

Zara didn't reply straight away. She wasn't sure how many questions he might have thought of on his way across the building to confront her. He may as well get them off his chest; then, she would decide which ones she chose to answer.

The silence stretched out between them. Then, finally, it appeared there were no more questions.

"I am off on holiday from Friday; I won't be returning to Portishead. My career has nosedived because of one error of judgement, and there isn't any point in me staying. I detest traffic duties and jobs nobody else wants; to be lumbered with that burden for the rest of my service is a demoralising prospect. I need a new challenge."

Zara saw Phil's reaction to her mention of an error of judgement; he couldn't disguise the discomfort her choice of phrase had caused.

"Don't flatter yourself," she said "my day out with Toby and Dave down at Shepton Mallet led to my downfall. I'd do it all over again. Saving Grace from drowning is the one good thing to come out of my career since I came south three years ago. Not that it's any business of yours, but I'm in a stable relationship and my partner and I will work together in the private security sector. I'm sure you understand the word 'private' means I can't divulge where I'll be working or with whom."

Phil slumped into the chair near the door.

"What the hell happened to us, Zara? What became of Cat and Mouse? We worked well, and I always hoped we'd stay together until my retirement."

Zara allowed herself a weak smile.

"Bristol happened; the Kelly family trial fiasco happened. Angela Chambers died; the baby Grace rescue took place. The criminals got stronger and stronger while we, the police, got weaker and weaker. What chance do a Cat and a Mouse have against the Lion or the Elephant? I can't stop to chat. I'm afraid. I need to prepare for my interview with the Divisional Commander. Goodbye, Phil. It was good working with you most of the time."

Zara Wheeler swept past Phil Hounsell and left the room. She headed for the Ladies, where she spent ten minutes taking deep breaths and getting her nerves under control. There were no tears. She realised how much stronger a woman she had become than that frightened little ingenue Phil first met up with at Durham.

DS Phil Hounsell sat alone in Zara's office; he had been stunned by her evident loathing for how the whole ethos of police work was heading. Phil sympathised with her on that score; he had been a vocal opponent of the softly, softly approach for years. Yet back in the summer of 2010, Zara insisted that they must work with the system rather than turn a blind eye to a vigilante killer such as Colin Bailey. Phil had wondered whether Bailey was a 'necessary evil' in the society successive liberal governments had created. How cynical and life-hardened Zara had become since then.

He was shocked, too, to learn that Zara was now in a relationship. Her colleagues had never said a word here at

HQ; he knew how difficult it was to keep anything quiet on that score in a relatively close-knit community such as Portishead police headquarters.

Most of all, he was gutted that their situation had become non-existent. How much worse could things get around here? Well, he would find out in a few minutes.

Phil strolled back to his office. He spotted new files in his in-tray and an urgent email from his boss. Something must have hit the fan at a high rate of knots. The all-important meeting his boss had summoned him to would give him more than enough to think about in the coming weeks. Indeed, it would stretch the entire Avon & Somerset police to the limit, and the repercussions would send tremors across the country.

Chapter Three

DS Phil Hounsell joined the rest of the team in the incident room. The Assistant Chief Constable was present. It must be something big, Phil thought.

The rumour mill he was not a party to these days had already filtered news to several officers in the room. A few of them were his superiors, and even his close colleagues appeared to know more than he did.

Phil could tell by their ashen faces that at least one death must have been suffered on their patch. Maybe being ignorant was a good thing. While a few late-comers drifted in, he wondered what this all-important incident could be. If it was another ram raid, they weren't talking about a few dozen designer bags or a couple of trays of jewellery.

As soon as the ACC began to speak, Phil sensed that sickening feeling everyone experiences when receiving terrible news. It was terrible.

The story began a few weeks earlier in Maidenhead, Berkshire, but the police were oblivious to that fact at this stage. Their officers were merely looking at the first violent attack the successors of the ram-raid gang had carried out.

The five members of that original outfit were English nationals who had been in and out of trouble with the law since they were teenagers. Year in and year out from the early nineties, they turned their hand to various sorts of thieving, mixed results — eighteen months in prison, two years on the outside, and another spell in prison. They are just thieving, never any violence against the person. They used a few harsh words, perhaps to keep the victims in line, but neither listed an ABH or a GBH anywhere on their CV.

They were on a slow road to nowhere. No qualifications to mention unless you count getting into your car inside ten seconds, quick getaway driving skills and being able to strip the lead off the church roof in the time you knelt indoors taking communion. Deep down, though, if you asked the police officers who regularly met up with them, they would tell you they might be career criminals who could be a bloody nuisance, but there was no actual harm in them.

The gang didn't deserve what happened.

They had disappeared two weeks ago, straight after the Taunton job.

Several pairs of eyes had been following them for a while. The watchers soon established the gang's *modus operandi*. They were impressed with the outbuildings they rented from a local farmer near Windsor. The farmer welcomed the money; it saved him from thinking of diversifying for a while. As usual, times were hard for farmers; if it wasn't the English weather, then the European Union and its constant interference were blamed. He didn't know what the lads used his outbuildings for, and he cared even less.

The gang assembled a fleet of stolen vehicles ranging from family saloons with quite a few miles on the clock to high-performance, top-of-the-range luxury brands in one building. They cherry-picked from their stock. They select an alternative model for each trip along the M4 to join the M5 and pay a lucrative visit to a different West Country town on each occasion. A trip to ram a shop front, first make a quick getaway, then switch to a more comfortable ride on the way home.

They used up two cars on every job, one left in the shop during the raid itself, and the other burnt out after the rapid transfer back to the motorway. They wanted a continuous delivery of expendable transport. That was where the second outbuilding came into its own. They kitted it out with everything they needed to run a 'chop shop'. There were always friends in the game that wanted to offload stolen cars. So the ram-raiders set up a ready supply from the London region. It proved to be a lucrative trade.

The gang did a rapid turnaround on cars left with them, and after good clean-up and welding, they generated dozens of untraceable vehicles. Several got sold on to contacts overseas in Poland or the Czech Republic; others became available for those quick trips to the seaside to snatch trays of bling or carry home an ATM to open in the outbuilding at their leisure.

Bulgaria has been a member of the European Union since January 2007; the British government placed transitional restrictions in force over the years, and now many thousand live in the London area. In its naïve appreciation of the real effects of unrestricted immigration, the English authorities imagined these newcomers to be either students or hardworking individuals seeking to improve their lot. Unfortunately, that naivety resulted in many innocent lives lost in this case.

Organised crime in Eastern Europe isn't something new.

Across the region, groups are involved in various activities, including trafficking drugs and humans, kidnapping, prostitution, extortion, car theft and the arms trade. For example, three years before the EU, in its wisdom, agreed to admit Bulgaria and Romania, there were more than one hundred organised crime groups in Bulgaria alone.

Among those who travelled to the UK for a fresh start were five men in their late twenties. Arriving separately in 2011 and 2012 with other family members, they soon got in contact with one another and resumed the activities they were involved in back home.

Dimitar Marinov, Iliya Todorov, Nikolay Iliev, Georgi Bonev and Zlatko Yankov were thugs. The five men bore the traditional 'look' of a 'mutra' or mafia mug. Sturdy and muscular build, they favoured close-cropped hair and wore expensive dark suits with lots of gold jewellery. They drove around in flash cars. These things don't come cheap, even in the UK, and somehow these five found the funds to manage this without apparently having full-time jobs.

By the summer of 2013, the gang became well-established in the trafficking trade of drugs and girls. They were amazed at the appetite for both that the British public demonstrated. Once a thug, always a thug, Dimitar Marinov decided that he wanted a bigger slice of the pie. He felt it was time to up the ante. After a couple of years in the UK, he considered the police and the courts ineffectual. Indeed, he learnt that the whole system was on a tipping point and on the verge of falling apart. He reckoned that he was ready to introduce the UK to a few activities that worked so well for his fellow criminals back in the old country.

Once Dimitar and his colleagues established the routine for the ram-raid gang using the outbuildings at the farm, they moved in on them. However, as the ram-raid gang prepared their vehicles for the next job, they were interrupted by the sound of the arrival of a JCB mini-digger. At first, they thought it could be the farmer and started to think of answers to his anticipated questions about what they did with his premises.

Four other men emerged silently behind them, and as the poor devils stared at the driver of the digger, checking out his suit and dark glasses, a volley of bullets from silenced automatics quickly dispatched them.

"Start digging, Nikolay," ordered Dimitar Marinov.

The compact mini-digger set to work; one advantage of having lots of spare cash, legally or otherwise, is that you can lay your hands on just the right piece of kit for the job you need. Dimitar knew that the one-tonne digger wouldn't attract much attention from the farmhouse, as that was quite a distance from the barns. He knew, too, that it was more than capable of digging two metres into the barn floor. So it was ideal for the task despite the space restrictions. Moreover, the bodies could disappear efficiently and with a slight delay.

Phase one of his plan was complete; he and his gang now controlled the transport section of the now-defunct ram-raid gang. Phase Two of his project could begin.

Clevedon is a beautiful Victorian seaside town overlooking the Severn estuary. It takes around one and three-quarter hours to drive there from Maidenhead. So Dimitar chose two high-performance cars now at his disposal, and he and Iliya Todorov drove the gang members towards their first target.

They weren't looking to visit the old Pier or stroll along the seafront; none of the many attractions entertained visitors to Clevedon throughout the year held any interest.

Instead, these day-trippers were interested in one particular spot, The Triangle, where branches of several banks stood within yards of one another.

The gang brought along extra enforcers for the ride. Anton Dobrev and Boris Tsankov were both experienced assassins. A little older than the rest of the gang, they were already responsible for over twenty kills between them in the mid-1990s back in Bulgaria.

They made the drive from Maidenhead to Clevedon in silence. When they got closer to Junction 20 on the M5, Dimitar Marinov checked with his passengers that they knew what to do. He then called Iliya Todorov and told him to brief his fellow gang members.

The two banks were struck simultaneously at ten-fifteen in the morning. Dimitar and Iliya remained outside in the cars while the enforcers separated. Anton Dobrev followed Zlatko Yankov into Lloyds Bank, while Boris Tsankov accompanied Georgi Bonev into the NatWest Bank branch a few yards further up the road. The four men donned balaclavas as they strode quickly to the doorways.

Nikolay Iliev stood on the pavement between the branches, poised, watching the cars, ready to act if a traffic warden or a policeman arrived on the scene.

As soon as the doors burst open and the gangsters burst into the bank, each man grabbed a customer and started shouting. They ordered the handful of other customers in the banking hall to lie face down on the floor. The men told them not to utter a sound. Next, gang members held guns to their hostage's heads and shouted at the counter staff to open the security door. They told them to stand away from the tills and that they would start shooting if anyone pressed a silent alarm.

Within two minutes, they had access to large amounts of

cash. Nobody behind the counter wanted to be a hero. It wasn't their money. Zlatko and Georgi left the two assassins in the banking halls to watch the panicked and frightened customers. The two thugs swept up as many notes as they could and prepared to leave. It wasn't about the money. Their orders had been to get in and out as quickly as possible. This raid's message was always the most critical element of this trip.

Zlatko and Georgi then stood at their particular bank's door and glanced out. All appeared quiet so far. Then, following Dimitar's instructions, they nodded towards their comrade inside the branch. The assassins shoved their hostages to the floor and opened fire.

The rattling sound of their Uzi's as they raked the banking hall was deafening.

Seconds later, the four men were leaving. The two cars purred into position to pick up their passengers. Anton and Zlatko exited the Lloyds branch when a girl from the jewellers around the corner arrived to pay in Monday's takings. She screamed as Zlatko cuffed her with his pistol and grabbed her cloth bag containing close to two thousand pounds. Every little helped.

Boris and Georgi left NatWest without anyone else getting in the way. Nikolay Iliev remained fully alert as he watched his colleagues piling into the cars. He saw a PCSO shuffling along the pavement and spotted that she started to take an interest in what was happening. Claire Ricketts was forty-three, overweight, and married with two teenage children that would miss her. She had been doing this job for only twelve weeks.

Claire took three bullets to the chest and fell against a charity shop window staring blankly across the road.

She found time to call for help; but she never worked

out why a young girl was sobbing her heart out on the steps of Lloyds Bank, wiping blood from her forehead,

A few morning shoppers stopped and stared when four hooded men ran to two waiting cars across the street. They watched as another big man in a suit, wearing sunglasses and waving a gun, ran towards the first car and got dragged into the back seat by a passenger. The vehicles were on their way out of Clevedon before Claire Ricketts was checked over by a volunteer staff member from the charity shop. The gang rejoined the M5 before any police vehicles or ambulances arrived on the scene. Local officers were shocked to find one of their colleagues dead on the pavement.

At Lloyds and NatWest, the banking halls were scenes of carnage. The walls and ceilings were pock-marked with bullet holes. The glass partition that separated the public from the staff lay in smithereens. Management and bank clerks wandered around, shell-shocked and traumatised. All they could see in front of them on the floor in each branch were dead and wounded customers.

When the emergency services finally entered the banks, they were as stunned as those inside, still standing at only a few minutes after half-past ten. Then, gradually, their training kicked in, and a degree of control was established.

Portishead Police HQ stood less than twenty minutes away. The local station received updates from their officers on the scene, and news of the double strike on the seaside town was eventually transmitted to the region's senior staff. As the full details passed to the ACC and others, Dimitar Marinov and his gang had travelled more than a few miles on their way back to Maidenhead. Finally, after eleven o'clock, DS Phil Hounsell and the others in the incident room heard the latest information on the casualties.

The ACC reported that a violent and ruthless gang struck two banks in The Triangle, Clevedon, around forty-five minutes ago. The cash stolen had been estimated at less than eighty thousand pounds. The men involved were heavily armed. Those inside the banks spoke with Eastern European accents; they wore balaclavas and dark casual clothing. Despite the staff from both branches cooperating fully with the shooters' demands, they murdered five customers and injured seven more. Another gang member in a dark suit and sunglasses shot dead an unarmed PCSO as he made for one of the two getaway cars. A BMW and a Lexus left Clevedon at speed in the direction of the M5.

Checks were being carried out in both directions, north and south. More searches would be undertaken in neighbouring forces to track journeys made by this vehicle heading for South Wales, the Midlands, or London via the M4. At this stage, there were no clues to the registration of either car. Nor did anyone have a reliable description for either of the perpetrators.

Phil Hounsell knew several things without venturing to suggest any of them to his overwrought ACC. Firstly the two cars would have split up as soon as possible. This crew wasn't going to be conveniently travelling in convoy, inviting the police to arrest them. Secondly, at least a million BMWs drove on UK roads, if not considerably more. Stopping each one that traffic spotted on the motorway network wasn't an option. You might be lucky to spot a pair of hoods in a Lexus because there were only a couple of hundred thousand of those currently on the roads. Even so, Phil wouldn't want to bet on traffic finding the right car. What a nightmare.

As Phil surmised, Dimitar Marinov and Iliya Todorov had kept well apart on the motorway. They only stopped on the highway until the next junction and headed across the country towards Swindon. Dimitar stayed on the A4 until he reached home territory. The BMW safely tucked away in the farm outbuilding well before one o'clock.

Iliya drove the scenic route via Cirencester and Oxford, which took somewhat longer, but the Lexus was extremely comfortable to ride in, so his passengers never complained; in fact, they slept most of the way home. Once they arrived back at the bar they used as a meeting place, Dimitar ran through their morning's work.

"The seventy or eighty grand we picked up will be useful," he grinned ", but the real payback from this attack might be the millions we could extort from the Head Offices of the two banks. We may need to find a computer genius to contact the main men at the top. Then we tell them what it will cost them to stop us from carrying out further attacks. They won't know where or when we will strike. What they know for certain is that we'll not think twice about killing people on their premises. Not paying up wouldn't be sensible."

"Do you believe it will be that simple, Dimitar?" asked Nikolay Iliev. "The police will lie in wait next time we go to Clevedon."

Dimitar laughed. "You fool, Nikolay, no wonder you only stand guard and dig holes for me; thinking isn't your strong point, my friend. We won't be calling on Clevedon again. We might hit Bridgwater or Cheltenham next. Somewhere with more money and more customers."

Dimitar told his team to enjoy their evening. To spend the money that he gave them wisely. He would contact them when he had planned the next attack in detail and everything was set to go. He told them not to worry about the police. They wouldn't be bothering them from the few scraps of clues they left behind.

At Portishead, the ACC emerged from the HQ's building to talk to the press around lunchtime. The media were all over the carnage, not just locally; this was worthy of national and international coverage. Personal stories of those that died were slowly emerging, with details of injuries suffered by those lying in hospital beds across the region. One or two were serious, others merely walking wounded and capable of being interviewed. None of the injuries appeared to be life-threatening.

Claire Ricketts' family sat at home grieving, with the League of Nations journalists on their doorstep. But, unfortunately, the nearest and dearest of the murdered PCSO weren't up to giving them any sound bites for their readers or viewers. Instead, the press hung around like vultures hovering over a corpse in the desert.

Zara Wheeler soon discovered that her interview with the Divisional Commander and the ACC was on hold. When she heard the reason for the postponement, she knew that it wasn't anything to get annoyed or frustrated over. What happened at Clevedon was horrible. Something that rarely occurred in the UK. Dunblane, Hungerford or a motorway crash in the fog created this degree of hysteria. The London bombings in 2005, the terror attacks at the Olympics, or the Royal visit to Bristol last November.

It was hard to accept that the death of one or two people practically anywhere in the country on any given day of the week didn't warrant too much media attention. But, once it started to get near double figures and beyond in an incident, the public sat up and took notice. On those days, life didn't get treated so cheaply.

Zara continued to prepare for Friday and her leaving

party; she contacted her closest colleagues and arranged a venue. It might have seemed callous to her friends if the men and women she talked with had been members of the public, but police personnel dealt with the emotions of loss and horrific incidents such as that being experienced a few miles up the road far too often.

Sometimes a few drinks with a friend leaving to have a baby did the trick. Maybe an old hand retiring after many years of service merited a trip to the pub. A few glasses to get over all the stresses and strains of the job was often the best tonic.

As the working day drew to a close, she walked to her car and drove home to Bath. She spotted that Phil's car remained on site. The bosses would be there for a while dealing with the fallout. Zara wondered whether Olympus might have an answer to a problem such as this. Would they be dealing with it already? She elected not to ask Rusty tonight; he was at Larcombe and unavailable for a few days. He was giving her space.

Zara rang her parents as soon as she got home. She arranged to stay with them in Durham for a short break. Zara decided to travel up to see them late on Saturday afternoon. There would be no point tackling that five-hour drive until her head cleared from the wine she would undoubtedly have on Friday evening. Instead, she wanted to use that space and time in Durham, with her loving family around her, to put her police career behind her and find out if she was ready to commit to an exciting, somewhat uncertain future with Rusty.

Chapter Four

Wednesday, July 10th, 2013

At the Olympus Project HQ at Larcombe Manor, morning meetings differed little from when Erebus was in charge. Athena and Phoenix were now at the head of the table, with Annabelle Grace Fox firmly in control.

The three senior Larcombe residents, Alastor, Minos and Thanatos, occupied the seats on the window side of the long table. They generally arrived earlier than the other attendees. As they lived in quarters within the old manor house, it gave them a head start, but it was more than that; Athena knew these three well. They enjoyed being in the appropriate position when Giles Burke and Henry Case turned up from the ice house loaded with data gathered over the past twenty-four hours. They aimed to continue to confirm their superior standing in the organisation, justified or otherwise. Phoenix watched this charade each morning with an amused expression on his face.

Athena understood what Phoenix was up to; she knew

what game The Three Stooges played. However, it was the five attendees of the meeting themselves who were nonplussed. When Phoenix wasn't scowling or deadpan, it unnerved them; it didn't seem natural.

"Good morning, gentlemen," said Athena. "Can I have your reports, please?"

Minos, the former High Court judge, opened the morning's business.

"The European Court of Human Rights has ruled that whole-life tariffs breach a prisoner's human rights. Eventually, such sentences have to be reviewed because the judges have declared that not having any possibility of parole was inhuman or degrading. But, of course, our government has criticised the ruling; the verdict stands, but they have six months to consider their response."

"Surely this wasn't what the authors of the human rights conventions envisaged?" asked Phoenix. "This is another asinine intrusion by Strasbourg on our ability to make the punishment fit the crime."

"On top of sticking their noses in over the deportation of Abu Qatada and giving prisoners the vote, it does cause you to wonder who's running the country," said Alastor.

"I think we have the answer to that," muttered Henry Case, "and they don't live over on this side of the Channel."

"If my sums are correct, the best part of fifty people might profit from this ruling," Giles commented.

"That is our understanding at this point, Giles," said Minos. "One can only imagine the public outcry when the names of those who might see the light of day outside a prison cell become general knowledge. Sutcliffe, Bamber, Brady and even Rosemary West might get parole hearings."

"Anything else on the legal front, Minos?" asked Athena.

"Not today," he replied and sat back in his chair.

Thanatos spoke next.

"I'm sure we were horrified by the events of yesterday morning in Clevedon. What we might imagine being a 'big city' crime carried out in a small seaside town less than forty miles from our doorstep is shocking. What data have we gathered so far on who may have been responsible?" He directed that question towards Henry Case and Giles Burke.

"Very little that one might call 'concrete' information, I'm afraid," said Giles.

Henry Case continued. "We are re-doubling our efforts to secure the relevant CCTV footage. All our attention in the ice-house focuses on this matter for now. Giles has access, for instance, to the number plate recognition programs used by our police services. We tracked no discernible suspicious mobile phone activity in the Clevedon district yesterday. The gang kept communication to an absolute minimum."

"This was well planned and professionally executed," said Giles. "If we have an Eastern European criminal organisation operating within the UK, they will have surfaced earlier. Somewhere in our data banks, we shall find the tiny threads of detail that will lead us to their door."

Phoenix glanced at the two intelligence officers. He hadn't thought about it previously. It might appear odd to an outsider that Olympus relied on a Burke and a 'Head Case' to run their intelligence section, but these blokes were good. He was confident they would find clues the police didn't. He longed for the day he led a group of agents to take these killers out. But, unfortunately, that day couldn't come soon enough; he'd spent far too long sitting around on his hands, waiting to get into action.

As he half-listened to Alastor, inquiring whether anyone knew what had happened to the ram-raid gang active in the same area over the past year, his mind switched to Zara Wheeler. Phoenix knew she was as sharp as a tack. Her brain added to the mix over in the ice-house would be very interesting indeed.

How would the boys take to having a female in their midst, he wondered? There was always something to consider when you held a position of responsibility. He craved the good old days when all he needed to think of was how to get rid of the next person on his little list.

Phoenix concentrated once more on Henry Case's response to Alastor's question.

"Regular forays took place somewhere in the Home Counties by a group of thieves, who used crude methods to obtain cash and goods over a lengthy period. We didn't pay them too much attention as they didn't commit crimes we consider to be within the Olympus remit. There's nothing to suggest this latest attack has any connection, whatever. This new outfit might even emanate from a different part of the country for all we know at this stage."

Phoenix now became fully engaged. He thought for a few seconds.

"Except for one similarity, Henry; the top of the range motors they used to get from A to B as quickly as possible. I appreciate that there are loads of Beemers on the roads these days, but coincidences bother me. So, Giles, can you look at the CCTV and ANPR data for the times this ram-raid gang carried out their raids and satisfy my curiosity?"

"Certainly. Phoenix," said Giles.

Athena decided the intelligence section needed to be back at work sooner rather than later. She suggested they return to the ice-house to follow up on suggestions the morning session yielded.

When the five senior staff were alone, she discussed the

first meeting in London with the top people in the organisation. That was on Friday, July 19th. It would be her first meeting as Larcombe's head. Plus, the first opportunity for Phoenix to be present.

"Do you know what's on the agenda?" asked Thanatos.

"It will mostly be a meet and greet," said Athena. "Erebus never received a written agenda; nothing is ever committed to paper. He received a phone call roughly two weeks beforehand inviting him to attend. He got another message twenty-four hours before his trip to London, relaying only a few keywords. Secrecy is paramount. I have learned the time and place, the dress code and that I may be accompanied by my plus one on this occasion."

Phoenix raised an eyebrow.

Athena smiled. "Sorry if you're miffed at being described as my plus one, Phoenix, but everyone here knows of our situation. Also, Erebus informed our superiors we were a couple and now shared the responsibility for Olympus matters here."

"No, Athena, it's not that when you mentioned a dress code. I hoped to wear the Rory Gallagher t-shirt and blue jeans you bought me for our Glastonbury weekend."

"Ah, you might need to keep those for another occasion. But, then, you will be suited and booted, and I shall wear one of my best dresses."

Phoenix groaned.

"Let's move on," said Athena. "Rusty is missing from this morning's meeting. We've sent him on a fact-finding mission this week and next. There are two reasons for this. First, his partner leaves her present job on Friday. She is taking a week's vacation; she will decide whether to throw her lot in with Olympus here at Larcombe during that break. If she does, she and Rusty will live in their quarters in the stable block, and she can start work in the ice-house. Second, her focus will be to develop our cyber-intelligence strengths together with Giles Burke. This mission is partly to take his mind off that situation and to give us a closer insight into the exploitation by landlords of migrants in areas such as Slough and Ealing."

"How much do we know about this woman?" asked Minos.

"How much does she know of Olympus, more to the point?" bridled Thanatos.

"Rusty trusts her," said Phoenix, "that's good enough for me. I prefer concentrating on what Rusty investigates in the big, bad world."

Athena allowed a few moments to pass before she continued.

"It is estimated that they have three thousand people living illegally in the borough of Slough alone. Our thermal imaging cameras have flown over that borough and several neighbouring council boroughs in the South East to confirm that the incidence of suspected illegal dwellings is fast becoming a significant problem. Outbuildings often don't need planning permission as long as they meet size restrictions and are *not* for sleeping accommodation. Snap inspections are forbidden. Councils must give twenty-four hours' notice before inspections, meaning landlords have ample time to remove evidence. If caught, the fines are only a fraction of the monies they can make from the rents they are charging. Any law-abiding residents who get fed up with such over-development in their area and seek to move away soon discover that their house value has been adversely affected because of the problem. The odds are that the only prospective buyer of their property will be a landlord eager to convert their home into another multi-occupancy money-making machine."

"If this is rife in the South East, then that suggests many individuals are involved. So how can direct action by Olympus be deployed to make a difference?" asked Alastor.

"The government position appears optimistic, even in the face of a hopeless situation. Local authorities want more controls placed on landlords. The response from the government is that the councils have enough enforcement powers to cope with matters. We believe that as councils face further stringent cutbacks, minimal constructive action will occur as things stand. Rusty will report back with what he discovers at the end of next week, and we will decide whether Olympus can remove a handful of the main players."

"Happy days," said Phoenix quietly.

After a few minor issues concerning the movement of agents around the country to carry out investigative sorties, Athena brought the meeting to a close.

"It's too quiet, Athena," said Phoenix when they were alone.

"Not in Clevedon, sweetheart," replied Athena, "that development concerns me. It begs the question when you consider the sum of money they might have stolen using different tactics. The violence was unnecessary."

"I see what you're driving at," mused Phoenix. "I was getting too snarled up with the ram-raid gang and how they fitted into this if indeed they did. Maybe the cash wasn't the main thrust of these attacks? Surely they don't think they can hold a major bank to ransom? So how would they send their demands? I suppose uploading a video to YouTube might be the modern method. More modern than sending a letter through the post made up of letters and numbers cut from newspapers and magazines."

Athena gave Phoenix an old-fashioned look. Why was he always so flippant, especially on such a serious matter?

Athena sighed and added, "My biggest worry is that if extortion is their aim, then an attack on two banks in Somerset won't be a powerful enough message to elicit a national response, even though it resulted in the deaths of six people. There will be more strikes, and the next one is only days away, another murderous raid that could occur anywhere in the country and on any target. We cannot assume that financial institutions alone are at risk. No matter how good our intelligence section is, we are as blind as a bat, along with every police authority in the UK."

Phoenix stood up and walked to the window. He looked out over the lawns and spent several minutes thinking.

"I wonder what Erebus would have done?" he asked.

"That's the first time we've resorted to that thought since the dear old gentleman left," said Athena, joining Phoenix by the window. She considered the photograph of Erebus with his wife Elizabeth that she had placed on the table. The picture showed them while they honeymooned in Ibiza.

"He would have demanded to know more than the police. Giles would have searched high and low for the tiniest of clues to the identities of these gangsters. Finally, he might have asked Henry Case to send a team out to lift a few known Eastern European criminals off the street so he could interrogate them."

"That's it," exclaimed Phoenix. "Let's assume that the activities of the ram-raid gang have ceased for now. Where did they get those cars that they used in the first place? Did they grab them themselves, or did they have another supply source, perhaps stealing to order? From what I've read, they drove a wide range of cars and vans, each being the right tool for the job. So I think it is more than feasible that they used outside help to get what they needed, don't you? If so, and they aren't making the West Country trips, what have their friendly car thieves been doing these past weeks? They're not the sort to go straight and apply for a retraining course or find a proper job. So I'm wondering whether this new outfit has diverted the ram-raid gang's delivery of vehicles for their purposes?"

"It's a long shot, Phoenix," said Athena, "but I agree it's worth pursuing. Let's ask Henry to search out a list of likely lads involved in this car trade sector. At first, we ought to concentrate on the London region. We can't be positive that this gang is operating from the capital, but on balance, it's the most logical home for our Eastern Europeans. That might seem facile, but we would have heard rumours before now if they had been in the UK for a decade. They're too well-organised and too ruthless to be new to the game. They must be relative newcomers and have managed to stay under our radar so far. My hunch is that we are searching for Bulgarians or Romanians. Those are countries whose people have been arriving in larger numbers every year since 2007 when they joined the European Union."

"I agree," said Phoenix. "They fit the vague descriptions of the thugs from Clevedon. Both in their appearance and the language."

Athena tapped the photo frame gently, "Thank you, Erebus; we've missed you."

Monday, July 15th, 2013

Athena's prediction that the next strike by the Eastern European mafia was only days away proved correct.

As she sat eating breakfast alone while Phoenix slept in, her phone vibrated on the table in front of her. It was the message she was expecting. The keywords that each Olympus leader would receive before Friday's meeting.

'Knightsbridge'. 'Churchyard regular'.

So the venue on this occasion was to be in Curzon Street, just a few minutes from her parents' London home, thought Athena. Then, a few moments later, Operation Yewtree popped into her head, and the jigsaw was complete. She decided to let Phoenix sleep. Plenty of time to fill him in on the details before Friday.

Athena finished her breakfast while considering what to do with him. She knew that he found this new phase in his life too quiet for a man who needed action to make him feel alive. It was a dilemma with which Athena was unfamiliar; she had to decide whether to send her beloved partner on a mission from which he may not return. How could she do that? Athena wanted him by her side now and in the future. The door opened, and a tousle-headed wretch slouched into the room.

"Ah, you've surfaced at last," she said.

"Is there any coffee left in that pot?"

Athena sighed; there must be a worthwhile task to find for the poor mite. Although, he would probably scare her half to death with the risks he'd take to complete a dangerous mission for the Olympus cause before he finally became helpful to her as joint leader.

As Larcombe Manor's residents eased themselves gently into the new week in Portishead, DS Phil Hounsell sat at his desk, arriving early, hoping for the best, expecting the worst.

He tried not to keep peering into the empty office where

Zara Wheeler had once worked. He had to face up to a future without Mouse as his sidekick. Naturally, he didn't receive an invitation to her leaving do. Toby Drysdale hadn't appeared yet to tell him how it went; Toby had less reason to be on this floor now that Zara had left. Phil realised there was little chance of hearing whether it had been a riot of fun and drunken laughter or a series of tearful farewells. Phil's career train was in the same siding as Zara had felt hers had been. Few people beat a path to his door to pass the time of day in amicable conversation. It generally involved a senior officer dropping by to chew him out again for failing to crack a case.

Phil told Erica on Saturday afternoon that Zara had quit her job. She asked where she would live and work next, but Phil couldn't help her. Finally, the couple agreed not to upset the children by telling them Auntie Zara wouldn't be around much anymore. Shaun and Tracey would be off school and on their summer holidays soon, so their active little minds were due to be fully occupied. With luck, the kids would have forgotten to ask after her by Christmas. Phil wondered whether he would be so fortunate.

Talking of good fortune, Phil thought, if he didn't get a break on the ram-raiders or this new bunch of thugs soon, he could be the next copper on this floor searching for a new job.

Dimitar Marinov shared none of the worries that Athena or Phil Hounsell faced that morning. Instead, he stood in one of the farm outbuildings on the outskirts of Windsor, checking that everything was in place for tonight. His team was heading for Cheltenham and a string of three supermarkets in the High Street. They planned on taking three vehicles on this occasion, each of them a seven-seater people carrier. The cars weren't particularly new, they couldn't get described as 'flash', but for this job, they were perfect.

Dimitar had no demand for luxury motors this afternoon; they would drive via Oxford, and if it took them ninety minutes or two hours, it didn't matter. They only needed to arrive safely and carry out the attacks. After that, they could make their way home more quickly if practical. After the raids, he planned to take the short route to the M5 from Cheltenham and head south to the M4 junction. Unfortunately, as they transferred to the London-bound highway, the three vehicles split up and lost themselves in plain sight as the busy summer evening traffic clogged the roads.

Dimitar had decided to leave Nikolay Iliev behind for this job. No need for anyone to stand guard on the High Street this time. Instead, they could use the Tesco car park and walk up the street to two other stores. He reckoned on twelve to fifteen minutes maximum to achieve their goal.

So far, he hadn't considered finding the right person to help him contact the bank authorities. He didn't want to risk bringing too many new people in on the campaign. There could be the risk of loose lips when you don't trust everyone in your group, like a brother. That was why he decided to switch targets to supermarkets for this attack. After that, there would be time enough to put other elements of his plans into operation.

Dimitar went through the evening's timetable for the benefit of the gang members, and then he added, "A summer evening means there will be plenty of shoppers. So there will be lots of easy targets, and it stays light later on mid-July evenings. There's little point in hiding dead bodies and spilt blood in dark corners. We want people to remember everything they see."

In the Lap of the Gods

With that chilling remark in their minds, the five men selected to join Dimitar on this raid knew what he expected of them. Andrey Pantev had been associated with Boris Tsankov in their home country and was rejoining his old ally. As a well-practised killer, he was on familiar ground. His driver would be Iliya Todorov. Tsankov was paired up with the head man Dimitar, while Konstantin Hristov had Zlatko Yankov as his driver. The men were heavily armed — the same as the Clevedon sortie.

After five-thirty in the evening, the three vehicles set off at five-minute intervals from the farm outbuildings. First, they cruised through High Wycombe and successfully negotiated the busy Oxford ring road. Then, one by one, they drove into Cheltenham, located the Tesco car park and parked in bays that gave them as speedy an exit as possible. Contact between the three vehicles must be by walkie-talkie only and kept to a minimum.

"We will leave at seven-fifteen," said Dimitar on the final transmission, "now... it's ten past seven. Check."

"Check. Check." Both drivers replied that they were in synch and their weapons equipped with full magazines and ready to go. There were no balaclavas on this job; despite the hot weather, the six men wore lightweight hooded jackets, dark glasses and baseball caps. The three enforcers hid their submachine guns in a bag for life that matched the supermarket they were visiting.

Dimitar Marinov left his vehicle with Boris Tsankov and headed for the supermarket doors at fifteen minutes past seven. Boris stopped at one of the stations and picked up a family-sized trolley, placing his bag at the bottom.

Andre Pantev and Iliya Todorov hurried up the High Street to the furthest target. Hristov and Yankov crossed the street to the doors of the smallest supermarket on their 'hit list'. The three pairs of gangsters used a family-sized trolley when they walked purposefully around the aisles. Each of the attackers raised the hoods of their jackets over their heads. They stacked high-value spirits, small electronic gadgetry and a few dozen CDs and DVDs in their baskets. Dimitar even found a stack of large bath towels that he threw into Boris's trolley.

Dimitar checked his watch. It was seven twenty-three; they would make their way towards the checkouts. He nodded to Boris, and the enforcer allowed Dimitar to push the trolley for a while. He retrieved his bag. Several staff members called for them to stop as they passed the checkouts and neared the exit. A security guard tentatively approached them and pointed towards the tills.

"You need to pay for those items, Sir," he began.

Boris Tsankov cut him in half with the burst from his Uzi.

Dimitar had been right about the aisles being busy with shoppers enjoying the warm summer evening. The locals came out in force, stocking up on drinks and planning for a barbeque weekend. He continued to push his heavy trolley out of the doorway towards the people carrier. In his wake, he heard screams and shouts. Then came the series of shots he'd been expecting.

"Music to my ears," he laughed. Inside Tesco's, Boris left three more people dead and seven wounded. He walked casually out of the store and joined his boss in unloading the trolley. Nobody attempted to stop him or follow him. Phones dialled furiously.

The local police station stood on the outskirts of town, and crime was low in this sophisticated corner of the world. It was why Dimitar chose it. He wanted people to experience the hell of living in a war zone and never know whether it was safe to go outside or not.

Dimitar ripped open the bath towel packaging and scattered a few towels over the goods in the boot. Then, he spotted his four colleagues trotting into the car park, their trolleys loaded with valuable items. He gave towels to each pair, and then he and Boris drove away. Within a minute, Todorov and Yankov drove behind them and headed for the M5 junction.

Dimitar Marinov picked up his walkie-talkie.

"Numbers?" he asked.

Zlatko replied first, "Five altogether. A couple might make it."

Iliya Todorov muttered into his unit next.

"We got loads of steaks and bottles of cheap wine. You gave us a crap store to rob. No TV's to pinch, nothing. Andrey visited two or three aisles to find someone to shoot. There was just one young girl on her own at the checkout. She screamed so much that Andrey put a bullet in her throat to silence the cow. No security, just a female manager in a booth. As soon as she picked up the phone, I shot her. So two dead definitely and three or four injured."

Dimitar grinned at Boris, "Poor Iliya."

He was still laughing as they merged with the traffic on the motorway.

They unloaded the people carriers in the farm outbuilding two hours later and wondered how much they had stolen.

"I reckon the goods from the three stores totalled less than eight grand," said Dimitar, "but the police and the citizens of Cheltenham won't sleep well in their beds tonight."

As they locked up and prepared to make their way back

to their homes in and around Maidenhead, Iliya Todorov remembered the steaks.

"Those steaks won't be any good if we leave them behind," he said, "we may as well enjoy them since we stole them."

Dimitar shrugged.

"Did you think to grab a bag of frozen chips while you hung around in Iceland, Iliya? No? I thought not."

Iliya carried the twenty-four sixteen-ounce steaks to his car, where his passengers waited for him. He had no idea what to do with them, but he wouldn't let good food go to waste. Finally, Dimitar Marinov and the others left for home. Dimitar was in a good mood. He wanted a drink and a woman. His passengers had to go along for the ride; nobody argued with Dimitar.

Tuesday morning promised another scorcher. Across the country, the sun shone, and temperatures soared. In Cheltenham High Street, there were few shoppers. Police had cordoned off most of the street. There were more members of Gloucestershire Constabulary in attendance than on Gold Cup day up at Prestbury Park. There had been police activity since around a quarter to eight last evening when phone lines had become unjammed long enough to contact the emergency services.

When they arrived, they faced scenes alien to the officers and paramedics unfortunate enough to be on duty.

The police officers' superiors at Quedgeley HQ had been called by their colleagues at Portishead as soon as they received news of the second attack. They had been expecting a strike on their patch. The officers knew precisely how they felt; hurt, angry and helpless. The supermarkets confirmed eight deaths, thirteen injured customers, three critical, and three serious. Public outcry gathered

In the Lap of the Gods

impetus. The local radio stations ran phone-ins throughout the day, and the local TV stations carried lengthy reports late last night and Tuesday morning.

"How can this happen here in Cheltenham?"

"Is it safe for me to take my kids to school?"

"Why? Why here?"

Nobody had the answers. Cheltenham and Clevedon weren't London, Birmingham or Manchester, where gang violence very infrequently surfaced on residential streets; this wasn't a large metropolis where terrorists from various quarters might concentrate a bombing campaign. Clevedon and Cheltenham, where the crime rate is low and rarely violent.

The question inevitably posed by one senior citizen from Minchinhampton who rang BBC Radio Gloucestershire summed up the mood: -

"What is this country coming to if gangs can turn up where they please, armed to the teeth to kill people without blinking an eye? Are we safe anywhere these days?"

If Dimitar Marinov had heard that broadcast, he would have laughed and clapped his hands. That was precisely the reaction he wanted; he was a psychopath. Instead, he had spent last night getting drunk and took two women to a hotel room where they partied until dawn. While the authorities and the media dealt with the attack on Cheltenham High Street, Dimitar was sleeping off the effects of his night into the early afternoon.

In the incident room at Portishead, DS Phil Hounsell listened to another debrief from the Divisional Commander. Avon & Somerset's police staff had committed as many of their depleted numbers as they could to tracking last week's attackers in Clevedon. They used every traditional method available to them. Plus, according to the TV shows that featured them, a few scientific tools were sure to get you the answers to the puzzle in front of you in less than fifty minutes. But, unfortunately, Avon & Somerset's detectives had come up with precisely nothing.

The killers had worn balaclavas inside the banks. Descriptions of the four men were vague and contradictory. However, there was a consensus that the main gunfire came from Uzi's; that was one helpful thing TV shows taught the man on the street to recognise. The ammunition used was standard 9mm, available in quantity through all criminal networks and possibly a few perfectly legal outlets.

Neither the car drivers nor the man in the suit who shot PCSO Ricketts was featured in any CCTV images. Interviews with the hostages and the injured victims yielded little. Sometimes a local copper can talk to a few contacts and come back to HQ and say, the word on the street is… In this case, these confidential informants could only offer a pathetic - they aren't from around here.

Phil gazed at a spot just above his Divisional Commander's head. Where would you look to find Eastern Europeans? Did they have a large community in Bristol that he had missed? Indeed it was logical to turn towards the capital. However, regardless of whichever country this mob emanated from, it was a good bet that most of them settled in London and the surrounding region. They had heard of streets paved with gold for donkey's years; it wasn't likely they made a beeline for West Bromwich or Exeter.

His boss droned on, but Phil was miles away. Why on earth might anywhere on the M5 be the starting point for the gang? That made no sense. If they drove from London and joined the M5, they could reach any destination in Somerset or Gloucester in a couple of hours. It might be possible for the ram-raiders if they were Brits, but not this mob.

"Do you have anything to add, DS Hounsell?" asked the DC, spotting that Phil was in a world of his own.

"In what respect, Sir," spluttered Phil.

"I propose we start patrols on the M5 carrying out rolling ANPR checks to see if we can't spot these cars the devils are using."

"An utter waste of time, Sir, with respect, even if we had the workforce, the vehicles and the budget for the equipment. They don't come from our patch or anywhere close. This mob comes from near London."

"Oh, really, and on what do you base this fanciful idea?"

Phil knew as soon as he opened his mouth, he would regret it. But he had committed himself. He was thinking on his feet as he had with Zara and, before that, with the ill-fated SOCA a decade ago.

"Because of their nationality. Since our borders have been open to more and more Europeans and other nationalities, three-quarters of every group that migrated here will have stayed in or around London. The gang has probably been there for around two years. They would have been arrested if they were active in day-to-day crime and not too clever. This gang has at least one member who is very clever indeed. I believe they've been establishing a criminal network, gathering strength as they recruit more migrants. We should work with the Metropolitan Police. See if they have any intelligence on gangs working with the trafficking and supply of drugs, trafficking, and supply of women; gangs that have been untouchable so far. We could check to see if there's any possibility there could be one gang they've suspected, but they have not identified so far. One rumoured to be hoping to branch out."

The room fell silent.

"Thank you for your input, DS Hounsell," said the Divisional Commander with a smirk.

Phil looked around the room. Most people stared at the floor; nobody wanted to catch his eye. But, strangely, the more he let his mind run loose on his ideas, the more he convinced himself he was on the right track.

The Divisional Commander had one more nail to drill into Phil's coffin.

"We will carry on with the actions I proposed. If these villains return to our patch, I trust we will find them. I am confident in our abilities as a team when we pull together in the same direction. The other neighbouring forces that may or may not have a part in this search will have to organise their response how they see fit."

The briefing ended, and Phil went back to his office. So that was how it was going to be on his patch. His bosses would cover their backsides by assuring the public they were doing everything they could to find the killers of Claire Ricketts and the others in Clevedon. But, for the Divisional Commander, the big picture only existed if he was on the front page of the Western Daily Press celebrating the news of a successful conclusion to this case.

That French phrase he struggled to remember a fortnight ago flashed in his brain. He wondered whether he should get a copy framed and hang it on the wall of his office.

Chapter Five

Friday, July 19th 2013

Athena chaired the morning meeting at Larcombe. It started promptly at nine o'clock and had to end within an hour. However, there were matters to discuss that couldn't wait. At ten, she and Phoenix would travel to London in one of the luxury cars from the Olympus transport section. The pair were then due to attend their first meeting with the others that comprised the twelve Olympians.

There were reports from Henry Case and Giles Burke on the Clevedon attack to be considered.

Rusty had sent a preliminary report on his investigation into the beds in sheds scandal in Outer London.

Minos had an opinion to divulge concerning the new threat that grew from the Clevedon and Cheltenham attacks. The number of dead and injured left the nation shocked and anxious. As the anxiety spread days after the second attack, the country took a deep breath and anticipated the next strike. Shopping centres reported footfall reduced by as much as twenty per cent. But, on the other hand, online retailers reported a surge in demand more akin to the run-up to Christmas.

Thanatos reported that the Prime Minister visited Clevedon yesterday morning and Cheltenham after lunch to reassure the public that these killers would get brought to justice. The local communities have the nation's sympathy as they cope with this tragedy, he said, and the public should not panic. 'This sort of attack is rare; it will not continue unchallenged.'

"Fine words and easy to say," said Phoenix, "but random strikes such as these are hard to stop."

"Anything further, Thanatos?" asked Athena.

"It is rumoured that with both attacks on their doorstep, the royal couple from Highgrove will be wheeled out for a visit sometime today."

Phoenix read through Rusty's brief report, and as Thanatos had exhausted his contribution for the day, he looked through his mate's primary findings.

'I interviewed a family who wished to move to a new house in Southall. While they viewed a property in one room, they discovered a young mother with two kids. They saw mattresses on the floor as there was no space to put in proper beds. Another family in a bedroom upstairs were in a similar position. Unfortunately, this overcrowding is happening across the boroughs. Walking around the streets near where they hoped to buy later that morning, I saw derelict outbuildings and a labyrinth of alleyways. I managed to scale a padlocked gate and follow one of the alleyways that led to three rundown garages. Each garage showed signs of being occupied, although nobody was home at that time of day.'

"I won't say I'm looking forward to Rusty's final report,"

said Athena. "But there's enough in this first draft to justify Olympus taking direct action against a few absent landlords. No doubt they're raking in the money while these poor souls live in squalid conditions. The risk of disease must be high; the safety aspect is not causing these landlords any sleepless nights. The chance of a fire breaking out in these overcrowded and dilapidated properties has to be huge. We cannot allow this situation to continue. We've got time to fit in a couple more items, gentlemen. What news from the icehouse?"

Giles Burke sat forward and appeared somewhat happier than earlier in the week.

"We found something of interest at last. I've lost count of the number of hours we've spent gazing at CCTV pictures of vehicles on the M4 and M5, plus any other main roads that adjoin them that may be relevant. We followed up on the suggestion that Phoenix made of the possible link between the ram-raid gang and the East European thugs; these two images might hold the answer."

Giles passed copies around the table.

"The first image is of a BMW 7 Series with a number plate issued at the end of the first quarter of last year. On the M4 close to Junction 15 on Wednesday, September the twelfth, it was around a quarter to five in the morning. The second image is a Lexus CT 200h travelling westward near Junction 10 on Monday, July the eighth, at eight thirty-two a.m. The dates are significant because a BMW of this description was involved in a ram raid last September, and the Clevedon attack last week included a Lexus. As you may make out, despite the grainy image, both cars carry the same number plate. It isn't possible because of the quality of the picture to identify the driver and front-seat passengers. What I would say is that the Lexus is carrying white males of the larger variety. The BMW has a short male driver with a large male passenger beside him with what looks like dreadlocks."

Phoenix was more than interested in this development.

"Brilliant, Giles. That confirms what I feared. The ram-raid gang were based somewhere this side of London and operating with an endless stream of cars they swapped around as they wished to cut the chance of detection. In the past six weeks, this Eastern European mob has taken control. God knows what they did with them. The two attacks show they won't have left any loose ends. Surely someone missed them? Families, friends, and even the local police, especially if they were career criminals. Can we follow up on that angle? I doubt it brings us any closer to naming the foreign gang, but if bodies are out there, finding them will, at least, bring closure to their relatives. When we return from this London trip, I want to go into this in more detail, Athena."

"We'll see, Phoenix," she replied, glancing at the clock on the mantelpiece. "We may have other more important things to follow up on after the meeting later today."

"It will need to be mind-blowing stuff to rank higher than wiping out this bunch of murdering scum," grunted Phoenix.

"We have very little time remaining," said Athena. "Alastor, we haven't heard from you yet this morning. Do you have any insight into the men who might be behind these latest violent attacks?"

"The raids suggested a high degree of detailed planning and were executed precisely and with zero compassion. That suggests a leader who is a sociopath or a psychopath. With so little data, one cannot decide which, but my hunch is that he is the latter. The rest of his gang will be merely puppets who will do whatever he asks. One interesting point I spotted on both occasions. Only one attacker was responsible for most of the gunfire in each theatre. That indicates their leader has several foot soldiers that have worked for him in other areas where violence is not the norm. Then, these attacks bring in extra assassins who have a long history of being paid assassins. It might help us to isolate the group's nationality and to piece together potential gang members from immigration records since 2011."

"There are a few things to follow up on from that, Alastor," said Athena. "Henry and Giles will add that to the list we're giving them."

"We'll cope, Athena," said Henry Case, "to bring you up to speed, I shall be receiving guests over the weekend. The men involved do not know they're coming to visit me yet. We've selected some dodgy car traders who may have dealt with our dearly departed ram-raid gang members. They will be able to shed light on the set-up; give us a clue when the ram-raiders disappeared, and with luck, what brand of Eurotrash we're facing here."

"You said 'will' not 'might', Henry," said Phoenix.

"Of course, Phoenix. I have total confidence in my powers of persuasion."

Phoenix prayed he never had to descend to Level Three in the ice-house for interrogation. He shuddered every time he recalled his first visit there with Erebus three years ago. He remembered that the dim ceiling lights died and flared with every metre he walked along the corridor to Hotel California. He stood at the end of the hallway with Erebus by the final door while everything remained in the darkness behind him. Phoenix would have gladly told Erebus whatever he asked. There and then, without Erebus needing to reveal the horrors within.

"Time for us to go, Phoenix," said Athena, bringing him back to the bright sunlit room and a haven. "Many thanks, gentlemen. Apologies yet again for having to cut things short but needs must."

Athena and Phoenix went to their apartment and prepared for their London visit.

"Will we be staying overnight, Athena?" asked Phoenix.

"Mummy and Daddy are enjoying the south of France sunshine at this time of the year. We can use the family home as our base. We can clean up there, get changed and take a taxi to Curzon Street for the meeting; then perhaps we can relax and enjoy ourselves over the weekend if there's no objection? I can get the transport people to pick us up on Sunday evening. I want to be back at Larcombe before Rusty and Zara move in together. It would be nice to welcome her personally, and it will give us a chance to debrief Rusty after his investigative mission."

"I have no objections to a day or two's quality time away with you, Athena; be aware that I know you're trying to occupy my mind to stop me from pining for proper action. But, unfortunately, Zara won't get the full tour when she arrives. Her key pass will only allow her access to the stable block, Level One in the ice-house for her work in the intelligence section, the cottages containing the canteen, and the swimming pool. As for debriefing Rusty, I should prefer to do that if I may; I think we should meet in the orangery where the old gentleman and I met. It's where we bonded, and I always thought of it as a special place."

"Certainly, darling, whatever you say. Yes, I agree with your thoughts about Zara. We can review her access restrictions in due course. As for the itch you need to scratch, please be patient. I am trying to identify a proper mission, but you must appreciate that I can't risk losing you."

"We'd better get moving; any more of that talk, and we won't be out of bed in time for the meeting tomorrow, let alone today," said Phoenix.

Within minutes, they were packed and ready to leave. The car waited for them outside the front door of the old manor house when they descended the stairs with their bags. As they drove smoothly along the long curved driveway towards the gates, they began to relax and sat in companionable silence. Both were anticipating their first Olympus meeting and what it meant for those that lived and worked at Larcombe.

Phoenix broke the spell first.

"What did you make of Alastor's interpretation of the leader of this foreign mob? You are undoubtedly more equipped to understand these things with your security services background than a simple man such as me."

Athens laughed.

"Let me see if I can answer that without upsetting you, my darling. A psychopath has a disregard for laws and social mores and a disregard for the rights of others. They fail to experience remorse or guilt and tend to display violent behaviour. Psychopaths cannot form emotional attachments or experience real empathy with others, although they often display charming personalities. They are manipulative and can easily gain people's trust. On the face of it, they appear normal to unsuspecting people and are educated and employed in steady jobs. When committing crimes, they carefully plan out every detail in advance and often have contingency plans."

"What are you trying to say?" said Phoenix.

"It's clear that you share personality traits, but we agree that you can form emotional attachments. Just because you are cool, calm and meticulous in your preparation for a mission, thinking of every eventuality, leaving few clues for the authorities to pursue, that does not mean you come from the same cloth."

"Thank goodness for that," said Phoenix.

As they travelled towards the M4 and London, Athena could not prevent her thoughts from staying to Alastor's other choice for the East European gang leader's classification. Was he a sociopath? How did that fit with Phoenix and what she knew of him? She understood that sociopathy is more likely the product of childhood trauma and physical/emotional abuse than nurture rather than nature. Because sociopathy appears learnt instead of innate, sociopaths can empathise in certain limited circumstances but not in others, and with a few individuals but not others.

What if the cocoon Olympus provided for Phoenix enabled him to form their relationship and develop a strong friendship with Rusty? Did he have any strong bonds that he shared with others at Larcombe? Not really; at times, he was dismissive of The Three Stooges or Three Amigos as he referred to them. Yet, she found herself thinking of them in those terms, something she had never dreamed of doing before Phoenix arrived.

There was no doubt that Erebus had penetrated that tough outer shell, and the two of them formed an unbreakable bond of mutual respect. Perhaps she worried unnecessarily. Something else more personal had troubled her lately, too; her period was late.

That was why she had suggested they stay over in town this weekend. But first, she needed to break the news to Phoenix. She had no idea whether he would welcome becoming a father again in his mid-forties, especially after the trauma surrounding the death of his daughter Sharron.

Athena didn't know how she felt about becoming a

mother for the first time in her late thirties. Until she started comparing those classifications for Phoenix that Alastor ascribed to the foreign gang leader, she hadn't remotely considered whether Phoenix might have the defective genetic makeup that a son or daughter of theirs might inherit. Her mind was in turmoil. So this crucial first meeting later today couldn't have come at a worse time.

Phoenix sat beside her with his thoughts. He didn't disregard the law; he believed in the rule of law. His problem lay with those who broke the law and then didn't get punished with what he considered the right severity level. He didn't feel guilty killing any of the people he had. Every single one of them deserved it. He took no pleasure in it; it needed doing. As for the meticulous planning, that was just common sense. If he planned his direct actions correctly, he guaranteed a one hundred per cent success rate. He wasn't prepared to accept less.

It was true he found it difficult to love someone after his experiences in his early years when his parents had denied love towards him, but he adored Sharron, his murdered daughter. He had loved Sue Owens, his second wife and cared for her when she got cancer until she died in his arms. He loved Athena now without question.

If someone asked him why he continued to want to risk death when he had a beautiful woman who loved him, Phoenix would grudgingly admit that it was because every person he had ever truly loved had died and left him. Yet, he kept putting his life on the line because he couldn't face that happening again.

"We've arrived, Phoenix," said Athena, nudging her partner

as he dozed quietly beside her. The car had arrived outside her parents' home in Vincent Gardens, Belgravia.

It wasn't the first time that Phoenix had seen the exterior of this house. Erebus had sent him to watch Athena just before a group of radicalised students had orchestrated a suicide bomb attack on Oxford Circus tube station.

Phoenix remembered only too well seeing Athena striding across the concourse and heading for a walkway that put her in imminent danger of being killed. She bought a few things to take to the hospital, where her mother was recovering from a major heart operation.

He hoped that this London visit would be more pleasant.

The Olympus driver carried their bags to the door, and Athena told him their weekend plans. He merely nodded and made a note to return to collect them at four o'clock on Sunday afternoon. With that, he set off on his way back to Larcombe Manor.

Athena and Phoenix freshened up and changed into their smart clothes.

"This collar's tight," moaned Phoenix, "are you sure I need to wear a tie?"

"I don't know why you complain so much," Athena replied, "look at yourself in the mirror. You're terrific. I'll have to watch the other female Olympians and ensure they realise you're off-limits."

"Oh, there are other women in the hierarchy, then? I imagined it as a mainly male domain," said Phoenix. He knew he was in trouble as soon as he opened his mouth.

"Why do you imagine this was a boy's only club? When Erebus made that first contact via the advert in the personal column of The Times, he focused on finding people with the same aims and ambitions as him. People who wanted

Britain to be Great again. The men and women who came forward were largely from families who could trace their ancestry back centuries and understood what Erebus sought. Although a few of the men who became our early financial backers have passed away, and their widows now hold the purse strings, the steel resolve required to regain the ground we have lost is as strong as ever, despite the gender change. A few of our numbers are those whom Erebus called the *nouveau riche*. I expect you to recognise their faces, but please don't ask for an autograph; that would appear crass. These people have amassed sizeable fortunes through the sporting or entertainment industry, and unknown to the public, they share the ideals of the Olympus Project. Erebus frowned on them somewhat, but the money they added to the coffers swayed his opinion over time."

"What makes Curzon Street so special?" asked Phoenix. "Why do Olympus go out of their way to get somewhere in a prestigious location if secrecy is paramount? Instead, we should hide in a gloomy old country house, miles from anywhere, so nobody suspected a thing."

"The London Executive Offices building is ideal for our purpose," replied Athena. "It's easily accessible for the vast majority of our leaders. Apart from one person who has to fly himself by helicopter from Scotland, I believe that we two have the farthest distance to travel. Remember, too, that the Project is ostensibly a registered charity to the outside world. So for a member of the public or a nosy journalist looking for a story, what more appropriate place could there be to see a national charity organisation holding their half-yearly meetings but in London?"

"We need to call for that taxi, Athena, if we don't want to be late," said Phoenix, consulting his watch.

"Yes, let's get over there and face the music. I'm nervous. I'm glad you're with me. Erebus gave me an insight into what to expect, how these affairs run, and who the other members are. But this is new territory for us, and it's scary."

"Did Erebus warn you of any potential enemies?" asked Phoenix.

"Why do you ask that?" Athena replied, looking puzzled.

"When we had those get-togethers in his rooms at Larcombe just before he retired, I sensed that he was implying there was opposition to us replacing him. That could have pointed to separate factions within the leadership. Perhaps not everyone around the table is singing from the same hymn sheet. I know you want me to be on my best behaviour today, Athena. Don't worry; I'll try not to disappoint. My role is merely to people-watch. I'll check for discord between certain parties and determine who might be for us and against us. More than that, in my opinion, Erebus subtly tried to point us towards the possibility that not everyone around the table still has the original Olympus goals at heart. I will look for evidence of that. We need to be on our guard."

Athena called for a taxi, and as they waited, she reflected on her thoughts as they had been travelling up from the West Country. Her life was changing in more ways than one if her suspicions regarding the pregnancy proved correct. She had hoped for a smooth transition from second-in-command at Larcombe and taking her place at the top table of the organisation. But, if Phoenix was correct, then intrigue and division might be what her future held; thank goodness she had Phoenix by her side to steer her through the stormy waters.

Phoenix gazed out of the window. A taxi pulled up near the pavement.

"Here we go," he said, and they left Athena's family home to make the ten minutes trip to Curzon Street.

Everything at the venue was as professional as you could ever wish. Phoenix and Athena followed the signs to the room Olympus had booked and entered to find a traditional boardroom layout that was furnished in an ultra-modern style. There were twelve comfortable high-backed chairs around the long, light-coloured wooden table; five chairs awaited each side and one at each end. The table had elegant small floral displays, water carafes, and attendees' glasses. Phoenix noted a total lack of any notepads, pens or pencils and no electronic equipment.

"This is very smart," he said quietly to Athena. He felt uneasy in surroundings such as this. However, it wasn't unaccustomed to such luxury.

"Check out the named cards on the table," she whispered back, "we're opposite one another at the far end from Zeus. Hera is next to us. Just remember that you mustn't reveal the identity of anyone who enters this room."

"Nothing to write with; nothing to write on," said Phoenix, "all electronic equipment removed. I suppose they will confiscate mobile phones in case I take a selfie with a pop star. Do you think they'll sweep the room for bugs before we start?"

"They did the sweep beforehand, I don't doubt," said Athena. "As for mobile phones, we'd better turn ours off now before anyone else arrives."

One by one, their colleagues gathered. They briefly welcomed Athena and Phoenix and made their way to their allotted chair as each person entered. The conversation was limited; once seated, the various leaders joined them, seemingly relaxed, and everyone waited patiently for proceedings to begin.

Phoenix studied the room intently to see where each arrival sat. Poseidon had arrived first. In myth, the God of the seas, Phoenix, couldn't believe he had ever sailed the high seas like Erebus. He was a refined-looking gentleman, well-dressed and in his late sixties. Poseidon had the demeanour of a banker rather than a sailor. His face was not familiar; his expression was so blank it was impossible to gauge what he was thinking. His hand had been icy and limp when they shook hands as he welcomed the two new arrivals to the Twelve Olympians. Poseidon's eyes were a piercing colour of blue, but no emotion showed in the briefest glances between them.

Hera and Zeus had arrived together. Athena was surprised by the warmth of Hera's greeting as she clasped her hand in hers and said how good it was to meet her.

"Erebus has told us so much about you, my dear Athena; we have high hopes for you in Olympus."

Hera merely nodded to Phoenix and swept away towards the others sitting at the table.

Zeus appeared much more cautious in his approach to both Athena and Phoenix. His welcome was cordial yet guarded. Athena chided herself for making snap judgements. Phoenix was in charge of the people-watching today; she should let him get on with it.

Phoenix found Hera and Zeus to be two peas in a pod, physically and in manner. He struggled to remember the particular attributes that Erebus had made him read up on for these characters from Greek myth. The supreme leader of Olympus and the lady who would be at the opposite end of the table to him were relatively short, perhaps five-foot-six and weighed in at around fifteen or sixteen stone. The couple looked no more than sixty years old. They gave the impression of being well-heeled bucolic farmers. Phoenix imagined they had vast tracts of land near the capital that had been in their families for generations.

A few details of the myth drifted back to him. Zeus and Hera were said to be both husband and wife and brother and sister. Phoenix shuddered. A simple tale of country folk indeed.

Phoenix did a double-take when the next woman arrived. She was a pop singer who had burst onto the scene in the mid-Sixties. A string of hit singles followed, and more than two dozen platinum-selling albums. She still performed today on worldwide sell-out tours. Phoenix had read she was worth seven hundred and fifty million. Husband number four was half her age and showing signs of fatigue.

When she approached Athena, you could feel the temperature drop in the room around them. There was the barest touch of a gloved hand on that of his partner, and then she turned towards him. In the seconds it took her to reach him, she had undressed him with her eyes. Phoenix swore he could hear her purring as she stroked his hand in welcome. It unnerved him.

"So, that is Demeter," whispered Athena as she slithered away, "I don't think she approved of me."

"Really? She appeared to take to me in a heartbeat," said Phoenix, earning him a look that should have turned him to stone.

The others came through the doors thick and fast, so introductions and welcomes had to be cut short. The meeting was due to start. Phoenix and Athena joined Hera at the foot of the table.

"You will have an opportunity to meet the remainder

later, Athena," said Hera, "Zeus will allow us to take a break later this afternoon for refreshments."

Hera turned to Phoenix.

"You must find this strange, Phoenix." she gushed. "You haven't been with Olympus long, and most of your time has been in the field, I understand?"

"Not strange at all," Phoenix countered, "it's very much as I expected. As you say, I have been active in the field, but I'm here today because Athena and I come as a package. So wherever she goes, I go from now on."

There was a distinct hissing sound from where Demeter sat further up the table.

"Time to get our meeting underway, ladies and gentlemen," said Zeus.

The following two hours flew by, and Phoenix soon found his mind in a whirl. Zeus controlled the schedule with a rod of iron. Phoenix tried as hard as he could to remember everything he had heard. He longed for a pen and paper or a tablet so he could take notes and refer to reports or financial statements later. Nothing said was recorded. No reports were distributed.

Zeus had the figures for the very healthy Olympus 'fighting fund' in his head and passed that information to his colleagues. Nobody questioned whether the data was accurate. It appeared that everyone took whatever Zeus said as gospel. The numbers were impressively large, and there didn't seem to be any shortage of donations.

Phoenix discovered there were still further contributors who stayed permanently in the background as well as the Twelve Olympians. They were never referred to by name. Their identifier was merely a number.

"Olympian number seventeen has transferred five million pounds into our accounts. We have sent her a message thanking her for her generosity." In addition, Zeus acknowledged several examples of extra funds donated to the Olympus Project.

Zeus moved on to give progress reports on direct actions around the world. These were brief verbal snapshots of what involved complicated and dangerous incursions by Olympus agents in Africa, Asia and Central America. Phoenix remembered how Rusty had schooled him in how to survive on missions such as those. If the need ever arose for him to work abroad. As it turned out, Erebus had kept him close by him at Larcombe. He had taken him under his wing. Today, listening to conditions in several theatres where other agents operated, he was very grateful to the old gentleman.

Phoenix wanted to ask Athena whether they had other centres similar to Larcombe Manor abroad. Although a few agents went on overseas sorties during his time at Larcombe, men such as Garry Burns and his team, for instance, were far from the norm. It suggested to Phoenix that there must be at least one, if not more, based on friendly foreign soil, from which direct missions could commence.

Athena hoped that the break for refreshments would come soon. It had been a while since breakfast. Neither of them had thought to grab something for lunch while they rested at her parents' home. She glanced across at Phoenix and caught his eye. Phoenix gave her a tiny grin and pretended to be falling asleep. As she turned back towards him thirty seconds later, as Zeus wrapped up the global review, she realised that Phoenix *had* fallen asleep. Hera was nudging him in the ribs.

"Let's take a break for half an hour, everyone. Refreshments are on the way to us in two minutes."

Whether Zeus saw what was happening or was alerted by the telepathic interaction between husband and wife, or brother and sister, was unclear. But the pause in proceedings gave Phoenix and Athena time to regroup, get coffee and cakes inside them and catch up with the people they hadn't met earlier.

Apollo was the sporting hero that Athena had intimated would be present. He was a former boxer who had fought for and won world title bouts in the Eighties. The enormous purses in the fight game made him a wealthy man. Apollo boxed smart with his money. Unlike many others who either didn't know when to stop fighting or to stop spending. He had invested in property and had amassed a fortune, at least ten times what he had earned in his career. Apollo was five or six years older than Phoenix, but he didn't show it. His handshake was painful.

A younger man approached Athena and Phoenix. He was in his early thirties; they recognised him from a string of funny TV adverts. As CEO of a mobile phone company, his worth was several billion.

"Hello there, I'm Hermes," he said, "it's good to meet you. I hope you're more comfortable now. The first time is the worst, isn't it?"

Phoenix shook his hand.

"You couldn't be anyone else, could you?" Phoenix said with a grin, warming to the young man.

"I'm glad there's fresh blood coming into the Project; the old fogies tend to plod along at a snail's pace. These meetings take forever to get through. I hope we get a chance to talk later. Are you staying in town tonight?"

Athena looked at Phoenix. She had been hoping for time alone. There was so much she needed to tell him.

"We are, Hermes," said Phoenix, "perhaps we can find

a place for an early evening drink and a meal. We won't stay too late tonight; we need our beauty sleep. We have plans for tomorrow."

Athena had to be content with that; thank goodness Phoenix had his sensible head on today. Zeus rounded up his flock. The meeting was to reconvene. Athena was eager to learn how Operation Yewtree had become an interest for the Olympus Project. What sort of characters Nemesis, Aphrodite, Heracles and Dionysus were and whether they were for them or against them must be put on hold for now. Their proper introductions might have to wait until the next occasion that Zeus summoned the twelve leaders.

Meanwhile, eighty-five miles away in Wiltshire, events were unfolding that would shatter the quiet Friday afternoon in the countryside and upset Athena's plans for the weekend entirely.

Chapter Six

Dimitar Marinov wanted to keep the authorities and the public in the state of high alert and panic that the first two attacks generated.

Families across the south of the country were winding down their working week, anticipating a great weekend enjoying the hot weather. But instead, Dimitar wanted to show them that no one could feel safe.

He and his crew gathered in their rented farm outbuildings and prepared to leave. Dimitar had never visited the county of Wiltshire before except to pass through it on the motorway. He imagined wealthy people lived there who enjoyed hunting, shooting, and fishing in the old days. The acres of green grasslands and wooded areas that flashed past his car window as he drove past influenced this impression. He could see few factory chimneys or palls of smoke to indicate signs of heavy industry.

Two four-person crews left the farm in battered old Land Rovers and headed west. Dimitar's driver today was Iliya Todorov. The enforcers Pantev and Hristov sat in the back as the miles clicked by, and Dimitar licked his lips at the prospect of delivering another murderous blow to the soft underbelly of the British people.

Five minutes behind them, Georgi Bonev had Zlatko Yankov as his front-seat passenger, and their firepower lay in the capable hands of Dobrev and Tsankov.

"Are you sure you understand what we need to do?"

Georgi eyed Zlatko as their boss's voice crackled through the walkie-talkie.

"Check," Zlatko replied.

"Are you happy with what we are doing today, Zlatko?" asked Georgi.

"We must go along with whatever the boss says," replied Zlatko, "what choice do we have?"

Georgi drove in silence the rest of the way via the M3 and the A303 to the small town of Amesbury.

The men behind him wouldn't think twice about putting a bullet in the back of his head if Dimitar thought he had stepped out of line. Or if he suspected one of his crew wasn't prepared to follow orders.

Georgi had been a gang member throughout his adult life. He knew no different, but there was a line he never wanted to cross. Dimitar had chosen the enforcers well. The men were as ruthless as he was, and neither of the four assassins had any line they wouldn't cross.

Dobrev and Tsankov, together with their counterparts in the rear of Dimitar's vehicle, would blindly follow whatever orders Dimitar gave.

The gang had been driving for over an hour when they pulled into a lay-by and drew up behind the first Land Rover. The final communication was by walkie-talkie as nobody left their vehicles. The summer sun left everyone in the cars boiling with no cooling breeze.

"There should be dozens of people drinking in the beer garden of the busy pub in the centre of town that I have selected as our target. You've seen the layout of the building from the drawings I showed you in the outbuildings. You will wear balaclavas. Make sure you keep the sleeves on your clothing buttoned to your wrists. It's hot, but we don't need survivors describing tattoos or other distinguishing marks. Is that understood?"

Dimitar heard nothing but grunts of agreement, as he had expected.

"Remember too that you ignore the staff and customers at the bars and eating areas. Move quickly to the rear of the building and attack the beer garden. Then you go straight over the fence at the rear, where we will be waiting in the Land Rovers to collect you."

"Yes, boss," came the response from the four gunmen.

A few minutes later, they pulled up in front of the large pub restaurant on the main street. Signs advertised the famous chain this old hotel belonged to in every window and on boards standing on the pavement. The pub was open from eight in the morning until midnight.

The masked men exited the rear of the Land Rovers and ran through the passageway that led to the beer garden — never looking left or right into rooms that contained many dozens of late afternoon customers. Plates of food were continuously delivered to tables by youthful staff members; the bar staff kept busy with regulars who stayed drinking most of the day.

Then there were the local self-employed workers who had quit grafting early today to swallow a few cold beers before going home. This summer weather needed enjoying while it lasted.

Seconds after they had left the Land Rovers, the men

burst into the sun's glare as it shone brightly on the crowded beer garden. Umbrellas festooned the grassy expanse of ground filled with ubiquitous wooden picnic tables. The tables held plates, glasses, bottles and cans. Everywhere people of all ages were having fun in the sun.

There were tables of young men swallowing pints of lager enthusiastically. Youths who paid no heed to the fact they would never get through to midnight unscathed at the rate they drank, even with the help of the burger and chips they were scoffing.

Elderly couples sipped glasses of something alcoholic with a mixer and several ice cubes. The conversation was much quieter than on the nearby tables, but most of it concerned the weather, and everyone wore a smile on their face.

Dotted here and there sat young mothers with children. Soft drinks for most of the mums, but with the occasional large glass of wine evident. The little ones had bottles or cans with fancy-coloured drinking straws. In between the tables, chubby little youngsters ran around without a care in the world. The children enjoyed the sunshine and fresh air until Mum decided it was time to get home after picking them up from school.

It was a scene repeated in towns and villages across the whole country that Friday afternoon. It had become something representing the British way of life. Dimitar Marinov planned to shatter this idyll forever.

As the Land Rovers made their way through side streets to take up their position at the rear of the beer garden, Dimitar and the others heard the initial bursts of gunfire and the screams. Forty seconds had passed since Pantev and his colleagues stepped onto the pavement outside the old pub.

When Iliya and Georgi reached their destination, the four masked men were clambering over the fence and preparing to jump into the back of the still-moving vehicles.

Dimitar looked pleased. As soon as Andrey Pantev and Konstantin Hristov safely climbed on board, Iliya drove them away from the devastated beer garden. The scene had been full of fun and laughter only ninety seconds ago. Then, as Georgi collected Anton Dobrev and Boris Tsankov, the driver offered a prayer.

A prayer for the poor souls murdered. A prayer of thanks, too, that Dimitar didn't ask him to join the assassins. Killing children was that step too far. There was no going back, even if there ever had been. The police would hunt them like dogs after this afternoon's attack. The nineteenth of July in Amesbury would become as 9/11 had become to the Americans: a date they would never forget.

His thoughts were interrupted by the squawk of the walkie-talkie. It was Dimitar.

"We will head for the M4 using the A34 to Newbury and should be home in ninety minutes. Andrey and Konstantin have reported a successful attack. Well done."

Georgi glanced in the rear-view mirror to check on Dobrev and Tsankov. They sat quietly, staring into space.

"A successful attack, yes?" asked Georgi.

"Carnage," said Tsankov in a guttural whisper, "the grass was almost red with the blood."

Nothing more needed to be said.

The name of Amesbury joined the catalogue of shooting atrocities in mainland Britain. It would rank alongside that of Hungerford, just twenty-five miles away and Dunblane, in far-off Scotland. In the meantime, Athena and Phoenix still sat in the Olympus meeting rooms on Curzon Street. News of the massacre filtered through to people around them in the outside world, but they were blissfully unaware of events in Wiltshire inside the conference room.

Zeus had switched attention to Operation Yewtree as soon as they had taken their seats after their refreshments break.

"Yewtree is an investigation into sexual abuse allegations, predominantly the abuse of children. Since last autumn, led by the Metropolitan Police Service, they assessed more than four hundred lines of inquiry. They identified hundreds of potential victims. These accusations cover four decades, from the late Fifties until the Eighties, and are national. There are many as yet unidentified predatory sex offenders. We have compiled a list of MPs and celebrities that warrant direct action. The Met are dealing with alleged abuse on an unprecedented scale. The high profile this Operation attracted encouraged victims to come forward to report the abuse they suffered during their childhood. As part of Yewtree, they questioned several people who have held public office and well-known celebrities. Criminal proceedings will undoubtedly follow, but sentences may not match the severity of the crime, and in many cases, their friends in high places will protect the abusers. We must not allow that to happen. We must find the guilty and mete out a punitive sentence."

"May I be permitted to ask a question?" asked Phoenix.

Zeus peered down the long table with disdain.

"I'm surprised someone with your field experience would query this course of action. You have a tremendous track record for Olympus of ridding the country of criminals who have persistently offended and somehow never faced justice."

"I have no problem with any men who are guilty of this

abuse paying the ultimate price, said Phoenix. "I have two queries. Firstly, Yewtree was a 'witch hunt' in a few quarters. Celebrities have been interviewed time and again. No concrete evidence has emerged so far to suggest they were ever involved in any cases of abuse. So are we one hundred per cent certain these people you mention are indeed guilty? Secondly, you stated you had compiled a list. That's an alien concept based on how we've handled things here. Athena instructed me that nothing should ever be in written form, yet what you said suggests Olympus has a 'little black book' of potential targets."

Athena saw that Zeus appeared flustered; perhaps, they had caught him. Both she and Phoenix were now on full alert. The two of them watched the reaction of the other Olympians to gauge whether their body language might show if they were a party to this breach of protocol.

Hera leapt to Zeus's defence straight away.

"I'm sure that was a slip of the tongue, Phoenix. Zeus merely meant that a few individuals had at first been implicated in this scandal and, for whatever reason, overlooked by Yewtree. After our exhaustive investigations, we identified those we were convinced were guilty. These men should face the courts; one might also argue that those who allowed them to avoid punishment should also suffer."

Nemesis shifted uneasily in her chair, and Athena noted that Poseidon was scratching the back of his neck and furtively glancing across at where Dionysus sat.

Hera's comments had given Zeus time to regain his composure. But, instead, he continued to press the case for Olympus to act against men not gathered in by the 'Met' under the Yewtree umbrella.

Athena knew that such action would be handed to

agents from Larcombe Manor to carry out. She wouldn't be comfortable with Phoenix and Rusty taking on such tasks.

One mission might not be hazardous in itself. For example, if a single guilty politician from the Seventies died in an 'accident', it was unlikely to cause much of a problem. However, a series of deaths of prominent people in a short period might be another matter altogether, and Larcombe and Olympus could find themselves under an uncomfortable spotlight.

The proposal involved too much risk, and she told Zeus so forcibly.

"Ah, the Goddess of wisdom has sharp teeth," snapped Demeter, "but perhaps her courage is tested where her partner is concerned?"

"The Olympus Project's true purpose at Larcombe has to remain secret at all costs," said Phoenix sharply. But, of course, he wouldn't let Demeter talk to Athena that way. "Athena is perfectly correct; this collective action would jeopardise everything you have worked for in the past seven years."

"I believe it's time for us to bring matters to a close," said Apollo.

Zeus spread his arms wide and smiled a smile that never quite reached his eyes.

"We can talk about this when we meet again. A lot of these men have waited decades for the axe to fall. We can wait a little longer to avenge those victims whose lives have been blighted by these animals. I'll be in touch with details of our next meeting."

Athena and Phoenix studied the others as they left the room. They noted who accompanied who; Hera walked close by Zeus, and Poseidon joined them. The female Olympians Demeter, Nemesis, and Aphrodite made a curious trio. Phoenix imagined they went their separate ways as soon as they got to the other side of the door.

Apollo left alone; Hermes made his way towards the end of the table to join them as arranged.

Heracles and Dionysus left the room deep in discussion. Still, Hermes had started chatting, so it was difficult for either Phoenix or Athena to tell whether they were in harmony or arguing.

"Right then," said the jovial Hermes, "where shall we go?"

Apollo re-entered the room. He seemed troubled.

"What's up?" asked Hermes, "forgotten where you parked the Rolls?"

"There's been another attack by this Eastern European gang terrorising the south of the country."

"Where this time?" asked Athena.

"Amesbury, in Wiltshire; they struck at a pub restaurant beer garden in the middle of town. They got in and out in less than two minutes. Eighteen men, women and children were killed; a further sixteen were injured, almost half severely. The youngest child who died was only fifteen months old."

"Evil bastards," said Hermes.

"We need to stop these guys," said Phoenix, "and fast."

"Sorry, Hermes, we're going to have to get back to Larcombe Manor," said Athena. She turned to Phoenix and gripped his arm.

"I'll arrange transport back to Bath, Phoenix and get up to speed on what the team has achieved so far in tracking these maniacs. Can you find us a taxi to Belgravia and we'll change our clothes there and then get packed and ready to return home? Everything else we had planned for this weekend will have to wait. Amesbury must be our top priority now."

Phoenix nodded and set off, Athena watched him leave, his jaw set, and she sensed his mind working overtime. He would be itching to get this gang as soon as possible. As Phoenix went outside the building to hail a cab, he was already ticking off a list of locations not to look for this gang. He had been right in assuming they came from the London region, almost certainly west of the city. For the third strike to be within ninety minutes of their likely base proved the clincher.

They just needed a break.

Athena clutched Phoenix's hand tightly when they sat together in the taxi.

"I'm sorry, darling, this weekend away hasn't turned out how I had planned it."

"Hardly your fault, Athena," replied Phoenix, "you weren't to know where and when this gang struck next. The sooner we get back to Larcombe, the better."

"The transport has already left. We'll have a couple of hours before it arrives. Let's discuss things while we wait."

Minutes later, they pulled up in Vincent Gardens. Once inside, it took them five minutes to change clothes and repack their bags. Athena stood quietly in the kitchen, brewing the coffee, when Phoenix walked into the lounge.

"What did you make of the meeting?" Athena asked as she joined Phoenix on the settee.

"Largely a waste of time," he sighed, "but there were a few interesting characters. I watched the dynamics of the group closely as we agreed, and there are distinct factions without question."

"I sensed a discord between certain members," Athena said. "Who stands in which camp, do you think?"

"Honestly? I don't understand as yet. Not everyone around the table is what they seem. At least two Olympians portrayed one face while masking their true intent."

"What on earth do you mean?" asked Athena.

"Let's put it to one side for now. It's complicated, and I need time to analyse every detail I spot. I just sensed, despite the positive way in which Zeus presented everything, dangerous waters lie ahead for Olympus."

"Go on, I'm intrigued," said Athena.

"Zeus is the unchallenged leader of the group. He has total control over the numbers," Phoenix continued. "When he reported on the Project's financial well-being, nobody questioned the figures at any stage. It's clear that whether it's financial, operational, or direct action proposals, Zeus has *everything* recorded somewhere. There's no way an organisation such as Olympus could operate without bank accounts for a start. There must be battle plans and lists of materials and budgets needed for missions across the globe; reports on their successes and failures must exist to improve plans for each subsequent mission. There has to be a black book of sorts despite Hera trying to pass off Zeus's comments regarding the list of suspected historical offenders as a slip of the tongue. However he has it formatted. As such, it has value. In the same way that if the financial or operational data fell into the wrong hands, the consequences would be catastrophic for Olympus."

Athena sipped her coffee and considered what Phoenix had said for a while. Then, finally, Phoenix stood up and walked to the window. They had ages to wait for the car to arrive. He was like a coiled spring. Phoenix wanted to act, not sit and talk about the people he had just met for the first time.

"I got the impression you warmed to Hermes?" said Athena, eager to discover what impression Phoenix had gained about the other attendees.

"Hermes is young and inexperienced. He's made a vast fortune in a short space of time. Whether he truly believes in Olympus and its ideals is up for debate. Zeus is happy for his money to be available for use by the Project, but I doubt he would take any notice of any comments or suggestions Hermes might offer. I think Hermes needs the adventure to balance the mind-numbing banality of the mobile phone business. Being an Olympian makes him feel he's arrived, that he's a respected member of the upper level of society. Nothing's further from the truth. Men and women like Zeus and Hera are from the landed gentry; their families have been on the top table of society for generations. They can spot new money a mile away, and no matter how big a fortune Hermes has, it won't help him bridge the chasm between them."

"I learn something new about you daily, Phoenix," said Athena.

Phoenix laughed.

"It's purely an observation based on what I saw during the meeting. I'm not a political animal or interested in waging a class war. I have no time for religion or sports, either. My focus is on one thing and one thing only. If people break the law, we must catch and punish them. The punishment has to fit the crime. The authorities should assume that responsibility. If they fail, then people like me are duty-bound to redress the balance. That's why I can't wait to get home to Larcombe. I want to start the ball rolling. I want this gang found and dealt with before they have another chance to attack an innocent target. The police aren't making any progress, as always. If they arrested them, the sentences the courts handed out would be derisory. What's the total number of dead in these attacks so far? How many do they have to reach before they reintroduce the death penalty? Hundreds, thousands? The number they killed is irrelevant because they're too weak to make the decision."

Athena joined Phoenix by the window.

"I couldn't agree with you more, Phoenix. Olympus is a necessary evil."

"Olympus is necessary, but I cannot accept what it stands for is evil. The people we kill are the evil ones. Most have been responsible for crimes so heinous that they defy description. We have to continue our work. That's why it's imperative aberrations such as the black book have to be managed so carefully. If the factions within the Twelve Olympians eventually result in an unresolvable rift, then we might be exposed. Together we are protected by the security blanket of the charity. The true purpose of Larcombe Manor and other similar establishments worldwide hides from sight. You were right to challenge Zeus and warn against direct action against a raft of men guilty of sexual abuse going back decades. One at a time, softly ticking the names off as we go, that's the only logical way to tackle the matter. A few might die before we can act. Our intelligence section should be able to help us in prioritising the missions so that we deal with those who are still active first."

"Why do you suspect a rift?" asked Athena.

"I can't go into the details until I consider everything fully, as I said before, but if I'm right that two distinct camps exist, then Zeus has a challenger for the leadership. Unless Zeus removes his opponents and replaces them with

In the Lap of the Gods

new blood, people he can rely on to support him without reservation, let alone downright opposition, then, in the end, the two factions will go their separate ways. At first, the Project will suffer a huge loss in financial support. Operations at Larcombe and elsewhere would necessarily reduce. The whole future of Larcombe Manor could be under threat. The bigger threat of danger comes from the splinter organisation. That faction would have significant funds but leadership with a different plan. If that plan involved widespread assassinations of public figures, they would become Public Enemy Number One as far as the police and the security services were concerned. If they're apprehended, they might uncover the Olympus Project's existence in return for a softer ride through the justice system. I'm unconvinced there's no more sinister threat; namely, those unhappy with Zeus and his leadership style may remove him and his supporters, imposing their aims and ambitions for Olympus. I don't think that either of us would be comfortable working for such an organisation. Today, we've seen that everything isn't perfect in the organisational structure. Yet the principles Erebus established and which persuaded me to come on board are still at the core of things so far."

"It's just over three years since I first met you at lunch that day at Larcombe," said Athena. "I hated you instantly. You appeared so arrogant."

"Ah, but my boyish charm won through," Phoenix replied, "do you know when I suddenly realised that we had to be together?"

"That first lunch?"

"Heaven's no. You frightened me to death in the first few weeks. Then, we swam in the swimming pool together, and I saw you in that grey costume. It took me a while to realise I'd fallen for you, but it was all over from that moment."

Athena and Phoenix stood by the window, kissing. If anyone had passed by and noticed, it didn't concern them. They were together, and that was all that mattered. Together they could ride out the dangerous water within Olympus; as joint leaders at Larcombe Manor, they would pursue the Eastern European gang. There was nothing they couldn't achieve as long as they were united.

Athena broke off the kiss but continued to embrace Phoenix. She needed to tell him her news. Together they would face that eventuality too,

In due course, their transport arrived, and they began the journey home.

Phoenix was asleep before they reached Reading. Athena knew this was typical of him. He seemed able to snatch an hour here and there. Later he could work through the night planning the operation to take out the foreign gang.

As they travelled west, she knew that once back at Larcombe, they would go straight into a meeting with Henry Case, Giles Burke, and Rusty if he had returned from his week-long survey. Athena imagined he might wish to get back to his room before Zara arrived. Not to make sure everything was shipshape. Rusty was a diligent ex-SAS soldier, and it went without saying that the place would be spotless. He would want to be there to greet her at the start of a new phase in his life. Athena appreciated only too well how much of a challenge that might appear.

She mulled over the things that Phoenix had noted during the meeting. For example, Athena found Zeus and Hera to be an odd couple but couldn't imagine they sat in different camps. Poseidon, on the other hand, felt like a cold fish. He was the archetypal banker; she wouldn't trust him very far.

What of Demeter, the still successful singer, a woman who was a man-eater with a vicious tongue? Did Poseidon and Demeter belong in the other camp? They seemed unlikely bedfellows.

Apollo, the boxer who avoided getting punch drunk and profited from the properties he'd bought with his world championship purses, had kept his good looks. Athena struggled to imagine the friendly image he displayed as belonging to an opponent to Zeus.

Hermes, the mobile phone genius, was young, amicable and engaging. But, nevertheless, Phoenix had been cautious; when he talked about him, he might have hinted to her that this friendly front hid a dark secret. Was he right?

That left four Olympians they hadn't met with before, during or after the meeting. What should she make of that, anything or nothing? She had recognised Heracles, the famous captain of industry. He appeared on television on many occasions. Whenever they needed a clear-headed opinion on the economic situation and its impact on manufacturing in the UK, the media wheeled him out for his views. He always gave excellent value for money. Heracles lived in his home country of Scotland and had flown himself south for the meeting by helicopter.

Athena's upbringing helped her appreciate the standing in society of the pair sitting next to one another on her side of the table. Aphrodite was the daughter of a Duke and one of those whose name appeared in the Top 100 line of succession to the throne. However, someone so far down the list was unlikely to be called upon to get fitted for the crown.

Her companion Dionysus was a Privy Council member; Athena knew there were currently six hundred privy counsellors. That number included former prime ministers, cabinet ministers as well as leaders of the opposition. In addition, there were members of the royal family, senior clergy, senior courtiers, and senior judges. They met on average once a month, and the Queen presided over meetings.

Details of its meetings, attendees and the matters discussed appeared in the Court Circular, so it wasn't a secretive organisation. The Privy Council's role was to advise the monarch of the day in exercising prerogative powers. Athena tried to recall where she had seen Dionysus; she was confident he wasn't a former politician and not a royal.

Athena's time with the secret services had taught her not to make assumptions. Yet, she found it hard to imagine Zeus and Hera at odds with these last two when they came from the same cloth. She tried to recall any comments they had passed during the meeting or refreshment break that gave her any clues. She struggled to remember them contributing very much.

As the car motored into Wiltshire, Athena was perhaps unavoidably wrenched away from the Olympus meeting to the horrors that had occurred in Amesbury earlier in the day. She couldn't bear to think of the pain the victims' families must be suffering; as for the young children, it was unbearable.

Athena looked across at the slumbering Phoenix and knew that his thoughts on capital punishment were sure to be echoed across the nation, at least for a few days. But, sadly, as he feared, too, our weak, liberal leaders were not capable of ever grasping the nettle. So instead, the politicians uttered the trite banalities we had become accustomed to and hoped that in a week or two, the families of the murdered men, women and children disappeared back into obscurity.

Athena thought that if she heard, we're sorry for your loss or, our thoughts are with the bereaved families at this time again, she might scream. But she knew her parents wouldn't appreciate hearing their privately educated daughter use such language. Athena longed to be able to go on TV and tell the public. But don't worry, leave it to us. We'll get the bastards.

She smiled to herself; then she remembered one final Olympian that had briefly slipped her memory. Nemesis, the goddess of revenge and retribution. She had said very little. Athena could only remember looking uncomfortable during Phoenix's discussion with Zeus about the black book during the meeting. When she left the room at the end, it had been with Aphrodite and Demeter. They looked decidedly uneasy in each other's company.

So, who was Nemesis? Might Demeter be the odd one out in that trio? Was Nemesis another titled female who might align with Zeus and Hera? She determined to research that when they got back to Larcombe, not just into Nemesis either, they needed to investigate the backgrounds of their fellow Olympians in their entirety.

As the car swung through the gates into the driveway that led to the old manor house, Athena thought of Phoenix's suspicions about several Olympus leaders and on whose side they were.

Athena reckoned that Larcombe Manor and its guardians should adopt an appropriate watchword for the foreseeable future.

Know your enemy.

Chapter Seven

Phoenix stirred as the car drew up in front of the main door.

"Are we home?" he muttered.

"We are, darling," said Athena, "please change your top before we meet up with the others. You've dribbled on that one. What am I going to do with you?"

"Just be thankful I changed out of my monkey suit."

The pair went upstairs to their suite of rooms and threw their bags on the bed. Phoenix got a clean top out of a drawer and changed.

"Happy now?" he grinned.

"A little better. Let's get to the meeting room and plan your mission."

When they entered, Henry Case and Giles Burke waited. Minos, Thanatos, and Alastor watched and waited too.

"OK, what have you got for us, Henry?" asked Athena.

"Late this afternoon, we picked up two dodgy car dealers from the London area we believe can perhaps help us with our inquiries. Our guests arrived twenty minutes ago. I normally leave them to sweat for a while and interrogate them over the weekend; this afternoon's events in Amesbury have altered matters significantly, so I will have to speed up the process. They will undergo an initial softening-up programme that is getting underway as we speak. I shall personally supervise the next stage once we finish up here, provided I have your go-ahead."

"Whatever you need to do, Henry, do it," said Athena, "this gang must be apprehended as soon as possible. We can't allow anything or anyone to delay us in achieving that result.

"Very well, Athena," nodded Henry.

"What's the latest from Amesbury, Giles?" Phoenix asked.

"There have been no further deaths so far. The speed and savagery of the attack stand out on this occasion. Can you believe they were in and out in a single minute? Hardly a chance for eye-witnesses on the High Street to identify the vehicles or the passengers. Nothing relevant to the raid showed up on any CCTV locally. Although, of course, that opinion might change if we only knew what prey we hunted. The shooters must have been dropped off on the pavement outside; they dashed through to the beer garden, fired indiscriminately for twenty seconds, and then scrambled over the back fence. While the attack took place, their transport drove to the rear of the pub. It parked, ready to pick them up as soon as they hit the ground on the other side of the fence. As I say, inside that first minute and a half, they had made their escape."

"So we have nothing in Amesbury itself and even less in the pub," said Phoenix dejectedly. "Just like the other raids, they left no useful clues."

"We don't yet know what the police CSI personnel will find at the scene. It's early days for us to hack into their systems to find out what they have collected. Perhaps one of the assassins will have cut a knee on the way over the fence. If they can retrieve his DNA, we can put a name on him. We're unlikely to get anything from the ammunition. A name and nationality will help us immeasurably find the gang's hiding place. Especially once Henry gets to work on our two informants."

"I didn't realise these two dealers were informants," said Athena, surprised.

"Oh, they're not, Athena," said Phoenix. "Giles is indicating that they will be by the time 'Head' Case has shown them the delights of Hotel California."

Phoenix walked over to where Giles sat and put a comforting hand on his shoulder.

"We desperately need a break on your side of things, Giles. So keep plugging away, mate," he said.

Phoenix sensed that Giles was a little depressed, but sometimes gathering intelligence took time. Luckily, they possessed the answer already, somewhere in the plethora of data they had collected over the past few weeks. If they did, Giles was the type to keep worrying away at the problem like a dog with a squeaky toy. On Christmas Day, the squeak got on your nerves; but it wouldn't be too long before the dog found the source and strangled it into silence. Giles was your man if you required the intelligence equivalent of a dog and a squeaky toy.

"Thanks, Phoenix," said Giles, "I'll get back to the ice-house if I may. I'll run through the reams of stuff we've got one more time and start collating the new material we've gathered. Then, perhaps in the morning, we'll be able to get a break."

"I'll get moving on finding out what my two guests can add to the mix," said Henry. "May I be excused too?"

Athena told her two ice-house agents to report back at nine o'clock in the morning. There would be no free weekend and no rest for the wicked. Well, that was the aim.

Phoenix glanced at the clock on the mantelpiece over the elegant Georgian fireplace.

"I think we've gone as far as we can on this today, Athena. So I suggest we finish, get a bite to eat, and have an early night."

The Three Amigos looked miffed. Finally, Minos decided he should be their spokesman.

"We understand the reasons for this emergency meeting regarding the Amesbury shootings and agree with everything decided so far; however, we hoped for a debriefing on your first session with the rest of our superiors."

"It was both boring and revealing in equal measure," said Phoenix with an exaggerated sigh. "Our financial position is very healthy, and we have achieved significant successes with direct actions carried out by our agents in many foreign places. But, on the other hand, we have several enemies around the table there who, without a doubt, will do us harm if they ever get given licence to pursue their ambitions. So it might have seemed good to sit with your backs to the window for meetings here at home. However, it would be more sensible if we jointly kept our eyes peeled in every direction over the coming months. There are dark forces at work; we must be on our guard and ready to defend ourselves against attack from three-hundred and sixty degrees."

Minos and the others turned their heads to Athena, seeking reassurance or punishment for Phoenix for misleading them. But instead, she smiled back at them benignly.

"What he said. We'll see you in the morning. Sleep well."

Saturday, July 20*th*, 2013

The morning newspapers and TV news bulletins were full of reports covering the Amesbury shootings. 'Outrage' was universal across banner headlines and news channels.

The image that featured most prominently that of a smiling, chubby-faced infant. At fifteen months old, a picture of little Kassie Paget, the youngest victim in the beer garden.

Much smaller images of the beer garden after the dead and injured bodies were tucked away on the inside pages or briefly shown on-screen. These were chilling enough; the full horror of the carnage was deemed too much to be seen by the nation's readers and viewers as they ate their breakfast on this glorious summer Saturday.

Millions of people saw the reports, and a tremendous outcry swelled up on social media. Understandably people were angry; they wanted answers. What were the police doing about these attacks? What were the government doing; was anyone safe?

Dimitar Marinov was content. He woke up to the furore that his orchestrated reign of terror provoked. Dimitar wanted this country on its knees, begging for these attacks to stop. But did he wonder if now was the time to make his financial demands? Perhaps another attack might be required to seal the deal.

Dimitar attended to his breakfast and scanned the newspapers. He didn't read about the Amesbury shootings; he examined the entertainment section, wondering which of Britain's favourite stars should die. Who might they miss the most?

He poured himself another cup of coffee and turned to the sports pages. Decisions, decisions; what a tough life. A Premiership footballer, perhaps? Dimitar had a busy morning ahead of him.

Meanwhile, in Bath, DS Phil Hounsell sat having breakfast, Erica and the kids seated around the table. He had anticipated a quiet family weekend. Instead, they planned a trip to the coast with a beautiful weather forecast, followed by a barbeque with friends this evening. Sunday morning was set aside for a few household chores, followed by a lazy afternoon in the garden and an evening meal on the patio. Finally, a bottle of wine to be chilled, ready to soften the dark thoughts of returning to work in the morning.

"How does this affect you, darling?" asked Erica, turning the newspaper headline towards him.

Phil heard the breaking news at Portishead before he left for home last evening. As he forecasted, his superiors breathed a massive sigh of relief that the latest strike didn't happen on their patch. They had scaled back the motorway patrols for the weekend as they didn't imagine many prospects of further attacks for a few days. However, the force's bean counters kept an eye on the dwindling budgets.

"It affects me deeply; I can't imagine what those families are suffering. This gang is ruthless. We must stop the swine. Professionally, I don't imagine I'll be called back to Portishead. There's no emergency on our patch. The bosses will send messages of support to the Wiltshire police; of course, you wouldn't expect anything less. I told them this would be bound to happen, Erica. I told them this gang is based in west London. Nobody wanted to listen."

The phone didn't ring. Phil, Erica, and the children prepared to get on with their weekend. It's not easy to relax when your thoughts are constantly interrupted by visions of Kassie Paget and the other victims.

Each successive hour's media bulletin reported the same almost static status. Just one of the drawbacks of 24-hour news.

Amesbury had been a one-minute attack. The police made zero progress in the first twelve to twenty-four hours, which left the public craving a time when the news came on only four times a day. Instead, you got to hear what went on in the world in bite-sized chunks crammed into a thirty-minute slot. The only escape from the continuous loop these days was changing the channel or switching off the television.

In Maidenhead, Georgi Bonev was not having a good day. He had returned to the farm with the other gang members and dropped off the Land Rovers after the Amesbury raid. He had been sick to his stomach with what had happened. Georgi never imagined that Dimitar would go so far as to slaughter innocent children.

When he had asked Boris Tsankov about events in the beer garden, even he had been affected by it, he could tell. As he talked of the green grass being turned red with the blood, just for a few seconds, the steel shell of the hardened assassin fell away.

Dimitar had roared off in his car to a party somewhere, leaving the others to travel back to their homes in a couple of vehicles. The same joy that followed the other attacks seemed to have evaporated.

Iliya Todorov offered to drop Georgi off at the end of

his street, but Georgi told him he wanted to make his way home. He said he would probably stop off en route for a drink. He didn't fancy an evening alone before he tried to wash away the memories of what they had done.

Georgi took one of the cars from the pool in the outbuilding. Dimitar would disapprove, but he wouldn't find out. He would be able to return it over the weekend. No problem.

As Georgi sat in the prison cell, he tried to recall what had happened. His head thumped. He remembered driving towards Maidenhead and stopping at a pub in the countryside. He had only drunk a few beers there. A pretty barmaid served him and seemed keen to chat. Georgi had eaten something there too, but he couldn't remember what he had ordered. A bar snack, perhaps; the trip to Amesbury had robbed him of any appetite.

He had left the pub by eight o'clock, or perhaps it had been half-past because it was still light. He'd got back into town and parked in the car park behind a bar he and the lads sometimes used. It was busy, but none of the gang had gone there. So he stopped drinking beers and switched to vodka.

The bar had closed at two o'clock; Georgi was almost sure he had been the last to leave. If you had asked the door staff if that was true, they would have told you they practically poured him out of the door; he was so full of alcohol. Georgi was a big solid man and not easy to shift.

When he stood on the pavement, he staggered off in the direction of his house, and then he found a set of keys in his pocket. What was this, he had thought? These weren't his door keys. Of course, he had driven a car to this bar. He had then made his way unsteadily to the car park and swayed as he pressed the button on the key fob. One of the cars replied with a flash of light and unlocked doors. He had stumbled to the car and fallen into the driver's seat.

He had seen the light within a minute of steering the car gently out of the car park, crossing the road and heading home at no more than ten miles per hour. Not a religious experience, just the local police doing an early morning sweep of the late-night drinking places to make sure peace reigned.

Georgi sat in the cell now, and his head thumped harder as the rest of last night's events came back to him. Shit. He was in trouble. He thought he remembered someone saying he had been four times over the limit. What do they know? He could have drunk more if the bar had stayed open. Limits are for pussies. Georgi felt sick. He threw up in the toilet. His head thumped even more.

At Larcombe Manor, the team assembled at nine o'clock for the meeting. Everyone was eager to get on with the job at hand — the task of identifying, locating and eliminating this murderous gang.

Athena and Phoenix had arrived early. They were already seated when Minos, Alastor, and Thanatos trooped in together. Henry and Giles made it just before the clock ticked around to nine. As Athena started proceedings, Rusty entered the room.

"A meeting on a Saturday morning? I'm guessing it must be about Amesbury; I spotted Henry and Giles trotting across the lawn from the ice-house with a load of files, so I thought I'd better put in an appearance."

"Welcome back, Rusty," said Athena warmly, "is your partner arriving today?"

"No," said Rusty. "I've finished my tour of duty in London and wanted to get back, have a shower and feel clean again. So I'll hold my report over until tomorrow or

Monday, Athena if that suits you. This matter has to be your priority, I'm sure. My partner will arrive later tomorrow. It's a decent drive south from Durham. In this weather, she'd be sensible to take a break, grab a drink and rest up for a while halfway through her journey."

"We must stop referring to the poor girl as your partner, Rusty. We have dozens of ex-military and ex-secret service people in the organisation who continue using their names. That's fair enough. We have to keep the illusion you are either recovering from PTSD or recruited after serving your country as part of that recovery. Those of us whose true identity it's wise to hide from the outside world have always received a code name to use here and elsewhere. We look forward to Artemis joining us tomorrow; I'm certain she will be a valuable asset to the intelligence section here at Larcombe."

"Thanks, Athena," said Rusty. "I'll christen her Artemis tomorrow when she finally arrives. It would be great if I could tell her what her name means. Give us a clue?"

Phoenix leant forward in his chair. Lately, he had done extra reading on the various gods and goddesses in preparation for yesterday's meeting. Phoenix wanted to see if the code name supplied to them matched their personality. He was amazed at the accuracy of most of them. Others had so many other explanations as to their meaning. He found it impossible to decide.

"Relax, Rusty," he said. "I should concentrate on the first attribution. Artemis was the goddess of the hunt."

"That sounds perfect for the ice-house," said Giles Burke.

"There are other things she was associated with then?" asked Rusty warily.

"Every breed of animal, the moon, archery, and virginity," said Phoenix, somehow managing to keep a straight face.

"She loves her cats," said Rusty, grasping at the first comment and ignoring the rest. "She told me she planned to leave Napoleon and Josephine with her parents after this week. It's not practical for her to bring them here."

"That's settled then," said Phoenix, "Artemis will join the hunt tomorrow."

"Back to matters for today then, gentlemen," said Athena.

Henry Case took his cue and started.

"We didn't have many problems with our guests once we got them settled. The car dealers had no idea where they were or which organisation or government department had lifted them off the streets. They worried we wanted to harm them; we soon corrected that assumption. We told them that they need not fear us. We stressed that the reason we invited them to visit us had nothing to do with their current business. Once they told us what we needed to know, they could return to trade in dodgy motors for as long as they wished. Once the preliminaries were over, we asked about anyone in the M4 corridor west of London that they supplied with numerous vehicles. One chap was adamant he only dealt in cars, never vans or trucks, and that his customers lived either on the continent or many miles from the capital. The second man was the most cooperative. He said his business was split fifty-fifty between home and abroad. He moved any model vehicle a client wanted. Several groups operating in the London region took stuff off his hands. We asked whether he had ever sold cars to the ram-raid gang. His eyes gave him away. The mere mention of the name made him nervous. I had to convince him that whatever he told us would be held in the strictest confidence and never spoken of to anyone. I felt it necessary to go back to stage one. I told him that when I said he didn't need to fear us, I meant that when I asked a question, provided he told me everything, he had nothing to fear. I left what might happen if he didn't comply with his imagination. This man finally admitted that he and his partners had enjoyed a good trading relationship with the members of the ram-raid gang. He stressed that at no stage did they ever suspect someone planned to use those vehicles for that purpose; I merely patted him on the knee and asked him to continue."

"You're all heart," said Phoenix. Henry continued his report without comment.

"A couple of months ago, they had received a phone call from a man with an accent. Their number's ex-directory for obvious reasons, so it was a shock to be contacted by a stranger. The man told them he had taken over the garage and its contents as their previous clients no longer traded. He wanted to continue the setup unchanged. The dealers began lifting cars and vans to order and delivered them to the site from which the ram-raid gang had operated. The men they saw there looked far more dangerous than their predecessors. I asked him to direct me to the site; again, he became agitated and reticent. I'm afraid I had to move to stage three. I returned to him after about forty-five minutes and asked again. The farm is near Eton Wick. I have the postcode. The farmer has several outbuildings he rents out that are remote from the farmhouse. His business is strapped for cash, so he doesn't ask his customers too many questions. The new occupants of the outbuildings are Bulgarians. As far as my chap knew, eight to ten live in or around Maidenhead, just five or six miles away. He said they were the meanest bunch of thugs he had ever come across in his life. He was scared to death of them. He said nobody from the ram-raid gang had ever contacted him since that day. He was certain the Bulgarians had killed them. He pleaded with me not to tell this gang that he had said anything. I told him not to worry. The gang would never hear a word from me. While he still felt chatty, I asked what he imagined these Bulgarians had been doing before they decided to trade in stolen cars. He thought they had started to gain a reputation in the region around two or three years back. Mainly it was drugs and girls with which they had connections. What they did with the cars and vans he sold in the last few months worried him the most. I asked him to explain; he talked to the floor. 'You know,' he said, 'don't you? It's them.'

Chapter Eight

Athena thanked Henry for the speedy results he had gained. He passed her the exact location of the farm and a map showing the buildings associated with the property. There were aerial photographs that an Olympus drone had supplied when it overflew the farm this morning at first light. The outbuildings looked deserted. The gang were at home in Maidenhead.

"What did you do with your guests?" she asked.

"I thanked them for their help and asked them to wait while we verified the information they had supplied. As soon as we were happy, we will arrange transport to take home our guests."

"Are you happy, Henry?" Athena asked.

Henry nodded.

"Giles, what do you have?"

"I've left my team working on Henry's new data. Now we know the exact location of the gang's hide-out, we can start to use the data we have to track the movements of vehicles. In addition, it might give us a clue as to the domestic arrangements of these devils.

Phoenix had been deep in thought.

"Do that, Giles. The more intelligence we have, the better. You need to be very lucky to link the gang on the motorway to the actual farm by CCTV; then, when they travel from the farm to their homes, we don't know what cars they drive. They wouldn't be so dumb as to use their stolen transport to drive around locally. So far as direct action is concerned, we need to get as many of them as possible in one strike. We can't pick them off individually. If we can isolate the gang members at the farm and remove them, it gives us the best chance of completing the mission without drawing attention to Olympus."

"I agree with you, Phoenix," said Athena, "but we've got two issues to consider. What if yesterday was the last raid? When will the next raid be; are subsequent raids planned in any case? Can we afford to have agents surrounding the farm, hoping they'll turn up, for an indeterminate time?"

"What do you think we should do then, Athena?" Phoenix asked.

"Why not have a chat with the farmer? Misdirect him into believing you are undercover police. Put him in the picture; ask him to contact the gang, telling them there's a small fire in one of their buildings. He could suggest they wish to remove something they wouldn't want to fall into the wrong hands. They could be there within twenty minutes from Maidenhead."

"Okay, what's stopping the farmer from calling the fire brigade?" said Rusty.

"Maybe he could tell them he'll leave the call until a quarter of an hour after he ends it. Suggesting they have around fifteen minutes to get everything out they need to save," offered Giles.

"That might work, but if Athena's first premise were correct, namely that the last raids have taken place, we would end up destroying loads of evidence," said Alastor.

"There wouldn't be a real fire, you muppet. We create lots of smoke by one of the outbuildings, so they had to keep driving towards the farm when they see it," said Phoenix.

Alastor had turned a shade of red that suggested he was about to blow a gasket. A mobile phone rang on the desk. Giles answered. He listened for a minute, then closed his eyes.

"Thank you," he said.

"Have they found something, Giles?" asked Athena.

"We intercepted a transmission early this morning from a traffic cop and his HQ in Maidenhead; he had stopped a drunk driver just after he had left a bar. It was around two fifteen. We have carried out further checks, and evidently, this guy failed the breath test, was kept in the cells overnight and will be released when he's sober. His name is Georgi Bonev. He's Bulgarian, aged 31, and arrived in the UK in 2011. His papers don't suggest a criminal past, but they may not be genuine. There's no record of employment we can trace, yet he has a property in the town. Our local agent visited the district near the bar and located the vehicle. It was parked and tagged by the officer for removal to the car pound this morning. When he sent the photograph of the car and the number plate, we had our first bit of luck. It's a Toyota Prius used on a ram-raid job, with a plate from a Vauxhall Zafira of the same vintage. Georgi Bonev is one of the gang members. A gang member dumb enough to use a pool car to drive home yesterday after the Amesbury attack."

"Bingo," said Phoenix.

"The agent will be trailing Bonev as he leaves Maidenhead nick. We can lift him if you think it might assist us going forward," said Giles.

"We could spook the whole gang if we bring Bonev here; we don't want them going to ground. So let's keep him under surveillance for now," said Athena.

Phoenix and Rusty were already poring over maps, plans and aerial shots of the farm. Athena could tell they wanted to get the planning stage underway as soon as possible.

"Why don't you two boys run away to the orangery? You can work on the plan of attack there. I'll arrange refreshments at lunchtime. Is there anything you particularly fancy?"

The two friends looked at one another. The pair recalled a similar occasion in the orangery with Erebus after a mission in the Cotswolds a few months back. In unison, they replied: -

"Coffee and a stack of bacon rolls, please."

Athena smiled briefly, then felt a little queasy. And so it begins, she thought. That conversation with Phoenix had to be sooner rather than later.

The two boys gathered the relevant items from the table and headed out. They were in their element. The planning and preparation were vitally important; it didn't match the adrenalin rush they got from a mission, but the success of those furious seconds of action depended on the groundwork done earlier. Nobody in their right mind tries to tapdance their way through a firestorm.

Athena instructed Giles to return to the ice-house to

start the long trawl through traffic movements in the M4 corridor. Each of the raids' start and finish points were known now; they had descriptions of a collection of vehicles used by both gangs and number plates they switched at will between them. Needles and haystacks sprang to mind, but knowledge was power. The more they knew about this gang, the better.

Alastor was a healthier colour now. Both he and his colleagues were waiting to hear what remained for discussion this morning.

"Phoenix can be brusque at times; even so, he has the best interests of Olympus at heart, so we must forgive his occasional odd turn of phrase. Moving on, you will recall last evening when we returned from London? You were all interested in the matters discussed at the meeting. Phoenix summed it up succinctly. He wasn't dismissive of your opinions; he merely paraphrased what happened. Our organisation's safety demands that the identity of the other ten Olympians sitting around the table is shrouded in secrecy. I would love to use your skills to carry out background checks on every one of them. Several of them work together against the principles prescribed at the birth of the Olympus Project. Whether they are aiming for financial gain, personal revenge or a more far-reaching influence on the governance of this nation, I don't yet fully understand."

"You suspect a coup, though, from what Phoenix suggested?" said Minos.

"Within Olympus, at first," added Alastor.

"As the new faction grows in strength, you are afraid it might be bold enough to attempt to topple the government and take control. Surely, they would need to have infiltrated and coerced the armed forces to agree with their new vision?" said Thanatos.

"It's not necessarily a new vision that's needed," said Alastor. "They could convince the armed forces, the police and security services that it was in the 'interests of national security.' It would follow the American response to 9/11 but taken to the next level."

Minos used his smartphone to call up the relevant phrases.

"Homeland security is 'the concerted national effort to ensure a homeland that is safe, secure, and resilient against terrorism and other hazards…so that our way of life can thrive…prevent terrorist attacks within our borders, reduce vulnerability to terrorism, and minimise the damage from attacks that do occur.' That could be enough leverage to persuade the armed services to come on board. You would be surprised how little it takes to flip a country from democracy to dictatorship. In these troubled times, people want strong leadership. Kowtowing to Europe over every aspect of our daily lives, the abject failure of our open door policy, and austerity piled on top of austerity are the main ingredients that encourage an ambitious person to seek power. If that is what we're facing, then as they begin to nibble away at the foundations, sooner or later, the whole pack of cards will fall."

"A little dramatic, Minos," said Thanatos, "don't you think?"

"Maybe," said Athena, "but we must be on our guard. I was listening to Minos and thinking it's odd for us at Larcombe to protect the authorities from a possible breakdown in democracy. Olympus operates outside the law while maintaining our main principles, ensuring people face justice when the current regime fails to act. We could not stand by and watch another faction usurp that ineffectual system—one which might not be acting in the best interests of the British people. No, we must stand firm on our principles and maintain the status quo while encouraging the authorities to find their lost backbone. I'm positive that would have been the course of action Erebus would have advocated. Let's return to my earlier topic: identifying those that may be plotting against us. I propose that we share the task among the four of us. You are intelligent men; you know that our benefactors have always been among the richest people in the country. If you set your mind to the task, the list of possible Olympians could be slashed to less than three hundred. For your protection, I shall give you three descriptions, with photographs where available. One of them is a current Olympian. The other two could be members based on their wealth and lack of criminal conviction or extreme political leanings. Don't think that your research is of no import for the two 'imposters.' If our fears are justified, we will face removing any cancer inside the organisation, and fresh blood will be required. At least, if we need to approach such people, we will know whether they have a clean bill of health."

"I think I speak for all of us, Athena," said Minos solemnly, "that we will carry out the research you ask for with due diligence and guard the information we uncover closely. However, would you prefer that we report on our findings privately, restricting meetings on this matter between just the four of us?"

"I think it might be wiser to meet with each of you individually. The fewer people who know about each investigation, the better. No disrespect to either of you nor Phoenix, Rusty and the others. They have more than enough on their hands. We will work on this alone. Once we have isolated the 'enemy at the gate', we can involve them, and at that time, we must act swiftly."

"Understood," said Alastor.

Athena closed the meeting and went to arrange those refreshments for Phoenix and Rusty. Life was going to be hectic at Larcombe in the future.

In the orangery, the agents formulated plans for the attack in Eton Wick. Phoenix and Rusty contacted agents from around the country to bring them on board. Rusty rang the farmhouse and talked to the farmer about the Metropolitan Police's suspicions concerning the people renting a property from him. The farmer soon recognised that the man he was talking to was an undercover officer working with a serious crimes unit; he was eager to help.

The coffee and bacon rolls had arrived and soon got demolished. The two friends left the orangery and walked over to the ice-house. The pair descended in the lift to the second level. First, they needed to speak to Bazza and Thommo in the armoury. After describing the scope of the mission, they left the two ex-SAS men to prepare a suitable list of equipment to execute their plans.

"I'd wait until they'd turned up and gone inside the building to sort out the fire, then send a rocket in and blow the place to kingdom come," said Bazza.

"Thanks for your input; helpful as always, Bazza," said Rusty.

"Don't dismiss the idea of an anti-tank weapon entirely," said Phoenix. "We can't be sure these guys haven't got an armoured vehicle, a reinforced one at least."

"What strength team are you taking on this one, Phoenix?" asked Thommo.

"There are at least eight of these thugs; if Giles and the guys upstairs can get more intel on who we're dealing with, I'd be happier. I expect Rusty and I can take that number out between us if they were run-of-the-mill criminals, but this gang is different gravy. I want to match them man for man, so we shall be a team of eight. I've contacted Jack Mould. The deadly duo from Shrivenham will be good to have stood beside us too. The others are from across the London region and split into two units. Three agents will form part of the hit squad, with nine held in reserve. They'll be called in to evacuate casualties and help finish the mission if we run into serious trouble. With the level of planning we've done on this job, we should cope with the initial squad. After the firefight, the backup personnel will sweep the area clean. When we hand the outbuildings back to the landowner, it must appear as if Olympus was never there."

"It sounds like you've got things well covered," said Thommo. "We'll take what you've just told us on board and add a few surprises to the package for you."

"We always wish you a safe trip, guys," said Bazza, more serious now for a change, "and usually after you leave here, we say we wish we were going with you. I don't envy you this mission; from what we've seen of the attacks, they're maniacs."

Rusty and Phoenix told the armourers to ring through as soon as the prepared materials were ready. Then they went back to the surface. A van from the Olympus transport section was pulling away, heading for the driveway out of the estate.

"I bet that's those two blokes Henry had in Level Three overnight; they're returning home in one piece with time to nick some more motors this evening. It's a funny old game, isn't it?" said Rusty.

Phoenix was keen to get back to Athena. He needed to know what he'd missed at the end of the meeting if anything; plus, he wanted to carry on talking about yesterday's session. So Phoenix left Rusty to follow up on getting the squad members finalised.

As his friend stayed in his refurbished and extended quarters to make the necessary calls, he walked across the lawn to find Athena. Phoenix realised that he hardly recognised his old stamping ground, which made it easier to manage.

Phoenix decided he needed a den within the apartments in the manor house; perhaps he could broach the subject with Athena later over dinner. It wasn't that he needed a place just to do his thinking and planning; he didn't have anywhere to listen to the music he loved.

No matter how much Athena said she had enjoyed the Glastonbury experience, Phoenix couldn't convert her into a lover of Judas Priest or Iron Maiden. When he lived in the stable block, he could lose himself in the music and block out the world.

As the hours ticked away until he headed off to Eton Wick and a potential bloodbath, he wanted time alone with his thoughts. Phoenix needed to shut out the images of the things he would leave behind if he didn't return.

Meanwhile, in the manor house, Athena sat alone with her thoughts. Phoenix was heading off on a dangerous mission within a day or two. He didn't know about the possible baby yet. Should she tell him before he left? As a leader, she knew she must do everything to ensure the enterprise was successful.

Pulling him out of the mission wasn't possible; even if there was a risk, she might lose him. She consoled herself with the thought that Rusty and Phoenix were together; he was so dependable; he would protect Phoenix and bring him home safe. Then she remembered Artemis. She was arriving later tomorrow. Rusty could be one hundred miles away in a firefight. What if it was he who failed to return?

As she heard Phoenix entering their apartments, she sighed. Erebus hadn't told her how difficult this leadership lark was, had he?

"Hello, darling," said Phoenix, "everything alright?"

For the first time in a long while, Athena felt the tears start to flow. Hell, her hormones were all over the place.

Phoenix sat beside her and held her close.

"In your own time," said Phoenix. "If it's Eton Wick, don't worry; we've planned every step, and Rusty will be there. We'll be back in time for tea."

"It's everything," Athena blubbed. "The meeting, Eton Wick, not having Erebus here to tell us what to do, those curtains, it's everything."

"The bloody curtains? What's wrong with them?"

"I liked them when we decorated this room but sitting here now looking at them through your arms. I realise I hate them."

"Okay, we'll change them when we finish up in Windsor. I'll have to come back now. You'll never manage to agree on the colour of the new curtains without me being there."

The two lovers sat there until Athena's tears disappeared, and the room grew dark. Neither spoke. One was thinking of the potential horrors of Eton Wick and how much he would miss moments such as this. The other person was thinking of the research she and her team were undertaking. Athena decided when she should take the test to confirm what she believed in her heart and realise how much she loved the man holding her.

Sunday, July 21st, 2013

Phoenix slipped out of bed early. It was fast approaching sunrise. He found Rusty waiting for him outside the icehouse when he trotted over the lawn. They had both dressed in dark clothing and were ready to roll.

As they descended to Level Two, Rusty told Phoenix he sent Zara an email telling her he might return late from London. He wrote and told her that when she arrived at Larcombe, she should find Athena in the main building. Athena could get someone to show her to their quarters and give her a brief tour.

"You didn't tell her you already got back from your working week in London? That might have been sensible," said Phoenix.

"No, I just said I'd make it up to her when I got back," said Rusty.

They found Bazza Longdon and Thommo Thompson in the armoury as arranged. Phoenix received the 'all set' message late last night, just after he and Athena ate a late supper and thought about going to bed.

"Transport should be up top when you arrive on the surface; I called as soon as the lift started down."

"Thanks, Bazza," said Phoenix.

"You've got everything you need to make a load of convincing smoke. The weapons and ammunition you usually prefer are there too. We added the anti-tank weaponry just in case. Rusty knows how to use it; Jack Mould will, too, no doubt. We'll give you a hand with it. There's quite a list you ordered for this job."

"Cheers, Thommo, you're a star," said Rusty.

The four men struggled to the lift with the equipment. Rusty and Bazza went up first. The Olympus truck stood outside, ticking over as promised. Phoenix and Thommo came up with the rest of the kit and made sure they got everything loaded securely.

The armourers turned to return to their home from home on the lower level.

"Aren't you going to stop to wave us goodbye?" asked Phoenix.

"You're coming back, aren't you? Just find out the bastard responsible for Kassie Paget and give him a round or two from me, will you?" said Thommo.

"You bet, mate," replied Rusty.

With that, they got into the truck and headed off towards the driveway and onwards to Eton Wick.

As the truck drove nearer the cattle grid between the stone pillars at the gateway, a curtain drew back in a room on the top floor. Athena watched as Phoenix and Rusty left. She offered up a prayer for their safe return. Phoenix didn't turn back towards the manor house. He glanced at his watch. The rendezvous point was due to be reached just after 07.00 hours. He closed his eyes as if he was asleep. He went through each step of the mission to keep it firmly set in his mind.

Rusty sat beside him. Rusty thought about Zara arriving later today. The seasoned soldier always planned to return from every mission he ever handled; this time, it was different; he had someone waiting at home for him.

Across London, the dozen Olympus agents selected for the task ahead were awake. The longest journey either of them faced was an hour, and it would be closer to fifty minutes on a quiet Sunday morning. They might have time for a few minutes in bed.

Kelly Dexter and Hayden Vincent waited in Shrivenham, dressed and ready to get cracking. Their mission timetable showed them joining the M4 and following the Olympus vehicle towards the capital. Kelly glanced out of the window. A black Ford Kuga pulled into the driveway and parked next to their van. Jack 'Jelly' Mould had arrived from Frome. She walked to the front door and invited him indoors.

"I'll transfer my kit to your van when we're ready to leave," said Jack.

"We've got to hang on until Phoenix calls to say they've passed the first Swindon junction, and then we head off to tuck in somewhere behind them. So we've got a while yet. Fancy a coffee?" asked Hayden.

"I'm dying for one, thanks," said Jack.

As Hayden made for the kitchen, he thought to himself. I hope not. Eton Wick might well turn out to be their most challenging assignment so far. The fight last November in Bristol looked like a piece of cake compared to this.

In Maidenhead, Georgi Bonev had a plan. He had avoided bumping into Dimitar so far. However, a rough time with his boss lay ahead; he didn't need the 'aggro' that his boss would give him because of the drink-driving charge.

At least his licence and insurance details checked out when the cop pulled him over. Unfortunately, whether the police slipped up or were just too busy to bother, it appeared they didn't check the vehicle he had been driving after they collected it.

Perhaps this was an effect of the cuts. No matter; it was Bonev's lucky day. He recovered the car from the pound late yesterday, and now he'd return it to the farm, with Dimitar none the wiser. Georgi never usually got up early on a Sunday; he didn't imagine that Dimitar surfaced much before noon on the weekend.

In the Lap of the Gods

At the farmhouse, Christopher Mellish, sixty-two years old, sat reading the Sunday paper. He didn't take in much of what he saw on the printed page in front of him. His mug of tea stood getting cold on the table; his fried breakfast lay untouched. He grew more nervous by the minute about what he had to do.

The undercover police officers would be arriving in the next forty-five minutes. What if the gang suspected a trap? How did they expect him to sound convincing on the phone when he warned them the outbuilding they rented from him was in danger of going up in smoke?

He was a simple farmer whose family farmed here in Eton Wick for four generations. The harsh reality of Britain's parlous state of farming hit home within a decade of taking him over from his father. His business became littered with regulations, red tape, and the bloody EU in every direction he tried to take. His wife left him five years ago. The children worked and lived in London. His kids wanted nothing to do with farming. Over the past couple of years, they increasingly wanted little to do with him.

Renting the outbuildings to the first group of men who approached him seemed easy money at the time. He suspected all the comings and goings meant something sinister but not enough to stick his nose into their business. Their cash was crucial to help him stay afloat. He had no choice but to go along with the latest crowd that took over the rent. The men sounded so threatening he kept as far away from them as possible. They always paid on time, so why worry?

Christopher knew the second that the police telephoned him, who he had been harbouring. The vicious foreign gang had been murdering innocent people all over the south of the country. He laid his unread newspaper on the table. In a few minutes, he must phone the leader of this group of killers and pretend that he didn't know what they had been up to recently; he must sound concerned and anxious to help. They needed to believe he was neighbourly. He didn't know if he was up to it.

While Christopher Mellish paced his kitchen floor, Georgi Bonev pulled onto the forecourt of a garage just outside Maidenhead. He decided to put a few gallons into the tank to pacify Dimitar if he discovered the car had made an unscheduled trip. He would think of something. Maybe the boss wouldn't notice. Georgi also picked up a couple of snacks; he hadn't eaten any breakfast yet.

Georgi looked at his watch; five to seven. He shuddered. Not from the cold. It was already getting warm. The thought of being up so early unnerved him. Sunday is supposed to be a day of rest. He would pull into the gateway that led to the farm outbuildings in less than fifteen minutes.

Five minutes later, he would have locked the car away in the garage. That old farmer might be in the yard or the nearby fields tending to his animals or whatever. As he drove towards Eton Wick, he thought he might hang around in the outbuilding for a while. He'd eat his snacks, check nobody was snooping around and then walk up the road for ten minutes. Then ring for a taxi. Georgi was happy with his plan. He could be home by eight at the latest — his comfortable bed was waiting for him.

At 07.00 hours, the vans containing the London agents pulled up in a lay-by a quarter of a mile east of the farm at Eton Wick. On the western side of the farm, two more Olympus vehicles parked in a lane a similar distance away. Phoenix and Rusty got out of the lead van and walked back to talk with Kelly, Hayden, and Jack.

"Good morning for it," said Rusty.

"Any more intel from Giles?" asked Hayden.

"Nothing useful yet," said Phoenix. "Remember the car Bonev, the gang member, drove last night? Someone collected it from the car pound late yesterday afternoon. As for traffic movements to help us spot vehicles that might be moving the gang into Eton Wick this morning, not a thing."

"The London agents are in position," said Rusty, viewing his smartphone.

"Call Mellish and give him a bit of reassurance; then a gentle nudge to call when we instructed him," Phoenix said to Rusty.

Phoenix called the leader of the London agents. Des Finch's squad needed to set up the materials to provide the supposed fire. Phoenix checked that the leader had the timetable clear in his head.

"Clear as a bell, Phoenix, glad to be working with you," said Des Finch.

"We'll be switching to the walkie-talkie now for communications; out," said Phoenix.

"Check," came the replies from his crew and the London squad leader.

The different teams collected their various pieces of equipment from the vehicles and moved into position. The battle of Eton Wick had begun, a campaign never recorded in the annals of history.

The reserve unit on the east side lay in wait around 250 metres from the outbuildings in a clump of trees. Any early morning traffic moving along the lane would never have suspected their presence. The trees held nine men, medical equipment and an impressive array of weaponry.

The advance unit, comprising Des Finch and two experienced Olympus agents, moved across the lane and approached the rear of the outbuildings. That earlier aerial reconnaissance had shown an ample supply of empty drums and flammable material to gather for their purposes. Christopher Mellish was not a tidy person. He had lost track of all the rubbish he had left lying around the place. The three men quickly assembled the ingredients for their fake conflagration and prepared to light it.

Des Finch contacted Phoenix on the walkie-talkie, "We're set; waiting for your orders."

"We've got company, Phoenix," said Kelly Dexter.

A Toyota Prius drove through the gateway of the farm and parked outside of one of the buildings. The driver got out and went towards the doors. Georgi Bonev had arrived.

Phoenix contacted the team at the rear of the building, telling them the thug was about to enter.

"Finch. Maintain absolute silence; hold your position for now. We have a visitor,"

"What the hell do we do now?" said Rusty.

"Mellish should be on the phone now with the gang leader. Provided he convinces them there's a big enough fire to make it worth jumping out of bed, they'll be roaring through those gates at half-past seven. How did Mellish sound when you called, anyway?"

"Just about holding it together," said Rusty. "I reminded him twice that he needed to call at ten past the hour. So I'll check now."

"We need to incapacitate Bonev swiftly," said Phoenix, "we can't afford for the boss to ring him. Then, instead of getting him out of bed to help remove weapons, ammunition and heaven knows what else away from the area of the supposed fire, he'll be telling him that there's no fire here at all."

Phoenix nodded towards Hayden Vincent; the agent

moved quickly and silently forward from his position. Bonev stood at the doors, trying to find the right key among the half-dozen on the keyring. Hayden slipped a knife from his jacket pocket and closed on his target.

Georgi Bonev finally found the key, put it into the lock and turned it. Then, as he slid the big right-hand door open to park the Prius safely inside, he felt a whisper of hot breath on his neck.

He hardly felt the knife as it crossed from the left-hand side of his throat to the right. Hayden lowered the lifeless body to the floor, then dragged Bonev inside the outbuilding. There was an awful lot of blood.

He needed to tidy up before the rest of the gang arrived in just over fifteen minutes. Hayden and Kelly formed an expert clean-up crew. This was just one of many messy tasks they had encountered since joining up with Olympus. Kelly was already by his side, handing him his kit. They got to work in no time.

Time was running out. Phoenix pressed the talk button on his walkie-talkie, "Phoenix to Finch; start the fires now. Make as much smoke as you can."

"Check," came the reply.

Phoenix turned to Rusty.

"Did Mellish make the call? Are they on their way?"

"He made the call; he sounded like he was hitting the bottle. Maybe he started before he picked up the phone. The guy on the other end was *not* happy," said Rusty.

The fires in the drums at the back of the building started to blaze fiercely. Then Des Finch and his team worked on maximising the volume of smoke. The grey-white plumes of smoke soared high into a cloudless blue sky. The group felt satisfied with their work. They retreated and split up to take their defensive positions fifty to sixty metres from the outbuilding. Seconds later, they disappeared from view. Their sabotage equipment would no longer be needed, so they stashed it in any spare shed or box available. The three agents were armed, locked and loaded.

Earlier in Maidenhead, Dimitar Marinov woke from a deep sleep disturbed by persistent ringing in his ears. He had been in his bed since just before five. Dimitar thought the person on the other end of the phone must have a death wish.

"What." he barked.

"It's on fire. You need to come."

"Who is that? What's on fire?"

Christopher Mellish had started drinking from a bottle of scotch after Rusty left him. He had opened the door to a man mountain with a face covered in war paint. His clothing didn't resemble anything the farmer had ever seen undercover police officers wear. So what happened to the TSG and their Kevlar vests and helmets he saw so frequently on TV?

After Rusty left, he continued drinking. Mellish rang two or three minutes later than Rusty had ordered. He needed a few sips more reassurance from the fast-emptying bottle. Now, making the call, Mellish became tongue-tied. Why didn't the fool understand what he tried to tell him?

Mellish took a swig of the scotch, then took a deep breath. He tried again.

"It's me, the farmer from Eton Wick. At least one of your outbuildings is on fire. I can see the smoke and flames from my window. What you have inside is none of my business, but you need to move anything valuable fast before you lose it for good. Do you understand?"

The farmer heard a grunt at the other end of the line. A

grunt followed by swear words in a language the farmer didn't understand.

"To help you out, I won't ring for the fire brigade for another fifteen minutes. By the time they arrive, you should have had time to get your stuff clear. I'm doing you a favour, you know. If the fire destroys the buildings, the insurance will help me overcome the pain of losing your rent money."

"Okay," said Dimitar, "we're on our way. Now get off the phone."

Dimitar sent texts to the various gang members. He ordered Iliya Todorov to pick up four, and he would pick up the rest. As he got dressed and went outside to his car, the return texts started pinging on his phone. All the gang members were ready to help except Georgi Bonev.

"Where the hell is that useless swine?" roared Dimitar, thumping the steering wheel with a massive fist.

The two drivers picked up their passengers and drove as fast as they could towards Eton Wick. Dimitar and Iliya knew that although time was of the essence, they needed to get there undetected. Everyone talked at once, asking how the fire started; which outbuilding was it? Where had Georgi got to? Why didn't he answer his phone? Nikolay Iliev called him every couple of minutes during the journey.

"Look," cried Andrey Pantev, "is that smoke from the fire? Shit, that looks serious. What do we salvage first?"

"We need to get the weapons and ammunition away. I have money stashed there too. We can try to fill as many vehicles as drivers with things we don't want firefighters or coppers to find. We will have to abandon the other vehicles. We can always get more."

The gangsters had almost reached the farm. Dimitar Marinov thought about what the farmer said. The fire could do a lot of damage to the buildings for sure. But he didn't have to let him know, so he had a chance to salvage things. So why do him a favour? Nobody did something for nothing, not in Bulgaria or Britain, from what he'd experienced so far.

Marinov mistakenly concluded the farmer must have started the fire deliberately. The bastard was going to claim on the insurance. Dimitar grimly smiled as he looked at the smoke still billowing over the farm at Eton Wick.

"Sorry, my friend," he muttered, "you won't live to enjoy the money."

Even though it had been an innocent mistake caused by the volume of alcohol he had drunk, that last comment he made on the phone could well have been Christopher Mellish's downfall.

Kelly and Hayden continued cleaning up the ground in front of the outbuilding. With his binoculars, Jack Mould kept watching from his position for any sign of the gang's arrival. Finally, he spotted the two cars moving at speed along the lane towards the farm.

"We've got company. Ten seconds."

Kelly and Hayden gathered together their kit and ran for cover. The large door was still partly open. Georgi Bonev's body lay on the dirt inside, and minor signs remained that a bloody scuffle had occurred. Phoenix cursed under his breath.

They had lost any advantage of surprise.

Chapter Nine

Phoenix rapidly reviewed the situation.

Two cars meant they had probably only eight or nine gang members left to confront. They had taken one out; that was good.

The doors to one of the outbuildings were open; that was bad. It gave the gang other places to take cover and access any vehicles, weapons, and ammunition.

Phoenix wasn't aware that Bonev had opened the doors to the building used as a garage. Apart from the vehicles and items associated with maintaining and altering them, there was nothing beneficial to the shooters.

The building next door held the arms, cash and other items that Dimitar Marinov desperately needed to recover. The plan Phoenix and Rusty put together had been to let the gang park, wait for them to get out of their vehicles, and identify the leader.

'Jelly' would then deliver his speciality; two taps to the head from his hide one hundred metres away in the trees on the edge of the property.

From that distance, he could have taken the wand from a fairy's hand on top of a Christmas tree. Jack Mould always said that provided he saw the merest twinkle of the star, it was history.

The plan had been for Des Finch and his two agents to clamber onto the roof. That allowed them to appear above and behind the gang. Then, with Phoenix and his team at the front, they hoped to finish the job quickly.

Phoenix and Rusty always prepared a Plan B. No worries. They had to slug it out for a few rounds with these gangsters before delivering the knockout blow.

After the quick dash from the outbuilding, Kelly Dexter prepared for her next role in today's action; she unpacked two drones and made them ready to launch. The drones would provide camera shots of the gang's positions, aiding agents on both sides of the buildings.

Hayden Vincent's task was to take part in the firefight. Kelly would be held in reserve and only brought forward if things got sticky. If the gangsters took out her drones, she would pick up her weapons and join the fight. Kelly was ready for whatever the next few minutes might bring.

Rusty watched the cars drive through the gate. The first car shot past the open door of the first building. The second car spun around in a tight circle, so the car pointed back towards the gate. When the driver's side of the car blocked the gap, the driver and his passengers exited the vehicle on the driver's side, and Rusty counted four men darting through the door. They quickly ran inside and hid from view.

The first car executed the same turn by the second outbuilding. The driver got out and went to unlock the doors.

"Do you have a headshot?" Rusty asked Jack.

"Negative; the height of the vehicle and the driver's door being open is blocking my line of sight," replied Jack Mould.

The drones buzzed overhead. The man in the doorway looked at the sky.

"OK, Des, get busy with those ropes, two and one. Good luck," Phoenix ordered

Des Finch sent an agent to the further outbuilding to start climbing. He and his colleague began to get to the top of their building, one at either end, leaving the still smoking bins doing their now pointless job in the middle.

The driver, who Phoenix had identified as the gang leader, was inside the barn. The door was open, but the gap was minimal. So the three remaining occupants started getting out to join him via the driver's side.

"Jack? Leave your position and come forward. We've lost the chance to cut the head off the snake. We need more firepower closer to the action now," said Phoenix.

"Check. I'll have to break cover from this stack of trees. I'll be visible to the enemy for four to five seconds until I find another hiding place in the old milking parlour. A little cover would be appreciated."

"No worries," said Rusty. "As soon as anyone pops their head out of those buildings, we'll give them something to occupy them."

Dimitar Marinov sensed trouble immediately after he spotted the open door. There were what appeared to be remnants of blood spatter. Someone had tried to clean it off. He barked orders to the men in his car. Nikolay Iliev phoned Todorov and told him what to do. Both car drivers lined their vehicles up for the gateway to make a rapid escape.

Once both groups of four gangsters got inside the two

buildings, it was clear; there was no fire. There had never been. Certainly not inside any of the buildings. Todorov told his boss that Georgi was dead. Someone had cut his throat.

"Professional job," he added.

"It must be SAS," said Dimitar, "the UK police don't kill anyone with a knife."

"What do we do, boss?" asked Todorov.

"What we do best," replied Dimitar, "we fight."

Dimitar Marinov ordered his men to begin arming and take up defensive positions. The heavily armed Andrey Pantev was ordered to lead the way. He could give covering fire so Nikolay could move weaponry next door for the others. Konstantin Hristov and Dimitar would stay screened by the car in the doorway, spot the attackers as they began shooting, and give extra covering fire.

"If I get a spare second, boss, I'll give those buzzing wasps up there a burst from my Uzi," growled Hristov, "they're not doing my hangover any good."

"At least you got more than two hours sleep," replied Dimitar grimly as he stared across the open ground towards the other farm buildings and the wooded areas beyond them.

"And so it begins," said Phoenix as he saw the two men burst from the furthest building. It was plain what they planned to do.

Kelly Dexter checked the camera shots from her drones as they buzzed to and fro in front of the buildings. If she sent them over the tops, the gang couldn't fire at them, and she could take the opportunity to confirm the London team's progress. Once the shooting started, there would be little time for conversations via walkie-talkie.

"Three on top, Phoenix," she relayed to her leader.

Phoenix ordered Jack and Hayden to keep the leader and his buddy busy while he and Rusty tried to take out the two running to the first building. During the first shots, Marinov was wounded, shot in the left wrist. Hristov hammered away with his Uzi, spraying in short bursts across the wide patch of ground that the supposed SAS men occupied.

Rusty and Phoenix successfully pinned down the two shooters. As Andrey Pantev reached the back of the car by the open door, a hail of bullets penetrated the wall surrounding him; he got hit, but he reached relative safety. He crawled behind the car's rear wheel. Nikolay wasn't so lucky. He stopped running when Pantev fell, and Rusty opened fire. Nikolay died instantly

Des Finch and his partner slid in a controlled fashion down the sloping roof above the doorway of the first building. They had secured the high ground, but it wouldn't stop the guns from reaching the men inside the building.

"One dead; one injured," said Rusty.

"Des," said Phoenix. "Make sure that gunman is dead; then stop anyone inside getting out to retrieve the weapons."

"Got it."

Des Finch decided to abandon the roof, and both men rappelled down the side of the building on the far west side. The remaining agent on the rooftop of the other building descended to the floor on the east side. He remained hidden, awaiting Phoenix's orders regarding the two men's exact position just around the corner.

Dimitar was still able to fire his weapon. Hristov kept a steady stream of bullets heading towards the Olympus positions. That annoying buzzing noise again overhead needed sorting out. Kelly Dexter was re-positioning her drones to pinpoint the enemy positions.

Hristov fired on the drones and hit one. Kelly Dexter aborted her mission and landed the other drone. She relayed the latest sightings to Phoenix and picked up her SA80 rifle, and waited for an invitation to join the action.

Phoenix kept watching the gunman behind the wheel of the car. He was severely wounded; so far, nobody had attempted to come out to help him indoors. Suddenly Phoenix spotted movement.

"Look out for the car, Des," shouted Phoenix.

Todorov had crept to the door of the car. He reversed it to where his friend Nikolay lay dead. Guns and ammunition lay on the floor by his body. Five seconds later, Todorov jumped out and quickly gathered the vital equipment. If Dimitar and Konstantin got to them, they still had a chance of getting out of this mess. He looked at his friend's body riddled with bullets and vowed to avenge him.

Des Finch and his partner ran around the side of the building. They became the first Olympus casualties as Andrey Pantev somehow lifted his body from the ground when he heard them approach. Pantev was still able to fire his Uzi despite his terrible injuries. At that distance, he practically cut the agents in half.

Hearing the awful noise, the agent at the far east end of the fight arena rounded the corner of the outbuilding. Two gangsters in front of him fired at will towards the Olympus agents in front of them. He opened fire.

Both Hristov and Marinov sustained injuries. The two men managed to crawl back inside the building. The agent suffered, too and slumped to the floor with his back against a tractor wheel. He could not see the shooters who had left his building. The cars screened them from him. Instead, he could see two bodies in Olympus gear at the far end of the first building. What a bloody mess, he thought before he passed out.

Todorov edged forwards. The car took lots of bullets, but he was close enough. Andrey Pantev was still breathing, but Todorov knew the enforcer didn't have long, minutes if not seconds, to live. So Todorov eased the Uzi from his grasp and beckoned for Boris Tsankov to help retrieve the weaponry he'd collected.

"Phoenix to Finch Squad B; we've got casualties at both ends of the buildings. Bring your medical team and firepower forward now. It's time to end this."

The remaining nine London agents moved forwards from their reserve position. As they neared the ground behind the outbuildings, they saw ropes and smoking fires but no sign of their colleagues. The group split into sections of three. One group went left, one right, and the others waited for further instructions.

Inside the outbuilding, the two gangsters assessed the damage. Dimitar Marinov was a tough cookie; it was only more flesh wounds.

"Konstantin, are you still able to fight?"

"Yes, boss, it's just a through and through; I've known worse."

"Can you take two Uzis? I can only fire one gun. I'll take an Uzi, and we'll try to get to the others. Anton and Boris will be feeling left out."

Both men tried to laugh, but it hurt too much.

"Did you remember to pick up the cash you stashed here, boss?" asked Konstantin Hristov.

"I've been busy," said Dimitar, "why do you want me to order a takeaway?"

This time, they laughed despite the pain. Both men knew the score.

They got to their feet with a struggle and collected as much ammunition as they could carry. Dimitar put a pistol in his belt and picked up one of the dozen submachine guns they had in their arms cache. Hristov lifted two to waist high and nodded.

"No problem. Let's go."

Phoenix watched and waited.

"Two thugs are leaving the furthest building heading for their friends. Jack and Hayden, can you move forward and take them out? Rusty and I will give you covering fire."

"Yes, boss," called Hayden.

The two men emerged into the open and started to zig-zag their way to new safety positions. Then, Rusty and Phoenix opened fire on the open door. As he heard the sudden increase in the shooting, Andrey Pantev struggled to raise his head, but it was over; a few seconds later, he breathed his last.

Jack Mould and Hayden Vincent lay prone, with the scopes on their rifles homing in on the running Marinov and Hristov. With the injuries they carried and the gear, their running appeared laboured, and both men stumbled more than once as they reached the doorway. Finally, Hayden Vincent had a head in his cross-hairs. He squeezed the trigger, and Konstantin Hristov fell, his two Uzis blazing away wildly in all directions. Then, for a few seconds, it was deathly quiet.

The agents at the rear had moved forwards stealthily, and at the east end of the farthest building, the team of three found their wounded colleague. He had several bullet wounds, but he would make it. Two agents moved him away to the rear of the building and treated him. The other agent trained his gun on the two doorways. Nobody in his line of sight ahead of him was still breathing.

The trio near the gateway tried to cope with their emotions rather than injuries. Silently, they laid the bodies of Des Finch and their colleague on stretchers and took them to the rear. Nothing more could be done. Phoenix told them to stand down and prepare for the clean-up stage.

There were four dead, one wounded; four left inside the first building with limited weaponry and no access to more ammunition. The Olympus losses were tragic but expected. The gang members were experienced fighters, prepared to fight to the bitter end.

That end was minutes away.

Phoenix and Rusty moved into more advanced positions. Jack and Vincent scrambled forward from a tractor to a cart, stacks of wooden pallets, and got cover wherever available. The agents soon found shelter twenty metres from the doorway and ten metres ahead of the Larcombe lads.

Phoenix called the remaining London agent forward from his position to the right of the doorway.

"We've got you covered; it's time to shake these buggers up."

"Check," replied the agent. He removed a flash-bang stun grenade from his pack and inched forwards, training his gun on the doorway ahead. Then he arrived alongside the door and began running swiftly past the entrance. He lobbed the grenade inside and kept sprinting to safety at the end of the building.

Jack and Hayden rose and moved forward as soon as the agent started running. They reached the doorway together and started firing.

Anton Dobrev and Iliya Todorov had been closest to where the grenade landed. The pair were out of action, at least temporarily. Dimitar Marinov was still alert enough to fire back, but his aim was poor due to his injuries.

Boris Tsankov had been loading the weapons that Dimitar had managed to deliver. He had seen the grenade as it arced through the air. He had hit the ground and yelled a warning. Boris returned fire towards the doorway, and the two men disappeared from view.

"What do we do, boss?" asked Tsankov, "they have us pinned down. We need to break out of here. Outside in the open, we have a chance of taking a few of the bastards with us. In here, we're sitting ducks."

Anton and Iliya were injured and dazed but recovering gradually. Finally, Dimitar looked around the garage and dragged himself to his feet.

"Open the door when I say," he ordered.

Boris Tsankov wondered if the boss was losing it. The other two thugs were up on their feet and moving forward. They stood ready to drag the big doors open. Their guns and ammunition were still on the floor, where they scattered after the stun grenade had exploded.

Outside, Jack Mould was helping Hayden Vincent back to a safe zone. Hayden had been hit in the calf when Tsankov had let fly. Kelly Dexter was concerned about her partner, but she retained her position. Her rifle with its thirty-round magazine centred on the doorway. Phoenix and Rusty were closer to the action, covering Jack and Hayden's withdrawal.

Suddenly the doors were dragged open, and the throaty sound of a vehicle chugged away in the dark interior. The JCB mini digger with Dimitar Marinov at the wheel barrelled out of the darkness and rammed into the car that blocked the doorway. With the scoop lowered, he shoved the car to one side. Marinov raised the scoop to give a measure of protection to him and the other three men directly behind it.

It was a comical sight. As Dimitar brought the JCB to a halt, Boris Tsankov and Anton Dobrev jumped onto the vehicle's tracks on either side. All three men opened fire with sub-machine guns. Hayden was on the ground being tended to by Jack Mould. Jack promptly picked up his weapon and ran forward to return to the fray.

Phoenix and Rusty were fazed by how the gang leader imagined they could make a successful escape. In seconds, they were locked in on the two gang members in exposed positions on the side of the tracked vehicle.

Tsankov was almost instantly hit in the stomach, chest and head by a volley of shots from Phoenix. He fell backwards onto the ground. Dobrev and Marinov were firing wildly; raising the scoop may have given protection, but it limited their vision, and when they hit Jack Mould, it was more luck than judgement.

Kelly Dexter aimed and fired. Anton Dobrev disappeared from where he stood on the track. Three shots to the chest drove him backwards; he was dead before he hit the floor.

Iliya Todorov had been cowering behind the JCB. On either side of him, he now saw a dead comrade. He had only had time to snatch up a handgun from the garage floor. He checked to find he had four bullets left. Iliya shouted at the top of his voice and charged off in front of the digger. Rusty put a bullet between his eyes to bring his brief part in the firefight to a close.

Dimitar Marinov was alone.

He thrust the JCB into gear and lowered the scoop. Then, standing up in the enclosed cab, he drove forward at the best speed the little digger could manage. Finally, he raised the Uzi to begin firing; the gang leader was an easy target.

Three Olympus agents fired at once, and Dimitar Marinov died in a hail of bullets. The battle of Eton Wick had ended. The firefight lasted just twenty-two minutes.

"Situation report?" asked Phoenix.

Kelly Dexter was tending to her partner.

"I'm fine, Phoenix; Hayden needs a doctor, but he'll live."

"All fine here," said the senior agent from the London squad at the rear of the buildings, "we've nearly completed the clean-up back here. Permission to start the clean-up inside?"

"Go ahead; take care of your casualty, and well, you know how we feel about losing Des Finch and his colleague."

"Thanks, sir," came the reply.

"Are you okay, Jack?" called Phoenix. He hadn't seen or heard from him for a while.

Rusty was on his feet, running back towards the sniper who had fallen to the ground between Hayden's position and theirs. A stray shot from one of the shooters, when they were firing blind, must have hit him in the head. He was beyond help.

"Jack didn't make it," Rusty told Phoenix.

"No, not Jack," said Phoenix, "he was probably the best sniper the army ever had. Of all the places he's fought for his country, he dies in a farmyard, and nobody will ever hear about it."

Phoenix knew that the clean-up was a vital stage of any Olympus mission. The London team were removing the Olympus bodies. Within a couple of hours, the team would cleanse this quiet corner of Berkshire. The presence of any involvement of Olympus in this direct action against the Bulgarian gang had gone. He and Rusty watched as Jack 'Jelly' Mould's body was taken away on a stretcher. Dejected, they walked to the far building.

Inside, they soon located the arms cache and an open safe.

"The leader must have emptied it. I'll check to see if there's anything next door or on his body," said Rusty.

"We don't usually loot the bodies, Rusty?" said Phoenix, somewhat puzzled.

"I thought we could recompense the farmer for the damage and disturbance caused by this lot," said Rusty.

"Not a bad idea, mate," said Phoenix. "It might help him to keep his mouth shut about what went on here this morning,"

Rusty returned a couple of minutes later. He had found a bag containing almost sixteen thousand pounds.

"Sounds fair enough," said Phoenix.

Rusty headed off towards the farmhouse.

As the firefight had raged on the other side of his farm, Christopher Mellish had finished the bottle of scotch long ago. He sat at his kitchen table. Then, he heard the approaching footsteps on the concrete path.

Christopher Mellish was agonising over who had won the battle. Was it the gangsters coming to kill him or the police to ask him questions about why he had harboured them, allowing them to kill so many innocent people? Either way, it was something he couldn't face.

Rusty knocked on the door.

There was a single gunshot from inside the farmhouse.

No one answered the door.

The clean-up ended at a quarter to ten. It took just over one hundred minutes. Finally, all the vehicles were back inside the garage, together with the dead bodies of the gang members. After that, everything outside was cleaned efficiently.

Kelly Dexter found her stricken drone and packed it away with its colleague. She helped Hayden Vincent limp to the van they parked earlier in the lay-by further along the lane. The flesh wound in his calf was now dressed and would keep until they got back to Larcombe. Then, the medical centre could tidy his injury correctly, and they could get home to Shrivenham.

Rusty and Phoenix checked the outbuildings and the yard one final time.

"Better lock up," said Rusty.

"What do we do about the farmer?"

"He's not going anywhere," said Rusty. "We could do one of those anonymous phone calls when we get back. What do you reckon?"

Phoenix shrugged. There was nothing inside the farmhouse or buildings to link this carnage to Olympus. When the police finally turned up, they might mark this as a gang war.

In time, if they dug around on the farm long enough, they should discover what became of the ram-raid gang. Unfortunately, what they made of Christopher Mellish's death didn't concern him.

The vital thing was that there was nothing to implicate Olympus.

They had avenged the families of Claire Ricketts and little Kassie Paget. The gang would never terrorise any other quiet towns around the country or continue with whatever other criminal pursuits they were involved in. His team had lost three men to achieve their goal but delivered a satisfactory result.

What he wanted to do more than anything was get back to Larcombe to be with Athena. Rusty must be itching to get home for Zara's arrival too.

Phoenix walked behind the outbuildings and saw that the London team was preparing to drive away. He admired the look of their vehicles. He was pleased with his excellent idea.

"Don't forget to pick up the notices, will you?" he said to the senior agent.

"All in hand, Phoenix," he said, "we'll be seeing you."

Phoenix stood and watched as the vans pulled away and headed up the lane.

"Ready to go home, boss?" said Rusty as Phoenix emerged from the side of the building.

"Do you want to remove the signage from the vans before we drive off, or do it when we get back to Larcombe?"

"Best to peel them off before we leave, I reckon," said Rusty.

Any cars or horse-riders passing the lay-by at that precise moment might have been confused. They may have wondered about signs advertising *Direct Action Film*s with the slogan, *The stories from tomorrow's headlines you can watch today* stripped away to leave blank surfaces on the sides of the vans.

All around the lanes approaching the isolated farm at Eton Wick, the London-based vans carrying similar signage, for now, stop off here and there to collect notice boards with the urgent message: -

Film scenes are being shot near here this morning.

Please accept our apologies for any inconvenience caused.
DAF

"Perfect planning prevents piss-poor performance," said Rusty as they began the two-hour drive back to Larcombe Manor. Kelly's van was barely in sight ahead of them in the distance.

"Not perfect though, Rusty; Plan A might have seen us clean the lot of them up inside ten minutes without a scratch with luck. As soon as we lost the element of surprise, we were bound to sustain casualties."

"Will Athena consider three dead and two injured, one seriously, as an acceptable price to pay?" asked Rusty.

"Don't ask Athena or the Olympus Project's leadership; ask the people of Britain. This gang has robbed and killed at will; they've caused panic throughout the country, with people scared to visit shopping centres or even to venture outside their homes. Of course, there will be shock and disgust at the violence at the farm today. But they'll be happy and relieved it's over if this gets marked down as gang violence. The shops will be busy again tomorrow."

The pair drove back to Larcombe Manor alone with their thoughts.

Death had been close to both of them today. But this time, it just passed them by.

Chapter Ten

Rusty steered the van through the gateway and headed for the ice-house. He longed to get to the stable block to be ready to welcome Zara. She wasn't due until late this afternoon. He needed time to get the sounds, the smells and the memories of this morning out of his head. If only for a while.

Phoenix helped Rusty unload the vehicle, and they began to move the equipment back underground to the armoury. A warm welcome awaited them from Barry Longdon and Pete Thompson.

"Good to see you made it back in one piece, lads," said Thommo.

"A messy business, boys," said Rusty, "we lost 'Jelly' Mould. Hayden suffered a bullet through the calf. He should be having that sewn up now."

"Did you know Des Finch?" asked Phoenix; the two armourers shook their heads.

"He and another bloke bought it, and a young lad was badly wounded but should make a full recovery."

"What was the final score?" asked Bazza.

"Nine-three to the good guys," replied Rusty.

"That's another bunch of murdering thugs off the streets forever. If the police had caught up with them, they would have got little more than community service," muttered Thommo.

"Don't be daft," said Bazza.

"Well, they wouldn't have served life; you can put your mortgage on that," said Thommo.

"That's not what I meant," said Bazza. "I meant, don't be daft; the police are so hopeless they would never catch up with them."

Rusty and Phoenix had to laugh at these two; despite the jokes they always cracked, they were passionate about justice. But, like sticks of Blackpool rock, if you cut these two agents open, they had Olympus running through them from head to toe.

After getting the equipment stowed below, they returned to the surface and headed for the stable block. The two friends dropped by the medical centre to get the latest on Hayden. They found him sat up in bed, being pampered by Kelly.

"Making the most of your little scratch, I see," said Phoenix.

Hayden gave a wry smile.

"I couldn't have made it away from the door of the building if it hadn't been for Jack. He saved my life, and within minutes, he was dead."

"A sad loss," said Phoenix. "I'm off to the manor house to report to Athena on the mission. Take care, and we'll see you both again soon."

Rusty left his friend and walked into his quarters. He needed to shower, change and rest up before this evening.

Phoenix walked across the lawn and wondered whether Athena saw the vans returning. He needed to report back to her on the mission, but he wanted to deal with the death of Jack Mould first. Phoenix wanted to get his family informed as soon as possible. Perhaps he should go to Frome as he had been in charge of the mission. He'd never done one so far; maybe Rusty could help, except his day was mapped out already.

When Phoenix reached the apartment, he found Athena wasn't there. So he rang security and asked her whereabouts. They told him she was in a meeting with Alastor.

"A cosy *tete a tete*, eh?" he thought. First, I may go for a swim to ease the stresses of the day; then, perhaps we can get together for lunch. Phoenix was starving.

Zara Wheeler left her parents' house later than initially planned. It took longer to say goodbye to her parents than usual and even longer to part with Napoleon and Josephine, her beloved cats. Her Dad waved her off and wondered why she bothered. Cats don't give a fig about humans; they're not faithful companions, not like dogs. Cats get up and leave when they feel like it. If they do come back, they're doing you a favour.

A few minutes before six, Zara reached the outskirts of Bath. She drove to her old house first to take a last peek. The home she had created after she bought it from Phil and Erica Hounsell will always hold a special place in her heart. It was the first home of her own. Hardly a year since that day, and now she was moving in with Rusty.

Zara made the short trip from the house she had sold within days of going on the market and approached the driveway into Larcombe Manor. Her last visit had been as a police detective; now, she would be here as a civilian.

A van drove past, heading for the exit; Kelly Dexter took

Hayden Vincent home to Shrivenham to recuperate. As Zara pulled up in front of the imposing front entrance of the main building, a member of staff crossed the courtyard to meet her.

"Good evening. You're Mr Scott's partner, I believe? I'm Martin; we expected you,"

Zara racked her brain to work out who this Mr Scott could be for a second, but she soon recovered.

"Is Rusty here?" she asked.

"So I understand, miss, he returned from duty at lunchtime. He's in the stable block; can I direct you?"

Martin walked to the end of the main building and pointed out the stable block on the left-hand side of the estate.

"Turn right here and follow the road past the walled kitchen garden on your left and the orangery on the right. I'll call ahead, and Rusty will be ready to greet you when you arrive."

"Thanks, Martin," said Zara, and she drove down to be reunited with her partner.

Rusty spent the afternoon going over the events of the morning. Losing 'Jelly' Mould had been dreadful. Phoenix called to say he wanted to chat with him before driving to Frome tomorrow to talk to Jack's family.

The ex-SAS man had never met any of the London squad on his travels, neither in the army nor as an Olympus agent, but it still hurt to lose fellow soldiers. Hayden had been fortunate, as had he and Phoenix; the gang they had been up against were professional killers who handled weapons with effortless skill. They had been no soft target; nightmares would come to him from this morning's battle.

The phone call from the main house disrupted his

thoughts. Zara had arrived. He went to the stable block entrance to greet her.

"Finally, we can be together," he said as he gathered her into his arms. "No doubts?"

"None," Zara replied. "I've spent my week's holiday wisely. I've walked in the hills to think things over. I talked to my parents about why I left the police, cuddled my cats and shed the guise of a police officer for good. When I started, I hoped to make a difference. While the police, the courts, and lawmakers work against one another, criminals will always thrive. In the future, I believe I can truly help to change things for the better,"

"Let's go inside, and I'll give you a quick tour of our rooms and the other facilities in the block. Then we'll get your things from the car and get you settled in properly. Looking at the piles of stuff in the back seat, it will take ages."

"Lead on," said Zara. "I agree; get moved in first, have a bite to eat and after that, bed."

"Sounds like a plan," said Rusty.

"Will I get to see the rest of the estate tomorrow?" asked Zara.

"I've got a meeting at nine, so no lie-in for either of us," Rusty replied, ruffling his partner's hair. "It wouldn't surprise me if you don't get a call soon from Giles Burke, your new boss. He'll want you to get used to the systems in the ice-house as soon as possible. As I understand it, Athena will give you the guided tour after the morning meeting. There are areas I'm afraid that you won't have clearance to enter. You shouldn't just wander off exploring, but Athena will explain everything."

"Athena? Is that Ms Fox, the lady in charge when I

visited here last year? I thought her name was Annette or Annabelle?"

They were at the door to their quarters, and Rusty ushered Zara inside. He was used to basic and functional. Zara suddenly realised that although this might be several steps up from the barracks she saw portrayed on film and TV, it was far from luxurious.

"All the comforts of home," said Rusty.

"It will do," said Zara, squeezing Rusty. "If this is the price I have to pay to be with the man I love, then I'm happy enough."

Rusty and Zara left their quarters, and Rusty pointed out the other rooms along the corridor that housed individual agents. They were the only couple in this part of the site.

"Beyond that, we have a medical centre. It has state-of-the-art facilities to treat injured personnel. We also perform cosmetic surgery on agents who need it to help hide their true identity from the outside world."

"Gosh, we didn't get shown any of this when we checked that Charity Commission query. Is the medical centre busy?"

Rusty drew a long breath.

"I can't go into many details, but we got involved in a mission this morning."

"Oh, that chap Martin said you returned from duty at lunchtime when he met me outside the manor house. What can you tell me?"

"It was hairy; I can tell you that," said Rusty. "We suffered casualties, and one of the wounded got brought back here. I think they discharged him a while ago. It was only a flesh wound. He's on his way home now."

"I passed a van on the way here. Don't the agents have to live in here at Larcombe?"

"We have people worldwide, Zara, with the majority in the UK. There are similar establishments to this one scattered around," Rusty began, but he paused and considered how much detail he should tell her. "Maybe that can wait until you've been here a while and settled in properly. Little bits will emerge as you work with Giles, anyway. It won't take long to build up the big picture. Let's move in your things; then, if you have more questions, we can chat over dinner."

"I've got a lot to learn," said Zara, "the first thing I must learn is to be patient."

Rusty put an arm around her shoulder and walked up the corridor towards the car crammed with Zara's belongings. Dinner would be a while yet.

Meanwhile, in the main building, Phoenix and Athena had found one another at last.

He had phoned Rusty and then spent an energetic hour in the pool and the gym, followed by a late lunch. Athena finished her meeting with Alastor. She was ploughing through the research he'd gathered on the Olympians when Phoenix wandered into the apartment.

"Thank God you're back safe, darling," she said, running to him and throwing her arms around his neck; Athena kissed him and clung to him for several minutes. Phoenix didn't have the energy or the inclination to move.

Phoenix eventually led her to the sofa and made her sit. He took her through the details of the Eton Wick mission. Athena was visibly upset that Jack Mould and the London agents had perished.

"What reaction has there been?" he asked, "I've been

too strung out to follow up; I needed time to clear my head."

Athena told him that so far, they had no news at all. Giles kept tabs on the media, waiting for the story to break. Since the farm at Eton Wick was relatively remote, and the farmer's family estranged, they may have a day or two's grace before the proverbial hit the fan.

"What did you get up to while I was gone? Anything interesting?" asked Phoenix.

There was so much she could tell him. But, for now, Athena wanted to enjoy the fact that Phoenix was home safe.

"Oh, just Olympus admin work, that's all, nothing but boring paperwork."

As they relaxed together, watching the clock tick around until Artemis arrived at Larcombe, Athena reflected on her meeting with Alastor. His progress was slow, but she remained convinced it would bear fruit in time. The pair had scheduled further meetings, meetings she needed to keep from Phoenix for the time being.

The phone rang. Phoenix answered. After he rang off, he said: -

"The security staff have informed us that Artemis has arrived; she's with Rusty in the stable block. Do you want to go over to greet her?"

"They'll be moving her things in and getting oriented in their quarters. So let's leave the lovers alone tonight. There will be time tomorrow to catch up with them both."

Athena stood up and walked to the bedroom door.

"Lovers should be alone. We can eat later; let's sharpen our appetites."

Phoenix pushed himself wearily off the sofa and strolled towards the bedroom. What time had that alarm sounded this morning? How many lengths of the pool had he swum this afternoon? Oh well, sometimes a man's gotta do what a man's gotta do.

It took two hours to get everything where it needed to go.

Rusty and Zara stood back and admired their handiwork. Her clothes were stored away, and a few ornaments from her Bath home made their quarters look more dignified.

"It's time to show you the old workers' cottages," said Rusty.

"What have you got hidden away in there, a ten-pin bowling alley?" asked Zara.

"Not much call for that here, but we have a staff canteen, a cinema, a swimming pool and a fitness centre."

"You're kidding," said Zara.

"Come and see," said Rusty. "If we're quick, we might have time to eat and watch a film."

"After the day we've both had, I reckon a meal and that early night might be preferable, said Zara.

"No argument from me," said Rusty with a grin.

While treating themselves to a three-course dinner in the staff canteen, Rusty asked if Zara had any more questions. She hesitated, then said that they could keep for now.

"There's one thing you need to know," said Rusty, "as from tonight, you will no longer be referred to at Larcombe as Zara Wheeler. None of the staff, including Martin, who met you on arrival, know your true identity. To protect that and Olympus, those agents who are not subject to the charity's headcount of ex-service personnel treated for PTSD are given a code name. As you thought earlier, Annabelle Fox is indeed Athena. You can never divulge that information to anyone. You must take that secret to the grave. From now on, you will be called Artemis. She was the goddess of the hunt. Athena thought it fitted your role in the ice-house perfectly."

"When I drove in through those gates this evening," said Artemis, getting used to her new name, "I knew my life would change. But I never imagined that change would be so dramatic. Do you have any more shocks in store?"

"Not tonight," said Rusty.

In the main house, the other lovers were in each other's arms. Phoenix was dropping off to sleep. Athena was battling with her thoughts.

"Phoenix," she finally began, "we've never discussed the future. Missions like today's show that nothing is certain. Jack Mould's family will never see him again; they could never have imagined that this morning. We're a couple, but we've never considered marriage or what might follow. What do you think?"

Phoenix was wide awake now.

"What might follow marriage? Divorce, I guess, but in our case, it's unlikely. Athena, we are a couple, and I want to be with you as long as I live. Missions such as today's show that I can't control how long I might be in my line of work. I've been married twice before, and if we did marry, I believe it would be third time lucky; but if we stay as we are, then I'd be just as content with that."

"What about what might follow if we're a couple, whether married or not?"

Phoenix thought for a while.

"Are you trying to tell me something?" he asked quietly.

Athena started to cry softly as her head rested on his chest.

"I haven't plucked up the courage to do the test yet, but I think I'm pregnant. I'm sorry."

"Sorry? Why be sorry? It's twelve years since my gorgeous Sharron died; I avenged her death three summers ago. That was a different life. My life now is with Olympus, at Larcombe with you."

Athena was still crying, but her tears turned to tears of joy.

"Perhaps I should amend that," Phoenix whispered in her ear, "at Larcombe with you and the baby."

Monday, July 22nd, 2013

Athena chaired the morning meeting at nine o'clock, where they thoroughly debriefed the Eton Wick mission. Giles Burke had heard nothing whatever. Nothing to suggest the so-called film crew raised more than a disgruntled eyebrow on the occasional passer-by in the country lanes.

The late Dimitar Marinov and his gang were allowed to rest in peace for a while longer. The tormented Christopher Mellish had to stay seated at his kitchen table. It was too early in the day to tell whether the patrols on the M5 had resumed. Or if a new initiative dreamt up by the Met would direct their search for the murderous foreign gang towards the Royal Borough of Windsor and Maidenhead. For now, everything stayed calm.

As soon as the meeting ended, Phoenix and Rusty discussed the impending visit to Jack Mould's family. Rusty provided his friend with the correct words and phrases that served him well over the years when breaking dreadful news to loved ones. Finally, Phoenix set off on the twenty-five-minute drive. It wouldn't be easy, but at least he had the tools for the job now.

Once Phoenix and Rusty left the room, Athena asked Giles if Artemis had visited the intelligence section. Giles shook his head.

"I rang their quarters at about half-past nine but got no reply; I assumed they were already asleep."

"Several of us decided on an early night, Giles. It was a long and busy day. I'll call her now, and we'll talk to you later."

Giles and Henry Case trotted back to the ice-house to watch their teams. Their team continued gathering scraps of data that helped them be a valuable resource to the Olympus Project.

Athena rang the stable block. Rusty walked through the door just as Zara picked up the phone. She had been expecting the call and recognised the voice. It was the well-educated, upper-class voice of the woman she interviewed last year.

"Good morning, Athena," she said, "I'm looking forward to meeting you."

The call ended without delay.

"She's picking me up from here in ten minutes; we're off on a walkabout," said Zara.

"Have fun," said Rusty, "I'll catch up with you later today. Undoubtedly, Athena will drop you off with Giles Burke after the tour, and you'll be pitched straight in at the deep end."

Athena had left the drawing room and was striding across the lawns towards the stable block. She felt a little anxious about meeting new people, particularly ex-police officers. Nevertheless, she and Phoenix agreed that this young lady must be welcomed and assimilated into the team as Rusty's partner in the New Year.

The two women met at the entrance to the stable

block. Rusty had suggested it might be better than making Athena knock on the quarters' door where she and Phoenix became lovers. Not that it was likely to be a painful memory, but it avoided any potential embarrassment.

"Artemis, welcome to Larcombe Manor," said Athena warmly, "it's lovely to meet you again."

"Thank you, Athena," replied Artemis, "we're on the same side this time."

"Rusty got you settled in last evening. I gather he gave you the tour of the stable block and the workers' cottages?"

"We were too tired to do much more yesterday. I want to see as much as I can today before I start working."

"Let's walk then; there will be areas you won't visit just yet. As we get to know you, and you get to know us, the access codes on the electronic pass you receive can be reprogrammed."

The two women set off towards the manor house.

"The orangery is spectacular, in my opinion. My old boss Erebus used to visit it almost every day. Rusty has meetings with my co-leader here at Larcombe from time to time; I'll walk you through to appreciate the building's ambience, but this area is off-limits after today."

Artemis admired the elegant structure, furniture and accessories; they oozed quality.

"It's beautiful," said Artemis, "but I feel out of place here. It's a gentleman's domain."

Athena laughed.

"I can't imagine what Phoenix will make of being called a gentleman, and we both know Rusty is a man's man."

As they left the orangery and walked across the kitchen garden road, Artemis filed away another piece of information about her new home. The co-leader was code-named

Phoenix; she wondered who he had been in his pre-Olympus life.

"We grow our vegetables and fruit, as you can see," Athena said as they skirted around the side of the walled garden.

"What a lovely selection of herbs, too," said Artemis as the various scents reached her nose.

"Rusty has told you that the charity is a cover for our true purpose. The garden and the veterans who tend to it are vital as a smokescreen for the outside world. When the commissioners visit, they see this and the men pruning trees and plants, watering flowers and shrubs, and mowing the lawns. That helps reinforce the message that they are recovering from the horrors they have experienced in war zones worldwide. The fact we have the fruits of their labour available to our chefs and housekeepers is a bonus."

Artemis thought how naïve she had been when she had been here last time. She had taken everything at face value. But, just as the Charity Commissioners had over the years, it was so plausible and clever. Athena led her towards the main building.

The two women stood on the patio in front of the Georgian manor house, and Athena briefly outlined its history. Artemis listened intently but knew that this was another 'no-go' area for her, for the present. She couldn't help thinking that her world was shrinking fast.

"It's a beautiful day, so let's enjoy the gardens. Erebus walked this way often. First, he and his wife planted the many trees and shrubs. Then, the loving couple sat on the patio, looked out over the estate, and watched their only daughter Helen riding her pony around the grounds."

"Is the daughter living locally then?" asked Artemis,

"won't she inherit this estate when this Erebus and Elizabeth die?"

"Elizabeth died only recently, but Helen was killed by a drunk driver years ago. That event proved to be one of the key motivators in creating the project."

"What happened to your old boss?" asked Artemis.

"He retired at Christmas; he's now living on the island of Ibiza. When he dies, the manor house and his estate will pass to Olympus."

Ahead of them now stood the old cottages.

"We'll skip this as you've seen the facilities on offer there," said Athena, "beyond the cottages, there's a wooded section. That forest extends to the edges of the property. There's little to see except an awful lot of trees. Erebus created a tiny pet cemetery in the woods over there at the rear of the ice-house. I believe it helped to soothe a young Helen when the family cats and dogs died. There are no headstones to read, I'm afraid. It's creepy if you ask me. I never go there." Artemis shivered; the pet cemetery didn't sound like a place she wanted to visit.

They stood at the entrance to the ice-house. Artemis had no clue how this insignificant folly of a building could be the same 'ice-house' Rusty described as her new place of work. She turned around, but this was their last port of call.

"I can tell you're confused," laughed Athena, "follow me."

Athena led her through the doorway. Athena pressed the call button. Artemis heard the lift rise for a few seconds, and then the steel doors slid open.

"Shall we?" said her tour guide.

Artemis followed her host into the lift and watched as she selected the button for the first level of three. When the doors opened, they walked into the command centre.

"This is where we track the movements of identified criminal targets, any possible terrorist threat and anything that threatens our national security. There are recreation rooms, dental surgery, and an operating theatre. Staff can take sleep here in shifts if we're under severe pressure. Those beds are at the far end. No doubt, you will prefer to walk back to the stable block. You will work on this floor. The two floors below us house the armoury, a shooting range and things of that nature."

Artemis glanced at Athena. Why take this trouble building a facility with three levels unless the other two were just as vital as the upper floor?

"Can we go to visit them?" asked Artemis.

"Sorry, they're off-limits," replied Athena, "oh, there's Giles Burke. How lucky. Giles, may I introduce your new operative Artemis. Artemis, meet Giles."

The two shook hands. Artemis saw that Giles resembled the archetypal computer geek, just as she did at school, university, and early in her police career. Nervously both of them pushed their glasses up on their noses.

"Welcome, Artemis. I hope that Athena has finished your tour and that you will stay with us now. There's plenty to learn; the sooner we start, the better."

"She's all yours, Giles," said Athena. "I'll head back to the house and wait for Phoenix to return."

"Still no breaking news to report, Athena," said Giles.

"Artemis is one of us now, Giles. You can tell her what she needs to know about yesterday's mission. I'm sure she knew what preceded it and why it became necessary."

Giles nodded. Athena left them, and Artemis began her induction programme in the command centre. It was lunchtime; her stomach told her that. Giles showed no signs of needing to take a break. They appeared to be in for a long afternoon. Her life as a huntress had truly begun.

Athena walked back to the manor house alone. Her thoughts turned to Phoenix, and her concerns over the baby and how he might react melted away as he held her last night. She thought too of Erebus. Just mentioning him and parts of his background to Artemis stirred many happy memories of her mentor. As she climbed the grassy slope to the patio and passed the table where he always sat, she wondered how he was enjoying his retirement.

Santa Eulalia, the third largest resort on the island of Ibiza, is little more than twelve miles from the airport. A quiet, working town welcomed William and Elizabeth Hunt with open arms when they honeymooned there. There were changes in the decades that followed. Much of the attractiveness remained unadulterated. When he arrived in January, William Horatio Hunt had been more than satisfied with his choice of a spot to spend his retirement.

Gavin, his crewman, and bodyguard had sailed 'Elizabeth' his yacht from the UK, to her new home in the exclusive marina. William had flown into Ibiza and taken a taxi past Eivissa, Ibiza's Old Town, and the town on the river. The taxi driver dropped him at the marina; Gavin helped William carry his small suitcase on board. Everything else had travelled over on board 'Elizabeth.'

William adapted to the switch from the challenges of running things at Larcombe Manor to being retired with little to occupy his mind quickly. After breakfast, he walked along the tree-lined promenade and admired the broad and sandy beach. There was no rush; the newspapers arrived mid to late morning; he picked up his copy of The Times from the kiosk at the top of the little Rambla and walked back to the seafront between flowering oleanders and hibiscus. Occasionally in the morning, tables were erected and filled with craft items. As the weeks ticked by the street, vendors recognised the arrival of an elegantly dressed elderly gentleman and called out a friendly greeting. William smiled and raised a hand in reply.

He loved walking the Calle San Jaime around lunchtime, too; he watched and listened as the locals came together for coffee and conversation at the tables on the pavements. The town was at its bustling busiest on these occasions.

When the weather was kind to him after lunch, and he needed the exercise from a 'constitutional', he walked from Calle San Jaime to the front. From there, he'd stroll along the promenade to Mariner's beach, where the only river in the Balearics flowed into the sea. Then, finally, he took the peaceful river walk that meanders up to the Roman bridge. He delighted in finding that they had carefully and faithfully restored the bridge since his last visit with his beloved wife. William spent several afternoons since his arrival sitting on one of the stone benches that overlooked the slow-running river, reflecting on those happy days with Elizabeth.

In the evenings, he had plenty of choices: he could dine in a restaurant yards from his yacht's mooring or be in one of several hotels or restaurants on the promenade in less than five minutes. Occasionally, he crossed Calle San Jaime and visited Calle San Vicente, famously known as the street of restaurants or, more commonly to the locals, as restaurant alley.

Now and then, he and Gavin took 'Elizabeth' for a sail, especially on sweltering days. They would sail around the island and visit Majorca or Menorca. The two men called in at little coves or busy resorts where splendid eateries served some of the best fresh fish dishes available. The cuisine was varied and consistently excellent. Life was good.

William had a favourite spot to sit and watch the world go by after lunch. With his copy of The Times under his arm, he headed back towards the marina and stopped at the Ring O'Bells on Calle de Mar. He would walk up the steps from the promenade and find a chair in the shade on the verandah. William never waited long before a friendly face appeared. He ordered his usual *café con leche* and began to read the newspaper.

By the end of his first week in Santa Eulalia del Rio, the owner and his wife had been on first-name terms with him. Then, when he folded his newspaper, ready to start the crossword, a voice would call out from the dark recesses of the bar behind him.

"Ready for your second cup, William?"

William would raise his hand in acknowledgement.

"Many thanks."

Then he took his fountain pen from the top pocket of his summer jacket and took up the challenge. He completed it before the coffee cooled. Erebus could well have been the pseudonym for a crossword compiler; William Horatio Hunt was a cruciverbalist *par excellence.*

As Athena reminisced about her mentor at Larcombe that Monday lunchtime in July, William Hunt sat sipping his first cup of coffee. It was a hot day. Gavin had stayed in the marina washing the decks and preparing 'Elizabeth' for a morning sail to Portinatx. The town's hotels were comfortably full of holidaymakers, and the bars and restaurants were busy. William had company in front of him on the lower patio; the wooden tables were full of new sunseekers, pining for all-day breakfasts and the first ice-cold lager of the day. The happy voices of children filled the air.

William sat on the verandah with his coffee and his newspaper. He hoped to read news from home about this terrible foreign gang terrorising the country. Surely Athena's Olympus agents *must* be on their trail by now? He scolded himself for caring about their progress on the matter; it was not his problem anymore. As he folded his newspaper to tackle the crossword, he thought of Phoenix. What a terrific find he had been.

As he reached for his pen in his jacket's top pocket, a shadow fell over the table where he sat. Someone loomed over him. He was about to raise his head when he felt a sharp prick in his neck. His attacker moved into the bar and pushed through the swing doors into the toilets. When he returned, he walked quickly out of the bar, down the steps and got swallowed up in the crowds of holidaymakers.

William sat in the chair, realising that he was finding it difficult to focus or move. He sighed. He took up his fountain pen and filled in a handful of squares on the crossword with a shaky hand.

"Ready for that second cup, William?" called Hayden from inside the bar.

William couldn't even raise a hand in reply.

Hayden and Yvette served customers for a while, and then Yvette went outside to take an order from a family that had just sat at an empty table. She glanced at William on the verandah; she could only see the top of his straw fedora. It appeared the older man had dropped off to sleep. It was a hot day, and he was in his seventies, after all. Bless him.

"I think I'll take a coffee out to William anyway," Yvette said to Hayden when she returned indoors. She gently nudged William as she placed it on the table in front of him on her return.

Commodore William Horatio Hunt OBE Royal Navy Retired (code name Erebus) slumped forwards onto the table. He was dead.

Chapter Eleven

Hayden telephoned for an ambulance. Then he went to the marina to find Gavin. The former naval officer ran up to the bar, but nothing was to be done. He searched for any signs of foul play. However, nothing came to mind. He knew he must call Larcombe Manor and inform them of his employer's death.

It was likely to be natural causes. At seventy-three, despite apparently being in good health, you never knew what effect the heat might have had on William's heart. On the other hand, maybe there had been something else. A ticking bomb was waiting to end things. He looked at Hayden and shook his head.

"The paramedics needn't rush; he's gone, I'm afraid."

Hayden rang the policia municipal, too; better to get everything moving as soon as possible. Things can move slowly at times on a holiday island. Yvette did her best to comfort the remaining customers and appease a couple of enthusiastic drinkers who didn't seem keen to move on elsewhere. It would take a while to get this sorted. It might be wise to close for a few hours. Customers dying on the premises had never been a great advert.

Yvette looked over to the now-covered body on the verandah. William Hunt had become a regular and a favourite; he was a real gentleman. She would miss him.

Gavin came up the steps into the bar. He made the call to Larcombe Manor.

Athena answered.

"Athena? It's Gavin. I'm the bearer of bad news. I'm afraid it's William; he sat drinking coffee, completing The Times crossword in a bar near the marina. It was very sudden. We're waiting for the emergency services, but he's dead."

Athena's lip quivered.

"Are you sure? Oh, the poor, sweet man. He didn't have long enough away from here. He deserved so much better; life can be so cruel. Phoenix and I will fly out immediately; we'll arrange to bring the body home."

Gavin reminded her of the law on the Iberian Peninsula and here on the islands. Repatriation required the negotiation of plenty of hoops to get authorisation. Still, no matter who you were, the body had to be embalmed within forty-eight hours and could not be transported home otherwise.

"Are you certain it was natural causes?" Athena asked.

"The paramedics have just arrived; I'll keep on top of things here and inform the consulate in Ibiza town. Come to the marina when you arrive, and I'll meet you onboard 'Elizabeth'. You can sleep on board for the nights you're here. I'll be able to pick up a UK-style death certificate from the consulate in due course. If the local forensic doctor certified William's death as 'normal', there might be no autopsy or inquest. Instead, the body will move to a tanatorio, a funeral parlour, and we need to get the relevant paperwork to them quickly. The embalming will go ahead, but we can inform them that the body will return to the UK for interment."

"He will join Elizabeth in the family plot; the arrangements are in place for that. It is so sad."

"When will you be able to get here?" asked Gavin.

"Phoenix isn't back from a trip yet. As soon as he arrives, we'll book our flights. Things are hectic in mid-July, so it might need shopping around. I'll be in touch. I'll let you get on with things out there. Goodbye, Gavin. I'm glad you're out there with him. I'd hate to think of him being alone."

Athena sat down in a chair. The tears came, but the memories of William here at Larcombe were all happy ones. Phoenix walked in an hour or so later.

"I'm glad that's over," he said, "I hope I don't have to do another one of those for a while. Are you okay, Athena?"

"It's Erebus. He's dead. Gavin rang an hour ago to say he passed away suddenly. We need to get out there to bring him home."

"That might be tricky," said Phoenix, "I don't have a passport remember? I was born Colin Bailey in 1968 and never needed a passport until I made myself scarce in 2001. I changed my name a year after marrying my second wife, Sue. I returned to the UK as Colin Owens early in 2010 and was brought here on July first. The next day Erebus christened me Phoenix, and none of my Olympus missions has ever taken me overseas. Erebus kept me on UK soil, not just because he had a soft spot for me, but because travel would likely throw up problems."

"Erebus told us everything he thought he needed to about you when he collected you from the river," said Athena. "There aren't many things I didn't learn about your past, and you know everything there is to know about mine. But, unfortunately, we've overlooked the smaller details during the past three years. There's a way around this, surely?"

"Is there any chance I might travel as Garry Burns? Although he's missing, presumed dead in Africa as far as Olympus is concerned, his status with the UK authorities remains intact. They must still have him registered as being here at Larcombe, recovering from PTSD. Last year, we told the police officer, formerly known as Zara Wheeler, that he'd left us and gone travelling. If I remember rightly, Giles covered our tracks with a false backpacker's trail in case anyone followed up on the story. If he set a false trail that never got followed, he can remove it just as easily, with no one being the wiser. Fingers crossed. I'll get on to Henry Case to see whether they can furnish me with documents that will get me out to Ibiza and back. Garry Burns won't be on a 'no-fly' list or wanted for questioning anywhere, will he?"

"Do what you can, Phoenix," replied Athena, "but make it quick because we need to get out there pronto. I would have preferred to leave this evening, but that's out of the question. Ryanair flies out at half-past six tomorrow morning from Bristol. We both need to be on that flight. Provided I can get us on it at such short notice."

Phoenix set off towards the ice-house. He suddenly thought of Artemis. He had to steer clear of her; they couldn't risk someone recognising him as Garry Burns *or* Colin Bailey. Not on her first full day. He went to his old lair in the orangery, called Henry, and asked him to join him.

Athena started to pack a few items in a bag and dug out her passport. If Phoenix got his details ready this afternoon, they could still be in Santa Eulalia by mid-morning tomorrow. She wanted to see the body for herself. She prayed that she could get there before the embalmer had done his work.

Why was she not convinced that Erebus's death resulted from natural causes? Did the impressions they had gained from the meeting with the other Olympians in London last Friday have anything to do with it? Were there indeed dark forces at work? Or was it that she couldn't believe the old gentleman she had admired so much had gone?

As she studied her passport, another thought crossed her mind. How would she ever be able to get married if she and Phoenix decided to go ahead? He was a non-person, as he had reminded her. His true identity must remain hidden if she wanted to keep him by her side, whether as her husband, partner or colleague.

As for any future birth certificate for their yet-confirmed child, would she be forced to put 'unknown' in the space reserved for 'Father'? God, what a nightmare. She laughed hysterically. Please spare me from going through life as Mrs Annabelle Burns, she thought.

Henry Case was his usual efficient self. After checking whether they had the details necessary to supply Phoenix with a passport to hand, the two men compared the latest photographs for Garry Burns and Phoenix. The latter was taken in his first few days at Larcombe.

"There's a passing resemblance, I suppose," said Henry.

"Burns's picture comes from almost ten years ago," said Phoenix. "If I wear glasses to alter my appearance a little, it should be good enough to get me through customs at Bristol. Nobody looks like their passport photo, anyway. They barely glance up from the desk at the other end, let alone scrutinise the document and verify the image. Our biggest headache might be on the way home; they're more alert on your way back."

"Leave it with me, Phoenix. I'll have everything ready later today. Is there anything I need to do in the meantime?" asked Henry.

"Pass the details, including the number, to Athena so she can secure our flights. Then, could you bring the finished article over to the main building when it's ready? Oh, by the way, how is Artemis settling into things here?"

"I haven't met up with her yet," said Henry. "Athena gave her the guided tour, and Giles set her to work as soon as that finished. No doubt we'll bump into one another in time. Safe journey tomorrow, Phoenix. I'll return to the coal face and pass on the awful news to Giles and the team about Erebus."

"Thanks, Henry," said Phoenix. "I must find Rusty and get him up to speed before we leave in the morning."

The rest of Monday was a whirlwind of mini-meetings to ensure that Minos and the others could assume control in their brief absence. They needed time to get Phoenix's things ready for the trip. Plus, the sad task of letting people at Larcombe know of their former leader's demise. But, like every good jigsaw, the pieces finally fell into place, and at six-thirty the following morning, their crowded plane taxied on the runway, cleared for taking to the air.

"Well, we successfully negotiated phase one," said Phoenix as the plane arrowed its way through the light cloud base and headed for the Mediterranean.

Fifteen minutes later, Athena was reading an article on her laptop.

"Cyanide," she whispered.

"Not sure this budget airline serves cocktails," said Phoenix.

Athena tutted.

"Don't be silly and listen. 'Cyanide poison is known to

cause harm to the heart and the central nervous system. Just a small amount of cyanide will prevent oxygen flow in the body if it binds itself to the iron element in the blood. So no circulation of oxygen will cause death to occur rapidly.' Gavin said there were no visible signs it was unnatural, but Erebus could have received a lethal dose with a pinprick. I need to inspect his body to put my mind at rest."

"Time isn't on our side, Athena," said Phoenix, "and you might be barking up the wrong tree. It's perfectly plausible for the old chap to have keeled over after a few weeks of temperatures in the eighties. He was getting on, you know."

The plane landed at Ibiza airport, and as Phoenix had suggested to Henry, passport control proved to be a breeze. The short taxi ride to the marina in Santa Eulalia confirmed the island to be both busy and uncomfortably warm. Gavin waited on the quayside by 'Elizabeth' to greet them.

"Let's get your bags on board the yacht, and I can start filling you in on what's happened in the past eighteen hours."

Athena seemed at home on 'Elizabeth' with all its nautical gadgetry and refined furnishings. Phoenix started to say he felt like a fish out of water, but he remembered the glare Athena had given him for the cyanide comment and held his tongue.

Minutes later, he was happy to be back on dry land and taking in his surroundings—no wonder the elderly gentleman had chosen this beautiful spot to retire. There were yachts of various sizes everywhere, and he lost count of the number of 'Sunseeker' logos. The water that lapped at the keels of the boats and up against the marina walls teemed with fish. He hadn't a clue what varieties. But the restaurants a few paces away wouldn't run short of fish for a long time.

"I've called a taxi to take us to the funeral parlour," said Gavin.

When they travelled *en route* to the closest tanatorio on the main road through town, Gavin got them up to speed with his progress so far.

"The consulate in Eivissa is working on the paperwork, which should be available tomorrow morning. Here in town, the authorities are putting the finishing touches on the documents they are responsible for. I'm hoping we can get the body released tomorrow or Wednesday at the latest. I'll pass the necessary paperwork to you, Athena, so you can arrange to fly William home. After that, I'll bring 'Elizabeth' back to the UK. That will take around three weeks. In that time, I can arrange for a mooring until it's decided what to do with her."

"Sorry this job didn't turn out as you had hoped, Gavin," said Athena. "We expected Erebus to sail around these islands, enjoying the high life for years."

"Me too," said Gavin sadly. "Maybe I'll find someone who needs a crewman on another vessel soon. I love the sea, and this yacht has been a joy to work on and sail. But, of course, William was great company too."

The taxi soon reached the funeral parlour, a reasonably nondescript establishment behind red-painted wooden gates. The three of them entered. Gavin explained in Spanish to a female staff member who the people he had with him had come to see.

"She told me to wait there while she gets the boss," Gavin said as the girl disappeared behind a curtain.

A mournful-looking middle-aged man returned with the girl, and he led them through to the back of the building.

Phoenix thought the undertakers didn't change a lot all over the world. Every one of them had that 'hangdog' expression. He guessed the job wasn't a barrel of laughs and after a while, their faces got used to what they thought equated to an appropriately sombre expression.

The casket with the body of William Horatio Hunt was ready to view. Athena knew that it was too late as soon as she saw it. Any hopes for forensic evidence had gone. She carefully inspected the face, neck and hands, searching for marks that might suggest a scratch or an injection. Did that look like a slight blemish on the neck, just behind the ear, up near the hairline? She urged Phoenix to take a look.

"It might be," he said, "but it's inconclusive."

Gavin took an interest now.

"What are you thinking? Do you think this was murder? I can't believe that. Nothing I saw suggested that. Okay, I'm not a doctor, but nobody here has any doubts about it being natural causes. His heart gave out, pure and simple. The local doctor tells me he always sees it; older people retire here from abroad and fail to cope with the temperatures. He signed the documents without a second thought."

After Gavin had discussed the arrangements with the undertaker, they took a taxi back to the road entrance to the port. He wanted to show Athena where her old friend had died. The three walked the twenty metres to the bar and up the steps into the bar. Gavin paused at the doorway and pointed to his left.

"That's where he sat every day after lunch. He had his coffee, finished a crossword, and then took a stroll along the promenade before returning to 'Elizabeth' for an afternoon nap. It had become his favourite spot. A place to people-watch and relax in the shade."

Phoenix walked into the interior of the bar.

Hayden recognised Gavin and assumed that the two newcomers were possibly relatives of the old gentleman.

"Hello there," he said, offering a hand for Phoenix to shake, "sorry about the old feller. He was a proper gentleman. Are you a relative?"

"William was our boss," replied Phoenix. "He had no family, but we were probably as close to family as he had. We can't get used to the fact that he's dead."

Gavin and Athena had joined them, and Phoenix ordered drinks.

"Might as well, seeing as we're in a bar," he said, "it seems rude to refuse."

"It was so sudden," said Yvette, who appeared from the other room. "He didn't have time to finish his crossword for the first day ever."

Gavin went down the steps to the toilets, pushing through the batwing doors.

Hayden came from behind the bar and walked to a wooden dresser. Photographs and odd ornaments adorned the shelves. He slid open a drawer, removed something and brought it over to Phoenix.

"Take a look at this; it's yesterday's Times. He had his first *café con leche* every day while he read through from front to back, then he folded the paper and started on the crossword clues. That became our signal to take him his second cup. He always finished the crossword in ten minutes or less."

Phoenix glanced at the precisely folded copy of The Times and the barely started crossword.

"What am I looking for?" he asked.

"We both stood at the bar and saw him fold the newspaper," said Yvette. "It was over ten minutes later I noticed he appeared to have fallen asleep. Yet he hadn't done any more than what you see there,"

Athena came to stand at Phoenix's shoulder.

"The answers don't fit the clues," she said excitedly, "he tried to leave a message. Notice how spidery the writing is on '4 Down'. That's strange; he would have been disgusted to have written so poorly. However, the first few solutions are correct in his lovely script."

"Something prevented him from carrying on as normal, that's for sure," said Hayden. "One of us always called out to him to ask if he was ready for his second cup. He usually waved a hand and answered in his very proper English tone. Like an old schoolmaster."

"Many thanks," said Phoenix to Hayden, "this will prove useful. We'll get to the bottom of it now, with the clues he's left."

Gavin trotted up the steps and picked up his glass of tonic water from the bar.

"What did I miss?" he said.

"Nothing much," said Phoenix. "We were hearing a few stories about Erebus from mine host here. Time for us to drink up and head back to the yacht."

"Come back soon," called Yvette as they left the bar and walked the short distance to the promenade. A few metres later, they descended the stone steps to the marina, and in minutes, they climbed on board 'Elizabeth.'

Giles had a few details to follow up in town and final calls to Eivissa to arrange times to collect the vital final documents. As soon as he disappeared, Athena asked Phoenix why he hadn't told Gavin what they had discovered.

"We don't know his exact whereabouts when Erebus died. He reckons he was washing down the decks and getting ready for a trip today. But, unfortunately, we haven't had that corroborated. He's been a familiar face in the marina and around town for six months; he could blend in easily enough. There are hundreds of visitors in the town at this time of year. Easy enough for him to mingle with the crowds, walk up from the marina, do the deed, and then hurry back to continue with the tasks he was supposed to be doing. He said Hayden came to fetch him when they realised something was wrong. That's the only time we know for certain he was here, on board."

"Motive?" asked Athena, clearly not impressed with his logic.

"Who knows? Money? Let's check the crossword and see if we can make sense of it."

Phoenix and Athena placed the incomplete crossword page on the table before them and began.

"We can ignore the perfectly written ones," said Athena, "which do you think he wrote after the poison first took effect?"

"This section here on the left-hand side seems less certain in how he formed the letters." said Phoenix, "The one that's off by a distance is the one you spotted. What did that '4 Down' clue say again?"

"It says 'school kid on vacation trapping brown bear'. Five letters."

"Are the answers in the back?" asked Phoenix.

"The answer is 'STAND' obviously," said Athena.

"Not obvious to me," said Phoenix.

"When they say 'on vacation,' it means that you 'vacate' the letters between the beginning and end of a word or phrase. The term 'trapping' suggests a word meaning 'brown' trapped between those two letters. So 'school kid' becomes SD, and a three-letter word for 'brown' is TAN. The word 'STAND' can mean to 'bear or tolerate'."

"Is our baby going to be as clever as you?" Phoenix asked.

"The answer that Erebus scrawled is 'DOLOS' not 'STAND'. So there's our clue."

Phoenix eyed Athena forlornly and waited for the explanation. That collection of letters meant nothing to him at first. Then he had a lightbulb moment. Something deep in the recesses of the mythological information he had studied when he arrived at Larcombe suddenly came to the surface.

"Dolos - the spirit of trickery and guile. A master of cunning deception, craftiness, and betrayal. An apprentice of the Titan Prometheus."

Athena looked impressed.

"Treachery," she sighed, "I was right. It was murder. The reference to a character from Greek myth points to the killer either being one of the Olympians or someone they hired. The Titans ruled the world before the Olympians in the so-called Golden Age."

"We may well be right to be wary about those faces around the table in Curzon Street," said Phoenix.

"Precisely," said Athena, "the battle for Olympus has just begun. The Titans have fired the first shot. That clue Erebus left us was the last act of a man who knew he was dying."

Phoenix vowed to take revenge on whoever ended the life of his mentor.

"Our first task is to identify them," he said grimly, "and destroy them before they gain control of the Olympus Project. Instead, they mean to turn it into something with a far more sinister objective."

Chapter Twelve

Wednesday, July 24th, 2013

Gavin managed to get the final clearance for William Hunt's body to fly back to Bristol around lunchtime. Athena checked carriers and flight times and to take her old boss home in style. She abandoned the budget company that had flown them out. They travelled back with British Airways.

Athena ensured everyone at Ibiza airport realised that she was the person accompanying the casket fellow passengers could see being respectfully wheeled across the tarmac to be loaded gently into the hold. She was smartly yet soberly dressed, thanks to her ability to forward think when she had packed her bag at Larcombe. A tearful dab of the eyes when checking in worked wonders.

Phoenix was one step behind her at all stages of the process. Casually dressed, he wanted to allow Athena to attract the most attention. With luck, he could slip under the radar on the return journey, as he had on the way out.

His one rebellious touch was the bright shiny 'I Heart Ibiza' badge on his carry-on bag.

Their plane landed at Bristol International in the early evening. Several holiday flights were landing in rapid succession, so Passport Control and Baggage Retrieval were both busy.

Athena soon left to rejoin her loved one. The pre-arranged Olympus van had been positioned on the perimeter so that the transfer went smoothly and efficiently. Athena sent the driver on his way and went to the gate in Arrivals to wait for Phoenix to appear.

He emerged unscathed after about twenty minutes.

"Remind me to buy Henry a bottle of champagne," he quipped as they embraced.

"I was getting worried when I had to leave you on your own," said Athena. "You usually get up to mischief if I'm not keeping you under tight control."

"There were enough tired and emotional kids in the queue in front of me to help me out. I spotted a few frazzled faces on the Border Control staff's faces and headed for the one that gave the impression she wanted to be anywhere but there. It was a doddle."

"Our car should be pulling up outside in a minute or two. Let's not keep the driver waiting," said Athena. "We need to get back to Larcombe to make arrangements for William's funeral."

"I wonder who will turn up?" said Phoenix. "Elizabeth's funeral was a quiet affair. Staff members from the home where she had been living were there. Plus a few of our people that could justifiably claim to have known him as head of the charitable organisation, but not many other family members, or people that he served with."

"You can't go to the funeral, I'm afraid," said Athena. "I

know you would want to be there, but we can't risk it. The main charity officers at Larcombe will go, plus a few of the house staff. As for other family and colleagues, we'll have to vet them closely before we go ahead. It's sad, but it's unavoidable."

As Athena and Phoenix travelled towards Bath from the airport, Rusty was snatching a piece of quality time with Artemis in their quarters at Larcombe.

"Giles keeps you busy, doesn't he?" he asked.

"There's a lot to learn," replied Artemis, "and so much ground to cover. I had no idea the scope of intelligence-gathering undertaken here."

"It all comes in handy sooner or later," said Rusty, "you'd be surprised."

"I can tell that you don't want to talk about the job you were on at the weekend, Rusty. But what were you up to last week? Anything interesting?"

Rusty told her what had happened on his trip to the London boroughs, investigating the beds in sheds scandal.

"It's the rich-poor divide that sickens you. I saw Jaguars and BMW's parked on driveways on one road, while around the back, there were as many as thirty garages. Those garages now have front doors with piles of rubbish stacked outside. Numerous streets similar to that exist across London where people live in appalling conditions only yards away from people living in the lap of luxury. The overcrowded and unregulated conditions are, at the very least, a fire hazard and potentially hazardous to health. As the migrants have kept flooding in sheds, garages, and derelict properties get used by people unable to afford to buy or rent housing and living outside the benefits system."

"It must be awful," said Artemis, "especially for the elderly and for children."

"I haven't given my final report to Athena and the others yet; perhaps we'll confront the problem of the landlords after she and Phoenix get back from overseas. It's not an easy choice. We can identify and locate the people making huge profits out of people's misery, but what happens to the tenants of these ramshackle properties? The councils could go in mob-handed and clear them out and destroy the buildings, so they don't get exploited, but you've still a moral duty to house these people. If they are illegals, fine, ship them back to wherever they were born, but if we accept them onto our shores, then we will have to find a place for them somewhere, aren't we?"

Artemis squeezed Rusty's arm affectionately.

"Your heart's in the right place, Rusty," she said. "But with budget cuts, I doubt councils in the boroughs can afford to commit resources to clear the problem. Let alone find a solution for the thousands of migrants that would then join the housing lists."

"Olympus may stick to its principles of making the bad guys pay. But, on the other hand, we may get told to take out the exploiters and force the government to tackle the issue of unfettered immigration."

"That sounds like a problem for another day," said Artemis.

"Mmm, I had better check with Minos to see when our leaders are returning home. If you want to hang on here for a while, we can get a bite to eat later."

"I'm sure I can find something to occupy my time while you trot over to the big house," said Artemis, "it would be nice to get an invitation one day."

Rusty smiled at her, "Patience, Artemis, patience. Everything will become clear in time."

Rusty left his partner and headed towards the manor house. He found Minos in the drawing-room.

"What's the latest then, Minos?" he asked, "have you heard from Athena?"

"The van that is bringing Erebus home has left the airport. Athena and Phoenix will not be far behind it. They should all be with us in fifteen minutes. A sad day."

"A sad day indeed," said Rusty.

The door to the drawing-room opened, and Alastor and Thanatos entered.

"As soon as Athena returns, we will have to discuss the breaking news from Eton Wick," said Thanatos.

"Not before time," said Rusty, "that farmer didn't deserve to be left like that for too long. So who discovered the bodies?"

"It seems that the postman had a registered letter to be signed for this morning. He knocked but got no reply," said Thanatos. "In towns and cities, they merely push a card through the door telling you where you can collect the item. In a few isolated places around the country, the postal staff knows who should be doing what and where. This chap thought it odd that there was no activity in the farmyard nor any sign of the farmer. So he looked through the kitchen window and saw what remained of the back of the farmer's head. The police were informed, and after a few hours on the site, they discovered several bodies, a significant amount of arms and ammunition and a veritable fleet of vehicles. The Met has already identified several of these vehicles as used in ram raids in the West Country. A couple were also present in Clevedon, Cheltenham or Amesbury. Identification of the bodies is ongoing; early reports suggest they were of Eastern European origin. The press conference has just ended on both major news channels, and the

Met is refusing to speculate on who these men were or how they died. The police are appealing for witnesses."

"Which suggests they haven't got a clue," said Rusty.

"We'll have to go through all of this again soon," said Minos, "the two vehicles have returned to HQ. Athena and Phoenix will be joining us shortly, no doubt."

"No doubt," said Rusty. "It might be better to let them update us on Erebus and what they found out in Ibiza. Then there will be his funeral to arrange. I would very much like to update you on last week's investigative visit to the capital, too, if I can. Covering those items should give enough time for the full extent of the fall-out from Eton Wick to become clear. We need to be on our toes, ready to react to any flak coming our way."

"Is Artemis settling in?" asked Alastor.

"She's fine, thank you for asking, she's learning fast, and no doubt Giles has got her collecting intelligence on the Eton Wick business as we speak. I'll look forward to what he and Henry have to say when they join us later."

So at Larcombe Manor, the evening was to be a busy one. Athena and Phoenix arrived in the drawing-room just fifteen minutes after their car had dropped them at the front door. Henry and Giles had been called over from the ice-house by Minos.

Athena told the team about the Ibiza trip in detail. When she revealed that Erebus had been poisoned, possibly with cyanide, there were audible gasps around the table.

"Who would have wanted to kill him?" asked Minos, clearly shaken.

"Too early to be sure yet," Athena said.

Athena and Phoenix had decided in the car on the way home from the airport that if Gavin was potentially involved, who *could* they trust? Erebus had trusted Gavin absolutely, without reservation. However, if he had gone over to the other side, then perhaps someone at Larcombe was a suspect too. The couple didn't want to believe it, but until they were sure, then they must keep their cards close to their chest. So they didn't tell them about the clue provided by the crossword.

"William will be buried alongside Elizabeth and their daughter Helen. We should know the details before the weekend. So what's next on your list Minos?"

"The bodies at Eton Wick have been discovered. The farmhouse and surrounding buildings have been crawling with police for the past six hours. Henry and Giles will have an update for us later. While they make sure we have the latest information available, perhaps Rusty could give us a brief report on his mission last week."

Athena nodded. She was glad the farm and its secrets had not laid undisturbed for too long. There was enough to occupy them at Olympus with the implications of the cause of William's death. Phoenix had assured her that they had done everything humanly possible to avoid the Eton Wick killings tracing back to Olympus. That was good enough for her.

The police would thank their lucky stars that the killings of innocent men, women and children were now ending. Their PR people would sow a few seeds that this rival gang would wipe out another to confuse matters. Inform the public that they needn't panic as this was an isolated incident and an infrequent occurrence on these shores.

The usual platitudes would follow. But, as further cuts bit deeper into the Met and other forces around the country, hopes of any progress in the fight against crime would disappear over the horizon.

Rusty was doing as instructed and briefly outlining what

he had uncovered when Athena returned from her daydream.

"Let's cut to the chase, Rusty," she said, "can we identify the most prolific landlords who are exploiting these poor devils?"

"Yes, Athena," he replied.

"Then dispose of them," she said firmly.

"What about the victims?" asked Thanatos.

"The government will have to provide the councils with the resources to cope with re-housing them. If they are sensible, they will move as many as possible away from the southeast. I don't envy them the task, but they have brought it on themselves. We will merely be removing people prepared to keep families in slum conditions and charge them exorbitant rents for the privilege."

Rusty knew he had made his point and that Athena was keen to move on to hear the latest news from Eton Wick.

"What intelligence do we have, Giles?" she asked.

"All the bodies have been removed. The army went in to remove the cache of arms and check the area was safe. The vehicles are still parked in the garage so far, and police officers stay on duty overnight. Police found an empty safe in one building. The possibility that this was a robbery that then escalated into a gunfight is also on their agenda. There appears to be a deal of confusion over how the farmer, Christopher Mellish, died. The Met is not sure if it was suicide. They don't know whether he was killed by the now-dead men or by a third party. CCTV images available from Clevedon, etcetera didn't help identify the gunmen as you will recall; the Met is certain; on the other hand, that the dead bodies fit shooters seen in those attacks. As you can tell, it's what Phoenix might call a 'bugger's muddle'."

"Have they found any eyewitnesses?" asked Rusty.

"Just before we came over here, Artemis traced a call to the local radio station. A lady horse rider called in to say she was surprised the film crew in the area on Sunday morning hadn't seen or heard anything."

"That's worth chasing up, Giles," said Athena, "make sure we keep on top of that angle. If you need to spread any misinformation over the airwaves, then feel free. Is there any indication that this lady phoned the police too?"

"Artemis is monitoring the police frequencies. At this stage, it doesn't appear that the police are aware of our deception. It might not take them long to join the dots once they pick up the information. We need to be ready to deflect their enquiries. Perhaps I need to create a history for Direct Action Films and show them as being financed from Eastern Europe. A few false trails might lead them to believe that the film crew notices were a decoy and that indeed a rival foreign gang was involved in removing the opposition."

"Good luck with that," said Athena, then added, "Artemis may have found useful input on that front. She understands her previous employers thought processes and their standard procedures; she may be able to supply you with the tools to create the most effective and plausible counter-tactics."

"Gamekeeper turned poacher?" said Giles. "That old saying flipped on its head in this instance, but you're right. Artemis being on our team should prove invaluable. She's as sharp as Rusty told you she was. I'm impressed with her insight even in the few days she's been with us."

Before long, the impromptu meeting closed. Athena and Phoenix went back to their apartments.

"We have issues to talk over in the morning Phoenix," said Athena as she slipped beneath the sheets to join her partner.

"Other people's actions will define our priorities," he replied, "never a great situation; it has to be said. But, ah well, tomorrow is another day."

Rusty and Artemis similarly reflected on a day full of action, change, and intrigue in the stable block.

"You never met Erebus, did you?" Rusty asked, "he was a real gentleman; old school. Hard as nails, but polite with it. It's terrible to think that someone might have wanted him dead. Athena was holding something back at the meeting this evening; I'm sure of that. The fallout from the Eton Wick episode is simmering. We may not have heard the last of that either. The only positive to emerge was the green light for direct action against the worst of the slum landlords."

Artemis was tired after a long day. She snuggled up to Rusty's broad chest and began to unwind.

"Nothing ever stands still in the ice-house. There are thousands of snippets of data flowing through every hour that might prove crucial or irrelevant. How Giles ever keeps track, I'll never know. He's a genius. Just a word or phrase, even the source of communication, can trigger his interest. Simply the time of day for a particular message. Giles Burke is that little boy at the Christmas parties we went to as kids; you know, the one we all hated because he thrust his chubby little hand into the bran tub and pulled out the coolest present every time."

"You love it, though, don't you?" said Rusty, "it's work at which you excel. We're both suited to our roles with Olympus; we're a good fit."

"Easy tiger," whispered Artemis with a yawn, "it's been a long day."

Gavin was in his bunk on board ' Elizabeth over a thousand miles away in the marina at Santa Eulalia. Everything was ready for his departure in the morning. His time on the island with his elderly employer was at an end. It had been a tremendous experience, and he was sad that it was over so soon. In three weeks, he would be bringing the yacht home. But, first, he needed to contact Larcombe and inform them he had arranged for a berth in Lymington harbour for her.

Olympus could arrange to collect William Hunt's belongings and decide what to do with the elegant craft. Gavin had already put feelers out among his contacts to find another wealthy patron who would allow him to continue sailing in the Mediterranean or the Caribbean. The sea was in his blood. Sailing was all he had ever wanted to do.

Before he drifted off to sleep, the last thing he thought about was who on earth wanted to kill William? Despite Athena's insistence that a third party was involved, nothing he had seen convinced him it was anything other than a heart attack. Maybe he had missed something? What had Hayden and Athena been discussing when he was in the toilet? Phoenix had dismissed it as banter, but Gavin resolved to have a quick word with Hayden before he left; to see if there was a sinister reason for his employer's death.

A few minutes after Gavin dropped off to sleep, the stowaway emerged from his hiding place. Silently he crept towards the bunk. The crewman was awake a second after the cloth pressed against his nose and mouth. He clawed desperately at the gloved hands that held it so securely, but the weight of his attacker on his chest eliminated any brief hope of escape.

Gavin lost consciousness without ever getting a proper glimpse of the man who would keep him sedated while they sailed out of the harbour in the morning. He would be bound hand and foot when two days out from Ibiza,

William Hunt's assassin callously slipped him over the side of the yacht. Then watched him sink below the surface.

Thursday, July 25th, 2013

While events in the Mediterranean unfolded, matters at Larcombe Manor concentrated on circumstances surrounding the death of Erebus. However, the team there were also considering the aftermath of the battle of Eton Wick. Over at Portishead police headquarters, DS Phil Hounsell sat quietly in his office.

He checked his in-tray. Either he was highly efficient in his old age, or people weren't forwarding so many items these past few days. It lay almost empty. He knew it to be the latter. Phil could pinpoint the exact moment that caused the usual constant flow of reports and requests to dwindle to a trickle.

His differences of opinion with senior officers had been an ever-present part of his career. That stretched back to his days as a police constable in Bordesley Green, his hometown's inner-city district in Birmingham.

Phil Hounsell recalled many fiery arguments that took place in London when he worked with SOCA a decade ago. What a disaster that had been. Hundreds of decent enough officers from different forces around the country were thrown together without any trace of dynamic leadership. If they had put a character in charge, every man respected and was prepared to follow into battle, they may have been successful.

In a few short months, the NCA replaced the broken wheel on the waggon. Only three letters to remember this time; that might help the wooden tops in charge. Why it took three years for a new initiative to get off the ground was anyone's guess. Phil Hounsell thought of last Friday's attack in Amesbury and little Kassie Paget. Might she have been alive today if SOCA had been helpful or if this NCA outfit mobilised quicker?

The NCA would become the UK's lead agency against organised crime, human, weapon and drug trafficking, cybercrime and economic crime across regional and international borders. In addition, it would absorb the body that handled child exploitation and online protection. It had many strings to its bow, yet its budget was half that of the agencies and bodies it replaced in these austere days.

Happy days for the criminals. They would be laughing as they strolled to their Swiss banks. Phil twisted around in his chair and found a file behind the filing cabinet. He checked a figure. Over five thousand known organised crime groups in the UK and approximately thirty thousand gang members. Who did they think would prosper?

The news of discovering the bodies of an Eastern European gang at Eton Wick in Berkshire yesterday was plastered over the media today. Phil should have been happy. Not more than a week ago, he had told his Divisional Commander that patrols and ANPR checks on the M5 would be next to useless. He informed them where he believed the gang would be based and suggested they had probably been involved in other crimes. That measured insight based on years of being a detective had met with scorn.

Phil's in-tray diminished day by day from that moment. Then, finally, everything panned out as he had imagined in that meeting. He had let his mind run free and built a scenario that made sense, given the facts in front of them. But, unfortunately, it fell on deaf ears.

They needed now to discover which crew took over the businesses run by the now-deceased foreign gang. If they left clues, the Met might find them, arrest them and get them to court in time. What happened after that would be a lottery.

As for the West Country, the patrols had been suspended over the weekend to save money. Patrols resumed on Monday morning. Nothing turned up, of course, because they were searching in the wrong place. But the ACC believed it essential to be seen to be doing something. He said their presence would reassure the public at the Tuesday morning briefing.

In the real world, the public was more concerned with the attack in Amesbury. They were much more horrified at the deaths of so many innocent people than police cars pootling up and down the M5. Soon after, the press started asking pointed questions about why they couldn't use this resource for urgent tasks, such as helping the Wiltshire police hunt for these vicious killers.

The ACC didn't handle pressure well, and his TV appearance on Tuesday evening had been an unmitigated PR disaster. Wednesday's local newspapers and one or two nationals gave him a terrible stick about handling the case. As readers caught up with that story, the Met began to uncover the carnage at the remote farmhouse. When that news reached the media, the relatively small local tale took on a life of its own.

Naturally, the public was relieved that the threat to their daily lives had gone. They could go to the bank or building society, trot around Tesco with a trolley to their heart's content. Wander to the pub again for a cold pint in the evening without someone wanting to blow off their head.

In the Lap of the Gods

Other quarters of the media concentrated on the gang warfare aspect. How can gangs of thugs be allowed to drive around unchallenged only fifteen minutes away from Windsor Castle? How can a remake of The Gunfight at the OK Corral occur on a Sunday morning, and nobody raises the alarm?

Here and there, the ACC still received an unwanted name check. Calls for his resignation appeared in newspaper articles and news bulletins. Phil knew the blame for this would end up at his door. It was the way of the world. The man might be useless, but he had the high ground with his seniority, and he would be frantically searching for a scapegoat, someone he could point to and say he received bad advice. Phil was pretty sure in which direction he'd look.

The Divisional Commander was the man sent to deliver the message. Phil had barely returned from lunch when there was a knock at the door. The DC came in and closed the door behind him.

"Good afternoon, Sir," said Phil, anticipating that it was anything but good.

"A messy business, Hounsell," said the Commander. "It's like this, you've got plenty of time served, and with the budget being trimmed year on year, we are looking for volunteers. So you'll be doing someone a favour. We won't have to force someone to leave. Well, the thing is, the ACC thinks you are a bad influence on younger officers. We need to be marching together in the same direction. Do you follow me? You always seem slightly out of step or, dare I say, walking towards us instead of with us. What do you say?"

Phil pitied the shambles of a man in front of him. How had he risen so far up the ranks? He thought about letting him squirm a little longer but instead decided to help him out.

"You're suggesting I take early retirement on a full pension, I imagine?"

The man opposite him sat back in his chair. The full pension option hadn't been on the cards when he had walked in, but Phil Hounsell didn't plan to go without a fight. He continued to sum up his interpretation of the Commander's garbled offer.

"As I see it, the ACC will be rid of the man who told him where the Eton Wick gang would likely be situated. He can save his skin if he tells the press we've carried out a 'root and branch' inquest. Tell them several unnamed officers have left the service after being found to have fallen short of the standards that the force expects. I imagine that if we could agree on my first comment, then the likelihood of anyone ever hearing the ACC knew the possible whereabouts of the gang earlier than last Friday would be extremely remote."

The two men stared at one another for a while. Phil didn't blink; the DC caved in first. He stood up and leant across the desk to shake Phil's hand.

"It wasn't my idea to come and deliver this news, Phil. He's got us jumping through hoops trying to save his backside. This place won't be the same without you. I'll sort out the necessary, and you can be off earlier than planned; good luck to you. There won't be anything showing on your record about this matter either; you can rely on me to see to that. He wants you away; I'll tell him you're going. How he explains it to the media is up to him."

"Thank you, Sir," said Phil, "that sounds fine. If you confirm things will go ahead as we agreed tomorrow, I'll tell the family at the weekend. If it's okay with you, I'll go on gardening leave next week, and the ACC needn't set eyes on me again. You can inform me when I need to return to sort out my financial details and return my things."

"No problem, Phil," said the DC. "I envy you mate, getting out while you're still sane. I can't wait for the chance to retire."

As the door closed behind the DC, Phil Hounsell got up and walked around his office. So this was how his career would end. He could forget about the sign on the wall with that favourite French saying of his. He would keep the news of his retirement under his hat tonight. If the Divisional Commander got a green light for retirement on full pension and no stains on his record, he could tell Erica at the weekend. He wondered how she felt about being married to a pensioner.

Thirty miles away at Larcombe Manor, the morning meeting had been brief but exhilarating. Athena wanted to get the items on the agenda cleared as soon as possible. First, she needed to meet individually with her three confidantes; events in Ibiza had brought the timetable forward. Second, Olympus had to uncover the identity of their enemies without delay.

As always, Olympus' affairs came before everything else. Once she was satisfied, she'd covered all the bases. Then and only then would she take that pregnancy test.

Athena, Phoenix and the others gathered in the drawing room at nine o'clock. Giles Burke was first in the firing line for her questions.

"What news, Giles from Eton Wick? Have the police linked the film crew and this gang? Are the police any further forward in identifying these men?"

"I'll take those one at a time, Athena, if I may. As you can imagine, the world's media has found its way to Eton

Wick since yesterday. The police still maintain a large presence, guarding the farm's perimeter, the garage, and the farmhouse. The police seem satisfied that Christopher Mellish took his own life. He had been drinking; they found an empty bottle of scotch on the table by the body. They took fingerprints on the fleet of vehicles in the garage. There is no indication that any of the gang entered the farmhouse. Indeed, they discovered little to suggest that anyone except Mellish had been inside the house for a considerable time. Formal identification will take a while. These men had no arrest records on UK soil. Artemis has trawled through police radio traffic, local radio stations, and the local press. So far, nobody has provided the police with a statement. Today, most media have moved on from Eton Wick to cover the naming of the Queen's great-grandson and doctors wanting double time for weekends. Nothing stays on the front page for long in this fast-moving world. We are on top of things for now. We are poised to spread misinformation the second the situation changes. I've almost completed the back history for DAF and covered my tracks sufficiently to outwit the vast majority of people who might carry out searches."

"Excellent, as always, Giles," said Athena, "let's hope things stay unchanged."

Athena then went through the funeral arrangements for Erebus. It would be a small family affair, where 'family' meant close Olympus colleagues who could appear publicly. However, there was no announcement in the press, nor had his former naval colleagues been contacted.

"He deserves far better," said Phoenix. "A state funeral would be more like it, considering what he has done for the nation over the years. But, unfortunately, nobody knows about it."

"We know, Phoenix," said Rusty, "and we'll remember him whether we go to the funeral or not. He knows we'll be there in spirit."

"What progress have you made on the direct action we sanctioned against the slum landlords, Rusty?" asked Athena.

"It's still in the early planning stages," replied Rusty. "I need a contribution from Phoenix whenever possible. A meeting in the orangery perhaps tomorrow morning? As soon as that's over, we can go ahead."

Phoenix was only too keen to agree to the get-together. He hoped Athena wouldn't deny him this early opportunity to get back into the action. Eton Wick had been tough, but missions such as that were what got his heart thumping.

"Agreed," said Athena, "but if you two are going to be involved in the mission, please take care. I need you here at Larcombe to help deal with the problems that have surfaced after Erebus's death."

"You are insisting that it was murder?" asked Alastor.

"We are," replied Phoenix, "and it may be the first step in an organised campaign."

"We must be on our guard," added Athena. "To that end, I should like to finish today. I wish to talk to Minos, Alastor and Thanatos for a few minutes about the funeral arrangements. So if you gentlemen have nothing urgent to raise, I'll let you get on with your business."

Phoenix and the others knew they weren't wanted and headed for the door. Athena gave Phoenix a reassuring smile as he left. He wasn't yet aware of the research that the Three Amigos had been carrying out for her. Although there was very little to add to what they'd already discussed about the funeral, the information concerning the ten Olympians was paramount.

The team needed to increase the intensity of their checks to uncover the faction working to overthrow the current regime. The Titans seemed as good a name for them as any. Athena wanted to discover who murdered Erebus or ordered his death, just as much as Phoenix did.

Her three colleagues who remained in the drawing room were eager to share their gathered knowledge since their last individual meetings. However, Athena still wanted to maintain the secrecy of each man's investigations for as long as possible. She assured them that everything would be made known to the whole team in time.

It was a delicate matter. Athena didn't realise that Gavin had been loyal to his employer. In her mind and that of Phoenix, there was a suspicion he was somehow involved. Time would prove otherwise. That time was not today.

It was something she could not bear to consider. One of the men she shared this table with daily could have tempted the opposition to change sides. But, the less they knew about the bigger picture they contributed to, the better.

Athena decided to work with the Three Amigos in alphabetical order. She asked the others to leave, and she and Alastor trawled through the data he had amassed so far. Meetings with the other two followed, and it was late in the afternoon before Athena returned to her rooms. Phoenix was nowhere around. She found a note that said he was spending his downtime in the swimming pool and then at the gym.

"Poor boy," she thought, "he's bored."

Athena sat and picked up the folder that Minos had presented to her. This one had spiked her interest. It was a story that only a handful of people were aware of, certainly not her adoring fans. It was the real-life story of the lady known to Olympus as Demeter.

Philomena Victoria Jacinta de Beauchamp Alexander, (code name Demeter)

Often described as a goddess of the harvest, she also presided over the sacred law and life cycle and death cycle.

Philomena was born in Surrey in 1950; her parents were from one of the oldest and wealthiest families in the country. She received private education in Surrey and Geneva. Aged sixteen, she ran away from her boarding school and returned to London. She wanted to be part of the Swinging Sixties and loved to sing. Within weeks, a record producer had taken her under his wing. Her first single, 'They Don't Have To Know', rocketed to the top of the charts and stayed at Number One for four weeks. Thus, the teenage phenomenon that was Honey B was born.

The record producer was to be her first husband, but that relationship was brief. He was thirty years her senior. He taught her everything she needed to know about the record business and opened many doors for her. But, in reality, he was merely a stepping stone as far as Honey B was concerned. He was cast aside within eighteen months. Philomena was aiming higher.

As the decades ticked by, her hits had not dried up like many other artists of her generation. Honey B was a chameleon; she changed her image and her style of music, but nothing prevented her from staying in the spotlight. Other groups and solo singers came and went. Honey B had fought her way to the top and intended to stay there. However, her reputation as being difficult to work with was legendary. She switched record labels and managers apparently on a whim, although without exception, it was because she anticipated a new trend or a slight dip in popularity.

Expensive and drawn-out court cases kept her name firmly in the media. Those cases cost her millions on occasion. Her victories came with the massive record sales and sell-out concerts that followed the free publicity. The public continued to love her as she became a new persona each decade. Her fans spread across all ages and all over the world.

Husbands two and three had been hand-picked. Honey B wanted someone younger, extremely good-looking and always in the media. She married an actor and kept him on a short leash for ten years before cutting him loose. After a career break, when she disappeared from the public eye for several months, she dated and married a sportsman. He was an international footballer fifteen years her junior who was never off the back pages. He and Honey B were never out of the headlines.

When he retired through injury, his usefulness was over. Honey B divorced him, and her present husband was a mere twenty-eight-year-old. Since he was eighteen, he had been a TV presenter and was popular with children and those youngsters who grew up with him on their screens.

Honey B was sixty-three years young and could afford cosmetic surgery to look a few years younger. Her entertainment star still stayed in the ascendancy. Her fortune was around seven hundred and fifty million. The money and property that Philomena Victoria Jacinta de Beauchamp Alexander had inherited when her parents died made that pale into insignificance.

Minos had done well. He had uncovered a history that explained more about the reasons for Demeter being at the top table of the Olympus Project. It also showed that

Honey B as a potent force. Everyone in her entourage was expendable; nothing would stop her from succeeding. Athena knew that she would prove a formidable enemy.

Athena put the folder to one side. One more potential enemy that she now knew far better. Athena was satisfied with her progress. She had time now to think of herself for a while. Athena searched in her handbag, found what she needed and headed for the bathroom.

At around half-past five, Phoenix wandered into the lounge. Athena sat on the sofa. She patted the seat, suggesting he sit beside her.

"We are going to be parents, Phoenix," she said.

"Happy days," he replied and kissed her.

Athena wondered why she ever worried; now, all she needed to do was tell her parents. That should be fun.

Epilogue

Monday, July 29th, 2013

A quiet weekend gave everyone a chance to reflect. The month of July was almost at an end. It had been a period of intense action and constant change. Phil Hounsell had bumped into an old adversary while on duty at Glastonbury but couldn't quite place who they were. His job satisfaction was at an all-time low. He counted down the days to his retirement.

Zara Wheeler had left the police service and committed herself to sharing her life with Rusty at Larcombe Manor for the Olympus Project. Working with Giles Burke, she had already established herself as a valuable asset in the intelligence section.

A vicious gang of Bulgarians had eliminated the ram-raid gang that frustrated the West Country authorities for months. But, over a few weeks, the gang led by Dimitar Marinov launched a reign of terror that left dozens dead and injured. Before those attacks could be escalated, their hide-out at Eton Wick was discovered by Olympus. Phoenix and Rusty led a successful attack to wipe them out, but not without losing one of their most valuable agents, Jack Mould.

Athena and Phoenix had attended their long-awaited first meeting with the upper echelons of the Olympus Project. It took place in London in the middle of the month. Since Erebus had retired, some sat around the table plotting to take control. Someone intended to take the organisation in a new, more sinister direction.

The murder of Erebus on the island of Ibiza demonstrated more evidence of the dangers posed by this splinter group within Olympus. Gavin, his crewman, was to be killed too by a mystery assassin sailing Erebus's yacht 'Elizabeth' home to the UK.

The ACC ignored him despite Phil Hounsell advising his ACC that he would be wasting his time searching for the foreign gang in his area. Later, when Phoenix and his team disposed of the gang, the ACC was under severe pressure to explain his tactics. But, instead, he wanted a scapegoat; Phil agreed to take the blame anonymously and took early retirement on a full pension.

Athena had started to research the other Olympians. She was trying to discover who was for them and who might be an adversary. Minos had uncovered that Demeter, the nation's favourite pop singer, was not the person the world imagined her to be.

As the month ended, Athena and Phoenix were celebrating the news she was expecting their first child. So everyone deserved a quiet weekend after that.

Next in The Phoenix series

vinci-books.com/the-price-of-treachery

Some enemies don't just attack. They infiltrate.

Criminal kingpins fall across London, as vigilante operative Phoenix dismantles a corrupt network of landlords. But a violent strike against a government figure exposes a mole deep within the covert Olympus Project—an agent tied to a shadow faction known only as the Titans, whose ambition threatens everything Phoenix has sworn to protect.

Turn the page for a free preview…

The Price of Treachery: Chapter One

Good luck in your new venture, the card read.

It was one of a handful of cards from well-wishers that had arrived at the Hounsell house in the past few days. Phil Hounsell was making a fresh start.

The Divisional Commander had been a man of his word. Phil had walked out of his job with his head held high and a full pension. He had cleared his desk on Friday afternoon, then spent the best part of August in the garden at home or on holiday with Erica and the children.

The ACC saved his career by the skin of his teeth. A gullible public swallowed his story that 'heads had rolled' at Portishead after the debacle of the hunt for the Bulgarian killers; in truth, the shrinking numbers were more to do with austerity cuts or fellow officers giving up the pointless struggle and quitting the service.

The identities of the murdered men emerged as the new month progressed. Dimitar Marinov and his cronies were a collection of career criminals and ruthless enforcers. The media questioned how these murderers just waltzed through immigration control without anyone wondering whether they were the calibre of person the UK needed.

As for the gang's killers, there had been little progress on that front. A few residents had contacted the police to ask if they knew about the film crew in the area that weekend. However, confusion reigned over the name of the company involved.

Memories were hazy; it seemed so innocent at the time. A trifle inconvenient to have gunfire in the background while serving breakfast or when fetching the Sunday papers. Not significant enough to remember every detail on what looked to be an official sign. The local police passed the Met police the information, and when added to the sum of everything they gathered at Eton Wick, it amounted to very little.

The media's attention switched to new matters; the killings had stopped, and the Met was following up on dozens of leads gained from the Bulgarian's homes. Dimitar Marinov was proven to have been a trafficker of drugs and young women. They raided dozens of properties, and the smiles on the Met senior officers were getting broader by the day.

The possible existence of a second ruthless gang of killers slipped to one side for the time being. There were five hundred gangs from which to choose. They could only tackle one thing at a time. As for the involvement of third parties, such as the one stationed at Larcombe Manor, for instance, it never crossed anyone's mind. Giles, Artemis and the team could keep their misinformation tactics in reserve for another occasion.

At the end of the third week in August, as Phil Hounsell and family were stepping off the plane from Marbella, news broke the Met had discovered the bodies of the ram-raid gang. At long last, their families learnt what had happened to them.

The press portrayed them as 'victims', which their criminal shenanigans suggested they indeed were not. But they were British rogues, slaughtered by foreign killers that should never have been allowed to enter the UK. Nevertheless, the headlines caught the mood of the country.

Phil had read the newspapers the following day and wondered at the mentality of people these days. His leaving-do and the finalising of his exit from Portishead took place on Friday, August 30th. The DC was there both in the office and in the pub later. The ACC and others were otherwise engaged. Phil arrived home in a taxi at about two in the morning, three sheets in the wind; Erica saw that he was tucked up in bed safely but also made sure he got up by eight o'clock so he could get used to going shopping with her.

Phil had thought about what he might do now that his police career had ended. What were his strengths? Detecting was his expertise, but he didn't fancy starting as a private investigator. So instead, he thought he would try his hand as a security consultant. Erica came up with the name; she suggested Hounsell Security Services, or HSS for short.

"What nature of security work do you think you might get offered?" she asked.

"I'll circulate my details around the regional companies and offer my services to help them avoid being robbed or defrauded for a start. We'll see what that generates."

It's odd how the supermarket run sometimes finds one bumping into old faces. Erica had Phil on trolley duty and piled stuff into the basket while he coped with his hangover. He knew better than to expect sympathy from his wife, so he looked at the other poor souls passing him.

"Morning, Sir," said a voice, "I don't see you in here very often."

It was Wayne Sangster, his companion from the Glastonbury weekend.

"It's not 'Sir' any longer, Wayne. I'm retired," he replied.

"Got out at last, then? Good for you. What are you doing with yourself?"

"I'm starting a security consultancy, offering advice to firms, that sort of thing," said Phil.

"You don't want to be pissing around with that caper, mate," laughed Wayne, "big money is in personal security. Looking after celebrities and Russian and Arab oligarchs."

"How do you know so much about it, Wayne," asked Phil. Erica looked eager to move into the next aisle. Wayne manoeuvred his small trolley around to follow the couple.

"I did a bit of security before I joined; I told you I'd done quite a few jobs, didn't I?"

"You did, Wayne. Are you still enjoying life?"

"There haven't been many laughs since the weekend we worked together, it has to be said. So I thought of looking around for something else. I've got a couple of mates in the security business that I might give a call."

Phil decided to make an executive decision; Erica was shelf-surfing a few yards in front, hunting for a specific brand of whatever they had probably withdrawn from production. That might take a while.

"How do you fancy coming to work for me, Wayne?" he asked.

"Do you have a uniform?"

Phil thought quickly.

"Of course, it will be a navy-blue shirt with epaulettes

and the HSS logo on the sleeve, black trousers, and boots. That sound okay?"

"You can count me in," said Wayne.

Erica returned from a fruitless conversation with a spotty staff member to find her husband and a strange man shaking hands vigorously.

"Good to have you on board, Wayne," said Phil, "would these mates of yours be interested in joining us? What do you reckon?"

Wayne agreed to check and start the ball rolling on getting himself out of the police service. Phil breathed a sigh of relief; the shopping run had ended. Erica still seemed miffed about the item she could no longer find. For his part, Phil was staggered that two adults and two children could demolish the loaded trolley he struggled to push towards the car in one week.

Monday, September 9th, 2013

Phil had rented office space above a dry-cleaning firm, far enough away from Bath city centre that the amount didn't make his eyes water. Wayne arrived at two o'clock on the dot, as he had agreed when he rang Phil earlier in the day. Wayne was off-duty until Wednesday and counting the days. With holiday entitlement, he would change uniform for the umpteenth time after Friday. His two mates, Dusty and Leggo, had been interested. The newcomers just wanted to know when Phil secured a decent-paying contract that made it worthwhile packing in their current jobs.

"Do we have the uniforms yet, boss?" asked Wayne, always eager to start dressing up.

"All in good time. Let's find work first," said Phil.

"I might have an idea, boss," said Wayne, "while we worked together at Glastonbury, I picked up loads of contacts. Dozens of people handed out cards and fliers. You never know when one of them might come in handy, so whenever someone stuck a hand out with an offer, I grabbed it. You've heard of that Honey B, the singer?"

Phil shook his head.

"She's older than you, boss; she's been around ages and upset many people too. A bit of a diva, I've heard. She's starting a UK tour next Monday. I've just read in the Sun that she's fired her security people. A car never turned up where and when it should have. Honey B was left standing on the pavement in Chelsea for ten minutes with the grubby public. She got recognised, and people started grabbing hold of her and wanting photographs with her and all that stuff. Now advising *her* on security would be a nice little earner."

"We don't have the experience for that, Wayne," said Phil, "she'd hardly employ a brand new outfit like us."

"Her first concert is in Bristol, boss. She doesn't have much time to get something in place, does she? I'll get hold of her management people and tell her we'll sort Monday night out, and if she's happy, we'll take it from there. What have we got to lose?"

"What, just the two of us?" said Phil.

"I'll get Dusty and Leggo to phone in sick if they're working. We'll be fine. It's personal security boss, and it's only her we have to look after; the venue will have its own guys. We need to liaise with them, collect her from the hotel, get her to the gig and return afterwards. All without the lady breaking a nail."

Wayne's confidence started to grow on Phil. Finally, he

asked him for the number of Honey B's management company and made the call himself.

"Good afternoon, I am ex-Detective Superintendent Hounsell; we have staff available with decades of experience in personal security. I understand you have a pressing problem regarding your client's security at next Monday night's concert in Bristol. We are based in Bath and are prepared to step into the breach. We will waive our fee for the night. If your client is happy with our work, we can negotiate a figure for the other dates on her UK tour. What do you say?"

Wayne looked impressed. Not with the waiving the fee bit. He enjoyed how Phil covered all the bases and didn't give the bloke on the other end a chance to breathe. Let alone pass comment.

Phil was listening to a voice on the other end of the line and making notes. Wayne watched intently. Phil ended the conversation.

"Well, boss?" asked Wayne.

"HSS have their first client; Honey B's people will be in touch later in the week with the arrangements we need to make on Monday," said Phil with a smile.

"What's next then, boss?" asked Wayne.

"What size collar are you? What waist and leg measurements? What logo should we have? Big boots at a guess?"

"Seventeen. Forty-two, thirty-three. A white horse. Size twelve, boss."

"Forty-two?" asked Phil.

"At a push, boss, honest," replied Wayne, "shall I ring Dusty and Leggo to get their measurements too?"

Phil sorted uniforms for the three lads and agreed to a logo that looked remarkably like the Ferrari prancing horse

In the Lap of the Gods

but white with HSS below. However, he decided to stick to a suit and tie.

The Bristol concert instructions arrived from the management company's London office. Miss Honey B wanted plenty for her money, which in this case was something for nothing. Phil sat in the office and went through the items, and set out a timetabled procedure. If Wayne and the others followed this to the minute, they should be fine.

It was like planning a raid and getting the resources to arrive on cue precisely at the right time. Again, Phil found he enjoyed the exercise; this time, they had a result. Even if raids he organised went off without a hitch, someone screwed up further along the line, and the criminals only received a caution or got off altogether.

He sent the schedule he'd prepared off to London and received a reply within minutes, saying his plan was acceptable. Honey B had given HSS the task of keeping her safe on Monday night.

Phil asked Wayne on Thursday evening to track down a reliable limousine firm. Naturally, Wayne had half a dozen cards in his possession. A car was secured. The flowers and champagne were ordered. The exact blend of aromas was on standby to be introduced via the air-conditioning to the interior while Honey B was on board.

Wayne was the designated driver for the evening. Dusty Miller and Jake Legg stationed themselves outside the venue's stage door on the pavement.

The limousine arrived on the dot, and Honey B swept from her Clifton hotel and into the back of her sweet-smelling stretch limousine. The door closed quietly behind her. The drive to the venue was smooth. It left not a smidgen to complain over, even for a diva. Wayne eased to a halt beside Dusty and Leggo. Phil tapped on the stage door.

Honey B waited until Dusty opened the door, and then she emerged to screams and flashing cameras and phones. Dusty and Leggo closed the gap to surround their charge, and she was inside the sanctuary of the theatre in seconds. The stage door slammed shut behind her. Honey B gave Phil Hounsell a head-to-toe appraisal.

"Mr Hounsell?" she asked.

"Yes, ma'am, Chief executive of HSS at your service. Your dressing room is this way."

"I've been here a dozen times before," she hissed. "I know the way."

The room also received the diva treatment. Phil was glad he wasn't paying for that lot, too; he thought this venue must be charging a fortune for tickets.

The concert got underway within ten minutes; a warm-up act played a short set, and then it was time for Honey B to take to the stage. The manager was praying nothing would go wrong.

"The audience will expect a two-hour show, but she can be fickle. If she gets it into her head that she's not feeling the love, she'll walk off after an hour. Another night she'll do an extra fifteen minutes."

"What will she do at the end, assuming she does the straight two hours?" asked Phil.

"Your guess is as good as mine. Honey B might run off the stage and collect her things from the dressing room. She'll expect you to be ready to whisk her straight back to Clifton. The last time she played here, she hung around in the room, cooling down and finishing her champagne, chatting to staff. She'll often have one glass before she takes to the stage, and the rest goes to waste."

Phil raised an eyebrow.

"Well, it would if the staff didn't look after it," the manager replied.

It was time for Honey B to sing to her adoring public. Phil stood in the wings and watched. He had to admit she sounded good. Phil recognised one or two tunes; his mother had several of Honey B's earliest hits on vinyl. However, he decided against mentioning it if she deigned to talk to him later.

Almost two hours had passed; Phil texted Wayne and told him to bring the car to the stage door. Dusty and Leggo lingered backstage, primed for action. Truth be told, they were having a coffee and nipping outside for a cigarette. Finally, honey B finished her set with one of her greatest hits. She left the stage to rapturous applause. She smiled.

Phil noticed that the smile didn't reach her eyes. As she made her way to the dressing room, her beady eyes appeared to be darting left and right. As if she was searching to find something to justify a tantrum. A strange woman and no mistake. He needed to tread carefully.

Honey B entered the room and went to close the door. She paused and turned back towards him.

"Will you drink a glass of champagne with me before we leave, Mr Hounsell? I hate to drink alone."

"I'll keep you company, ma'am," he said and took the proffered glass.

Honey B threw a wrap around her shoulders and sat in a comfortable chair. She studied Phil over the top of her glass as she sipped her drink. Phil didn't enjoy how she looked at him; not a pleasant inspection, more like a surgical dissection. He looked at the photos and cards adorning the table in front of them. The room was full of roses, dozens of them, all splashes of red and yellow.

Near her handbag lay a photo that didn't fit. The rest

looked like signed pictures of Honey B alone or unsigned shots with a fan at an exotic location worldwide. This one was a hastily framed shot of a man and a woman, snapped, leaving a building. Phil's heart almost jumped out of his chest. It looked like the two people he had met at Glastonbury at the end of June. He was sure of it. So why on earth did Honey B have a photograph of them?

Behind the public mask of Honey B, Demeter spotted the security consultant's sudden reaction; her mind raced. How could this ex-policeman know Athena and Phoenix? Her colleague had taken these pictures in Curzon Street as they left the Olympus meeting. Shortly before he travelled to Ibiza to carry out a small task for her and her friends, she hoped to unmask the true identity of her male opponent. Could this man hold the key?

Honey B soon switched back to her day-to-day persona. She drained her glass and told Phil she was ready to leave. Honey B caught hold of his sleeve as he moved to the door to summon Dusty and Leggo.

"Thank you for tonight. Call my office tomorrow; name your price, and you can be my security people for the rest of the tour."

Phil Hounsell thanked Honey B, trying not to sound too grateful. He didn't want to overdo it. She could be fickle, and the chill that ran through his arm as she touched his wrist unsettled him.

As she swept away from the stage door in Wayne's stretch limousine, he thought they must be doing something right. HSS was up and running.

Demeter was purring gently in the back of the car; what a stroke of luck to stumble across someone who recognised Phoenix.

"I believe we are hunting the same man, Mr Hounsell,"

she muttered. "I shall have to keep you close by my side. What fun we might have."

Monday, August 5th, 2013

While Phil Hounsell wrapped up his police career on one side of the county, matters in August had started on a more sombre note at Larcombe Manor.

Athena and a handful of mourners attended the funeral of William Horatio Hunt. Erebus was laid to rest between the graves of his beloved wife, Elizabeth and their daughter Helen. They could now seal the family vault. The generations of the Hunt family that had occupied Larcombe for five hundred years would see no other coffins arriving to join them.

Athena shed tears for Erebus, her mentor, as she stood in the vault beside Minos. Her cheeks were dampened by the showers that had greeted the small congregation as they followed the coffin onto the hillside cemetery that overlooked the Hunt family estate.

The gods expressed their displeasure at the manner of Erebus's death; as the mourners left the dark recesses of the vault, they emerged to violent claps of thunder. Seconds later, sheet lightning illuminated the hillside on the opposite side of the valley.

"I understand," said Athena quietly, "but you can rely on me. I will discover who was responsible for his death and take our revenge."

Minos placed a hand on her shoulder to comfort her.

"We owe Erebus a tremendous debt of gratitude. Olympus could never have existed without his vision and drive. This nation has no idea how many lives the missions our agents have carried out saved over the past six years. A simple ceremony such as that was a scant reward for his true significance."

Athena nodded. "We will each of us remember him in our way, Minos. But, the integrity of the Project had to be maintained. As much as we might wish to proclaim his name from the rooftops and demand the headlines he deserves, that would never be possible."

The party of mourners from the Olympus Project HQ gathered in the car park at the entrance to the cemetery. Athena stood for a moment and gazed across the hillside to the mausoleum. No one spoke.

Athena turned and walked to the cars from the transport section. Time to return to Larcombe. There was to be no wake nor no maudlin recollections of a life well-lived. It had to be back to business, battles fought, and debts paid.

In the orangery, Phoenix sifted through the reports Rusty prepared following his recce into the 'beds in sheds' situation in Outer London. Phoenix had missed the opportunity to attend his saviour's funeral, like many others who worked here at headquarters.

His true identity had been closely guarded since his arrival at the beginning of July three years ago. The day Colin Bailey ceased to exist and the Phoenix was born. The struggle to keep that knowledge hidden was doubly tricky now that Artemis worked in the ice-house. Zara Wheeler and Colin Bailey had a history.

The young ex-policewoman lived at Larcombe with Rusty Scott, his closest friend. Disillusioned with the current role of policing, she joined forces with Olympus. Phoenix had no idea what she might do with the knowledge of his past life should it ever be uncovered. Until Artemis could be trusted one hundred per cent, Phoenix had to resort to creeping around the estate. He moved between the rooms he shared with Athena and the orangery, which became his sanctuary. Trips to the ice-house and the other facilities needed strict control. Phoenix felt like a caged animal. Not a feeling he relished.

"Concentrate, man," he scolded himself as he leafed through the reams of intelligence that Rusty had gathered.

The background of the rent crisis in London was plain for anyone to see. The city had built new homes at around half the pace needed to satisfy the intensifying demand. Moreover, its population surged past nine million before the decade's end. As a result, average rents rose by over fifteen per cent in the past two years. As a result, the poor devils forced to rent the roof over their heads to live in the vast, sprawling metropolis parted with an average of over twelve hundred pounds per month.

Phoenix looked at his surroundings. He and Erebus used the elegant, refined orangery for their private meetings for over two years. He knew just how much he owed the old gentleman. How different his life might have been if Erebus hadn't marked him out as a potential recruit for Olympus.

After Sue Owens died, Phoenix became a wealthy man, but money was no substitute for family. Larcombe was now his family home. Erebus had been the father figure he never knew as a child. Athena was his partner for life, and she carried their child. Phoenix felt at one with his surroundings for the first time in his life.

Phoenix knew the direct actions he planned were challenging. The capital held thousands of families and individuals who wanted nothing more than to experience the sense of calm and 'belonging' he experienced. But, unfortunately, whenever an opportunity arose to profit out of ambitions such as those, unscrupulous people always stood waiting to take advantage.

Rusty identified two targets as meriting special attention.

Hounslow, a West London Borough, had its share of rogue landlords. Oscar Friedman, a grocery shop owner, started to expand his property portfolio twenty years ago. Oscar was a quiet, attentive grocer in his mid-sixties who charged over the odds for his fresh produce to the customers that visited his shop every day.

As far as anyone knew, Friedman merely rented out the rooms above the shop. Oscar and his wife lived in the more sophisticated climes just over the borders of the Borough in Richmond. Retirement beckoned, and they were sure to have put enough by to see them live out their days in moderate comfort.

The truth behind the public face of Oscar Friedman proved to be far more sinister. He employed an agent to look after the properties that provided his primary income. Sylvester Read, a former estate agent, was single and in his late thirties. He spent his leisure time watching or participating in his favourite sport. Sylvester was a cage fighter. Violence is his answer to most problems. If the problem needed extra muscle, he called Frank DeAngelo.

DeAngelo was a thug for hire. He had spent more than half his adult life in prison. Frank wasn't the brightest senior citizen on the planet, but he came from an Italian family that came to London in the 1920s. Since then, there had been a DeAngelo family member filling the role of 'enforcer' in nearly every organised crime gang in the capital.

Rusty had gathered evidence on the Borough and the impact of uncontrolled immigration. He identified the long list of properties Friedman owned and the methods Read employed to continually improve the returns on his employer's investments.

Hounslow had been a rural area in the not-too-distant past. Now, many areas resemble shantytowns. Twenty thousand gardens held ramshackle sheds or outbuildings of different sizes. Many of them rented out illegally. The census showed the official population at a quarter million two years ago. Only two years later, that number stood closer to three hundred thousand.

Shed renting had reached a crisis point. So the council set up a squad to tackle the problem. The squad now carries out dawn raids; properties that break planning rules face severe sanctions. Too often, though, the landlord only receives a warning.

The knock-on effects of the housing crisis are easy to see. Local schools have to accommodate hundreds of extra pupils. Many are the children of newly-arrived migrants, while others are from families who moved out of Central London to cut housing benefit costs. Doctors' surgeries, dental practices, rubbish collection and the sanitation system, are stretched beyond capacity.

Criminal landlords, such as Oscar Friedman, made huge profits from the most vulnerable people in society. Families trapped into living in filth in little more than shacks, yet paying hundreds of pounds a month in rent.

Sylvester Read's response to questions from inspectors from the council squad was as flimsy as the fabrications that Friedman's tenants occupied. Yet, it was tough to prove that many buildings were places people lived. The council squad needed to give the landlord notice of an inspection visit.

Oscar merely phoned Read, and when the inspectors arrived the next day, the families were at work; the children attended school. If a wife stayed home with an infant, she moved up the street to another house. The grocer owned more than a dozen properties on one street alone. The council might have suspicions, but obtaining the proof was as elusive as a winning lottery ticket.

Phoenix read page after page of escalating harassment and intimidation. Sylvester Read and Frank DeAngelo dished out racist and homophobic abuse regularly. The pair made frequent late-night visits to properties with no prior warning. Tenants complained locks changed while they worked. Services such as hot water and heating often got disconnected.

Repairs and maintenance on properties withdrew to the level where they became uninhabitable. That happened most often with single-occupancy apartments. Once the tenant had to move out, Friedman had a ready supply of families prepared to pay more rent. Overcrowding wasn't a word in his dictionary.

Rusty talked to a disabled lady in her fifties, who had lived in one of Friedman's flats for eight years. She kept herself to herself and always paid her rent on time. Despite her physical limitations, she kept the place clean and tidy. Read visited her.

He forced her to sign an agreement that reduced her rights. Then, two Somali men moved into the attic space above her flat. They tried to break into her flat to rob her on several occasions. The poor woman was terrified they might do far worse than rob her. So she quit the flat, and within a week, a family of seven migrants occupied the place she had called home.

Phoenix spotted another familiar story in the file. A young bank worker in her twenties moved into Hounslow from Brighton. Read told her initially; he had nothing available for someone wishing to live alone. He suggested she shared accommodation with a group of professionals, as the young girl was away from home for the first time. He persuaded her to at least meet her potential housemates.

Read picked her up after work and drove her to the property, a five-bedroomed Victorian house converted into flats. When they pulled up outside, he explained that each apartment already contained three tenants. As they climbed the stairs to the top floor, Sylvester Read pointed to a newly installed set of stairs leading to the loft.

"We're installing an apartment up there. Will you feel more comfortable being on your own? If so, this could be just what you need. You can still enjoy the company of the others in the communal areas."

The young girl was ecstatic; even though the rent was high, she grabbed the chance and arranged to move in soon as the flat became ready. Within six weeks, Oscar Friedman had decided rents needed to increase across his property portfolio. The young bank worker was distraught. The actual costs of living away from home had started to hit home. She called Sylvester Read to ask if he knew of anywhere cheaper on his employer's books. Was it possible for her to move into one of the other flats in the house to help her new friends with the extra burden they had to stand?

Read called around in person. Well, of course, he did, thought Phoenix. The slimy agent turned up at the loft apartment late at night. The young girl told Rusty 'his breath reeked of alcohol. He apologised; of course, he said he appreciated the financial impact of a rent rise was unfortunate. However, it wasn't easy to see a way forward. The landlord insisted on three occupants as a maximum and a minimum. He believed it resulted in less unwanted interference between the sexes with that arrangement.'

Read then suggested a solution to her problem; he could waive the rent increase in exchange for sex. The young girl had been horrified and ordered the agent out of her flat. Read merely shrugged his shoulders.

"I'll pop round tomorrow night, sweetheart, to see if you've come to your senses. If not, the extra money will be due in full for this month and next. If you can't pay, then you'll be in breach of our agreement. I will tell my boss you're a flight risk and might disappear without paying what you owe. He'll want you out of here in days. After that, it's up to you."

Rusty had detailed the sorry tale. The girl had opened the door to Read the following night. Sylvester Read visited her regularly for the next eight months while she hunted high and low for a flat outside the Borough. The violence that typified his lifestyle continued in the bedroom. She was depressed and withdrawn. Her haunted look when being interviewed shocked even Rusty, a hardened soldier. She was still battling to mend her broken life in a woman's shelter in Chiswick.

"This direct action is going to be a pleasure," said Phoenix as he moved deeper into the file. Friedman bought property after property in the same style as the semi-detached Victorian house he had just studied. Most were for multi-occupancy letting, and the tenants were white, middle-aged to elderly business people. Read and DeAngelo carried out Friedman's orders as the years passed. First, they moved these people out so that large migrant families could replace them.

Not everyone wanted to leave. DeAngelo called around late at night and used his fists to mete out a mild beating. Read and DeAngelo returned together if the message hadn't been received loud and clear by one visit. Then, the beatings became more severe.

The violence continued to escalate as the number of immigrants flowing into the country increased. Many of these new arrivals arrived here illegally; others had outstayed student visas and evaded deportation orders. It's not difficult to find a hiding place in a city of over eight million souls. As soon as there was any sign of trouble from one of these tenant families, Friedman reacted. Complaints about the state of the dilapidated properties they occupied resulted in Friedman getting his lackeys to pay a visit.

They warned that their illegal status could become known by the authorities if they didn't pay up and keep quiet. If they didn't heed the message, then Read forced himself on the wives while DeAngelo subdued the husbands and made them watch.

Fewer and fewer of Friedman's properties remained in the hands of the tenants living there at the outset. Indeed, the turnover was rapid. There was evidence in Rusty's file of dozens of tenants living in fear, too frightened to seek protection from the police. So instead, the thugs targeted anyone that didn't fit their twisted idea of normality.

Read and DeAngelo terrorised two men in a civil partnership. They suffered verbal abuse for months. Then, when the thugs wanted to persuade them to leave the flat they shared, they arrived on a Sunday afternoon and tried to force the pair to agree to go. The older man tried to argue with Read. He insisted they had rights. He had arranged to see a lawyer in the morning to end this harassment.

DeAngelo grabbed the younger man's wrist. He forced the palm of his right hand flat on the tabletop in front of his partner.

"Rights?" he bellowed. "You ain't got no rights."

With that, he pulled out a knife and stabbed it into the man's hand, pinning it to the table. The screams echoed around their apartment and the other flats in the house for days. There was no visit to the lawyer, and the whole property became available for new tenants within days.

Phoenix looked at his watch. Athena should have returned from the funeral. He was sick to his stomach with what he had read so far. He identified the first targets and confirmed the punishment. There would be time to read stories of the Irish mafia in Ealing later. He needed a breath of fresh air.

Phoenix checked there was nobody in the vicinity of the orangery, and the pathways were empty. Then, he headed to the main house with a glance towards the stable block and ice-house for signs of Rusty or Artemis.

He found Athena sitting by the window, looking over the manicured lawns. She held the silver-framed photograph of Erebus and his wife Elizabeth against her bosom. Phoenix could see her tear-stained cheeks. He wrapped her in his arms and kissed the top of her head.

"Hard saying goodbye to those you love, isn't it?" he said.

"Even harder when you know they died before their time," said Athena.

"We'll find out who was responsible and avenge him soon enough, Athena."

"Have you kept busy while I was gone?" she asked.

"I feel dirty," he growled. "After reading Rusty's reports on the vermin living in the big city, I need a shower."

"I think I might join you," Athena smiled and took his hand. "I have a favour I need to ask."

"Lead on," said Phoenix, trying not to appear too eager.

"Mummy and Daddy are home soon from the south of France; we need to visit them. I want a united front when we tell them they will be grandparents in the New Year."

"Ah," said a deflated Phoenix.

"You're going to be there, so that's final," said Athena,

The thought of interrogation by her father inside the Fox family home in Vincent Gardens, Belgravia, was terrifying to a simple West Country lad.

"How do you think they'll react to having a vigilante killer as a prospective son-in-law?"

"One step at a time," replied Athena, "we'll tell them our news of the baby first. Then we can let them get used to the idea we're a permanent item before we mention the 'M' word."

"Oh, they know we're a permanent item then?" asked Phoenix, surprised.

Athena blushed. "They know we work closely together for the charity; I always catch them looking at one another whenever I mention your name. With them being abroad most of the year and Mummy's heart problem always having to be taken into account, I haven't confirmed their suspicions in so many words."

"Awkward," said Phoenix as they reached the shower in their en-suite bathroom.

"Maybe we should discuss what we're going to say to them?" said Athena, slipping out of her clothes.

"Later," said Phoenix.

The Price of Treachery: Chapter Two

I never imagined myself as a sailor. My parents enjoyed the sea-going life while they lived together as long as it came with a crew and plenty of bottles of champagne. We could be found on the Isle of Wight in August for Cowes Week with monotonous regularity when I was a teenager. My mother left on a cruise ship for the Mediterranean or the Caribbean not long after we returned home in those days.

My stepfather didn't want me hanging around while they wined and dined with the yachting fraternity. So I got packed off with an old local fisherman every afternoon of our three or four-week stay. He took his boat out to the lobster pots and pootled around the coastal waters, teaching me how to steer his tiny craft. When we were lucky, and I wasn't bored out of my skull, we even caught a few fish with a rod and line. I still recall the occasional flounder or bass I managed to land unaided.

My guardian didn't worry about success with his fishing expeditions; my stepfather paid him well. As the summers ticked past and I grew older, Michael Woodford passed on more valuable information than I realised at the time. He was a man of few words, for which I was grateful.

The silences were heaven. Life at home had become one screaming match after another. It was only a matter of time before my parents parted ways. Michael explained the vagaries of the tides, vectors, and races in the currents around the island. I thought it went in one ear and out the other, but by the time we made our ferry trip from Yarmouth to Lymington, I had subconsciously absorbed enough information to help me through what lay ahead.

Michael Woodford had retired. My stepfather was adrift. Not literally, of course, but he no longer travelled the ferry crossing in August after I turned seventeen. I accompanied my mother to social functions during Cowes Week for the first time.

Although she was at pains to point out I was her companion, not her toy boy, I spotted a knowing look on several faces we met. Those faces belonged to upper-class clientele in the clubs and harbourside restaurants we visited that summer. They thought after her last husband went that, my mother had hunted down his son as her new partner.

Mother had her reasons for denying my existence. Of course, I didn't fully understand them as a child, but I appreciated the logic behind her misdirection at seventeen.

The links between a mother and son and vice-versa are more robust than in marriage. We stayed in close contact no matter where she went or who she lived with. I owed her everything. I could refuse her nothing.

When I moved to London at eighteen to seek my fortune, I did so with a generous allowance. However, she promised that capital was available should I identify a market opportunity that helped me make my fortune.

When that opportunity arose, I grabbed it with both hands. A decade later, I still reaped the benefits. From time to time, my mother needed a favour in return. How could I refuse? She had made other similar requests to the one she made in January. So I flew out to Ibiza for a weekend visit.

I watched from inside a café on the marina as Gavin helped William Hunt carry his small suitcase on board the yacht 'Elizabeth.' I followed Erebus as he walked along the tree-lined promenade after breakfast. I stood twenty feet to his left, leaning on the black-painted iron railings as we both admired the sandy beach.

I strolled up the Calle San Jaime around lunchtime as he whiled away an hour with this blessed newspaper under his arm. I thought of ways to dispose of him on his river walk up to the Roman bridge, but the waters were too shallow to conceal the body. So, in the end, I decided to stick with what I knew best. I have taken risks throughout my business life, doing things my competitors never dream of doing. So I decided to do the deed in plain sight. Risk everything on the roll of the dice.

I flew home on Monday morning and called my mother. She was in Australia with her latest husband. Even younger and less appropriate than the last. She was in no immediate rush. William Hunt wasn't going anywhere, and she had other things on her mind. I didn't ask what they might be; I knew better than to question her motives.

We met for only the second occasion that year in mid-July in London. A few words passed between us, enough to get me on a flight out to the Balearics early the following week. I visited the marina café once more and watched the comings and goings on 'Elizabeth'. Gavin, the crewman, fetched supplies, started the regular clean-up and looked to be kept busy for the next couple of hours.

William Hunt sat on the verandah of the Ring O' Bells with a cup of coffee. His copy of The Times was neatly folded in front of him on the circular table. He was too preoccupied with his preparations for his crossword to notice my approach.

I bounced up the steps, eager to fulfil my mother's wishes. I stabbed Erebus in the neck and hurried past the pool table into the restroom without breaking stride. I waited for thirty seconds. Then hearing no cries of alarm from the bar or outside, I calmly walked out, descended the steps and escaped into the town to find a taxi.

I disposed of the syringe in San Antonio, as far away from Calle de Mer and the pub as possible. But unfortunately, drug paraphernalia was not an uncommon find around the club capital of the Mediterranean. On my way back to my hotel in Santa Eulalia, I sent mother a text.

'Bellringer silenced.'

The next few days proved interesting. Poor Gavin appeared distraught. A nice cushy number cruising around the Balearics had ended abruptly. I knew I didn't have long before someone arrived from England to claim the body. I called from the hotel lobby to the company dealing with William Hunt's mortal remains.

The embalmer and I rapidly came to a financial agreement. He pushed the older man's name to the top of his list in exchange for a year's salary. I followed him home that evening and dropped the envelope containing the cash off at his shabby first-floor apartment. No chance now of anyone tracing the exact cause of William Hunt's demise.

Two familiar faces arrived in town the next day. Very subdued and with lots of tears. I smiled as I watched them from what had become my favourite spot on the island. It appeared that Erebus was flying home with an escort, and Gavin was getting things ready to leave the sheltered haven of the marina. As he finalised things with the harbour master, he left 'Elizabeth' unattended. I crept aboard and stowed away until we were well out to sea.

The more people you kill, the easier it becomes. I was so relaxed I slept an hour or two longer than intended. Gavin was fast asleep when I slipped from my hiding place. The crewman awoke a second after my chloroform-soaked cloth pressed over his nose and mouth, but he was too late. He clawed in vain at my strong hands and soon lost consciousness. I tied him up securely and regularly added to his sedative. I sat and watched over him until morning as I read through the manuals for 'Elizabeth' and the rest of her class. By dawn, I was confident I knew which buttons to press.

I dressed in fresh clothes from Gavin's closet, A tight fit, but the ploy was only necessary while I negotiated the narrow channels in the marina. I managed this without mishap and soon motored out into the open seas. From there, three weeks of hopping from harbour to harbour around the coast of mainland Europe lay ahead of me.

Two days out from Ibiza, I got rid of my unwanted passenger. He was alive, if only just. Trussed up like a mummy, he didn't suffer long as he dropped to the bottom of the ocean, unable to move his arms or legs.

The weather remained kind throughout my journey. My GPS and Gavin's technical wizardry at his disposal on 'Elizabeth' were simple enough to master. My birth father didn't pass on many attributes in my genes, but I am always in awe of his innate skill at anything he tackles. Mother had been attracted by it once.

I received more than my fair share of her cold demeanour, which precluded any emotional attachments, male or female. She soon sensed I had inherited her dark side. That was what made us such a formidable pair. There were no limits to what we did to achieve our ends.

I was to deliver 'Elizabeth' to the Lymington Yacht Haven during Cowes Week. I was to arrive within a day or two of the time Gavin expected to steer her into her berth. When William Hunt's friends came to visit from Larcombe Manor, they would find her secure and undamaged.

A note from Gavin showed he had found another post, sailing a yacht in a far-flung Pacific paradise. They had no reason for suspicion. Mother had decided this option was much safer than scuttling the craft in the Atlantic. She frowned at my suggestion of rigging 'Elizabeth' to explode into fragments of wood, glass, and metal when someone from Larcombe entered through the cabin door.

"Far too dramatic, darling, and too remote. I want to be there when they die. Much more satisfying. No, do what they expect Gavin to do, return the yacht to its home, and after that, they can keep it, sell it, whatever they wish. It's of no consequence. We can wait."

Wednesday, August 14th, 2013

Today was the day I left my final safe harbour at Barfleur. I was going to negotiate the English Channel. This journey may seem foolhardy for a novice, if not downright dangerous. That morning I thanked Michael Woodford and the skippers who took me under their wing during that final summer we visited the Isle of Wight together.

In the less frantic weeks that followed the social whirl of the regatta, I crewed for various sizes of boats. Then, my mother disappeared to tour Greece and Italy, so she dumped me on Michael Woodford and his family for the rest of the summer.

I discovered that Michael spent his retirement days drinking cider and chatting about days gone by with locals and incomers. I learned the ropes on the craft that skimmed through the Solent or tackled the busy shipping lanes between the island and the French coast. When I left for home, bronzed by sunny days and balmy breezes, my education for what was to come today was complete.

To make a solo crossing of the English Channel is a daunting prospect. One is sailing out of sight of land, crossing busy shipping lanes and tackling ripping tides. These are stern challenges, but not impossible ones. If your preparation is meticulous – passage plan, weather, tides and boat checks – there's no reason you should fail. Confidence is a hurdle, but not something in short supply as far as I'm concerned; besides, Gavin had already done that work for me in his spare time in Santa Eulalia.

It's the skipper's job to ensure the boat's paperwork is in order. The chances are it won't be needed today, but if it wasn't at my fingertips, I could be in a lot of trouble. I mustn't draw undue attention to myself. Gavin's certificates, licences, and insurance were in order. I had my passport and EHIC.

Gavin meticulously collated the right charts and reference books for easy reference. He even owned one of those handy zipped-top holders full of rulers, dividers, pencils and an eraser. The last time I saw one of those was when I sat my A-Levels.

I had to give Gavin a gold star for his planning. He realised the necessity to use a single time zone and made adjustments for tides and heights. I checked the forecast with our dear old Met Office just in case; if things went wrong, any enquiry panel used their version as gospel on every occasion.

The forecast was southwest Force 3, becoming variable. I could always use the motor if the wind died. Visibility was excellent, and I had a green light. I ensured I was stocked with plenty of easy-to-prepare snacks and drinks. I filled the water and fuel tanks and brought emergency jerry cans of fuel, bottles of water, and odd spares for the engine.

'Elizabeth' possessed a decent toolkit and sail repair kit. I checked engine oil, gearbox oil, fresh water in the header tank, drive belt tension, and saltwater filter. Once I got moving, I ensured I had cooling water in the exhaust.

Gavin's diary confirmed he checked the rig thoroughly a couple of days earlier, and the winches, too, had only recently been serviced. So, a few minutes after five, I eased 'Elizabeth' out of her berth. I focused on every tiny detail. I had courses to steer from buoy to buoy and sails to set — no time left to be nervous.

For that first couple of hours, I found it difficult to judge the range of oncoming ships and altered course very early. Better safe than sorry. I soon settled into the rhythm and spent the next few hours gliding between tankers ploughing majestically on without a care in the world. I took time out for a drink and a bite to eat.

The wind was perfect. 'Elizabeth' skipped along at six knots for a spell; I sensed the wind veering, and we slowed to under four. Finally, it was time to lower the spinnaker and switch to the motor for a while. My nerves endured a severe test for the next few hours, but at last, we emerged on the other side of the shipping lanes without even a near miss.

As we entered the Solent, the wind picked up enough for me to revert to sail. I was in familiar territory now. So close to the shore, there were dozens of smaller craft. I wondered whether they had someone with the experience of a Michael Woodford to tell them where the dangers lay. It is sometimes hard to manoeuvre through a race in a small boat. How large a race could that little craft ahead cope with and not get mangled?

On my trips alone, close to shore, I avoided races as far as possible. Either by going at slack tide or by staying well out to sea. A very calm sea can give you a false sense of security; the race is cunning and leads you into it; before you know it, the tide accelerates, and you must commit. On the other hand, you can go from smooth calm with a slight swell to a white-knuckle ride in less than a minute.

These experienced kayakers came prepared; it wasn't long before the waters calmed, but I bet their little hearts were beating faster than an excited puppy's tail. A race often forms by headlands where the moving water is compressed, speeding up and causing rougher conditions. If the turbulent waters meet waves in the opposite direction, the water is more likely to break, with short sharp waves collapsing.

Where two streams converge, this results in rough water, as in the tides off Hurst Point, over to my left. I avoided this by keeping close to the Isle of Wight. So I could look up at the cliffs to enjoy the comparative wildness of this part of the island. Occasionally I could see people walking the coast in the early evening sun.

Every so often, the sea became less smooth as I passed a hidden ledge, but the generally calm sea meant it posed no problem. I skirted past Crooked Lake and turned towards the mainland, allowing the stream vector to take me into Lymington port. On the way, I felt the sea become rougher as I passed over the Fiddlers Race. Finally, it smoothed out as I looked for the series of navigation lights leading into Lymington Harbour. It was just before ten when I arrived at the Lymington Yacht Haven.

This last part of the journey took two hours. I had to watch several dangerous rocks and hidden reefs closely. Imagine damaging this beautiful yacht on one of these semi-submerged rocks. I wanted 'Elizabeth' to be in pristine condition when Athena and Phoenix came calling. We didn't wish Athena to be upset, not in her state. She won't know that the mother is aware that she is 'with child'; our colleague is careful not to show their true colours; what a blessing to have someone on the inside these days.

I had to remind myself that I still needed to thread my way alongside the marina and get 'Elizabeth' into her reserved berth. After an exhausting journey, I was losing concentration. Before long, though, everything sat in its rightful place. Time to print off Gavin's note, tidy up, collect my things and get ashore. All that remained was the final paperwork.

With that completed, I set off on the twenty-minute walk into Lymington and the excellent room I reserved at Stanwell House. After ten hours of sleep and a hearty breakfast, I took a taxi to the station. I arrived at London Waterloo before noon. I sent my mother a text while I sat on the train.

'HRH is in residence. Can't wait to meet again.'

My summer break had ended; the business world called

me back to its bosom. Deals hammered out, millions made. My phone vibrated as I walked into the atrium that led to my London HQ. Mother had replied.

'Rest. Gather your strength. Difficult days lie ahead.'

**Grab your copy…
vinci-books.com/the-price-of-treachery**

About the Author

Ted Tayler is the international best-selling indie author of the Freeman Files and Phoenix series. Ted lives in the English West country, where his stories are based. He was born in 1945 and has been married to Lynne since 1971. They have three children and four grandchildren.

His thought-provoking mysteries appeal to readers of Sally Rigby, Joy Ellis, Pauline Rowson, and Faith Martin. His action-packed thrillers are a must for fans of Mark Dawson and J C Ryan.

Gus Freeman's cold case investigations are carried out with reasoned deduction rather than bursts of frantic action. In each of the 24 books, unsolved murders are accompanied by romance, humour, and country life. The core message in the 12 Phoenix novels is that criminals should pay for their crimes. Unfortunately, the current system fails to deliver the correct punishment, so Phoenix helps redress the balance.

Acknowledgments

The love and support of my family; without them, this would have been impossible.

www.ingramcontent.com/pod-product-compliance
Ingram Content Group UK Ltd.
Pitfield, Milton Keynes, MK11 3LW, UK
UKHW040119190326
469155UK00004B/1232